# The Death of GOD

## and Other Stories

Timothy Reynolds

Cover Art & Design by Timothy Reynolds
Author photo: Cometcatcher Media

First Edition: 2015

Reynolds, Timothy G. M. 1960-
The Death of GOD / Timothy G. M. Reynolds

ISBN: 978-0-9813478-3-7

1. Horror.2. Science Fiction. I. Title. II.
Title: The Death of GOD and Other Stories

Cometcatcher Press
Calgary, Alberta. Canada.

This collection of stories is dedicated to
the late André Golding.

André was my English teacher at
Don Mills Collegiate Institute in the late 1970s,
and not only did he introduce me to
*The Lord of the Rings*,
but he made us each write a full page, every day.
André didn't care what we wrote,
just so long as it was coherent.

W. O. Mitchell made me want to be a writer,
but André Golding showed me that I could.

Thank you, both.

# Contents

# Introduction

Hugo Award-winning author Robert J. Sawyer once told me that short stories are a great way to build writing credits before—and while—writing novels. Published short stories show editors and publishers that a writer can tell a story, see it through from concept to final polish to sale. Well, I'm a novelist at heart. I started—but never finished—my first one in 1981. Since then I've started and finished at least a first draft of five more. Two are completed and one of the two is published. I even competed in the Pulp Press 3-Day Novel Contest in which writers must complete a novel within the 3-day long Labour Day weekend, starting with no more than an outline. I wrote 39,000 words that weekend...on a manual typewriter. I didn't win, place, or even show. But I did it, and that's all that matters.

In 2007, friend & publisher Gwen Gades asked me to edit *Podthology: The Pod Complex* for her Dragon Moon Press. Through that project my friend Jennifer Rahn introduced me to editor/author Emerian (Emz) Rich of Horroraddicts.net. Then, when Emz was putting together her anthology *Horrible Disasters* she contacted friends and strangers alike to submit horror stories that take place during or in the aftermath of real disasters. The project was a fundraiser for international disaster relief and in light of the various hurricanes, earthquakes, and tsunamis that had recently occurred, I thought that was as good a reason as any to finally write a short story for something other than a class assignment.

**"Shut Up & Drive"** wasn't my first short story ever, but it was my first new one in close to twenty years. Emz loved it, accepted it for *Horrible Disasters*, and I was hooked. I heard about another anthology, a steampunk-Jules Verne tribute. The creative side of my brain kicked in and **"Hawkwood's Folly"** was written for Kindling Press' *20,001: A Steampunk Odyssey*.

Not long after, I discovered Duotrope, a free-at-that-time online listing service for writing markets. Ooh, what a wealth of information that was. The short-story ball got rolling, and for 18 months I couldn't stop writing and submitting. Eighteen stories later, twelve were 'sold'. "**Hawkwood's Folly**" was selected as one of 2012's best pieces of speculative writing by ChiZine Press and reprinted in *Imaginarium 2012*. "**Dragons in Suburbia**" received an Honorable Mention in 2013, and "**Why Pete?**" received an Honorable Mention in *The Writers of the Future Contest* of LA. "**Why Pete?**" was also the last of the short stories here to be published, in *Tesseracts Seventeen: Speculating Canada From Coast to Coast to Coast.* T17 is Edge Science Fiction & Fantasy Publication's annual collection of select Canadian speculative fiction.

Then Duotrope started charging an annual subscription fee and I moved away from short stories and back toward the novels that were still itching to get out of my head and on to paper. But people have been asking where they can read my 'shorties'. Some of the stories were only online, some were only available through obscure small presses, and some were only available in eBooks. After I self-published my novel, "**The Broken Shield**", I decided that a collection was in order. Collections don't sell well, and even big names like Stephen King never see sales numbers from short stories like they do with novels; but even if I sell one or two online and a handful at conventions each year, I wanted *one* place where my words can come out to play in all their forms.

In *The Death of God and Other Stories* you will find humour, horror, hard science fiction, fantasy, superhero, and some dark, nasty stuff you might not like at all.
Enjoy.

# Uncle Julius

**First Published:**
*Podthology: The Pod Complex*. Dragon Moon Press. 2009.

I am a writer today because that's what I decided to be after reading W. O. Mitchell's *Jake and the Kid* in high school. After meeting Mr. Mitchell at a reading in Waterloo, Ontario, and nervously telling him that he inspired me to be a writer, he told me "Don't ever quit." So I'm not. And **"Uncle Julius"** is my tribute to Bill and his wonderful style.

~~~

## Uncle Julius

We buried my Uncle Julius today. He was 72, and, yes, he was dead when we set him in the ground. It's only noon, but I've had a couple drinks already and right now, while I'm waiting for them to get the wake buffet set out in the dining room of the farmhouse I grew up in, I'm trying to decide what a fitting tribute would be for Julius.

Maybe I should get out my long-ignored, dust-covered brushes and finally paint the portrait of him that Mom wants, based on a couple of the published photos taken of him when he was in the heart of his own personal media hurricane (my favourite is the one from the Topeka Capital Journal where he's facing down Jack Happer's prize bull and smiling!). Also under consideration is finally finishing composing the song about him that I started back in college when he was on some Wichita morning show trying to roll an egg across the host's desk with just the power of his mind. I finally digitalized the old videotape we have of the show so maybe it's about time I finish the song.

Then again, although the painting and the song both need to be done at some point in time, based on the massive influx of emails that's bombarded me in the last twenty-four hours, I think I'm going to have to at least address his hundreds of thousands of fans he found through my odd little podcast, RS: RELATIVELY SPEAKING.

Although possessing strange planetary popularity now, RS started out a few years ago with really, really limited appeal, since I was just getting my feet wet in the new medium to see if it was a good fit with the material I wanted to get out on the Net. I'd always wanted to host my own radio show so once a week I put together a podcast involving my strange relatives, usually starting each half-hour 'cast with a short interview with Mom's lawyer-cousin, Leon. Leon and I chatted mostly about the legal ups and downs of incorporation and contracts within the farming community and I'll be completely honest and straightforward and tell you flat-out that no one could ever describe those early podcasts as either riveting or captivating. That all changed, though, the week after I upgraded my portable digital recording gear and was started taping and podcasting a couple of the Wichita County Fair performances by my infamous singing aunts, The Warbling Wrens.

Infamy is far too easy to achieve in this day and age, but my aunts more than earned theirs. For as long as I can remember, Fair Time meant that they were often either half in the bag from judging the entries in the home-made cider competition or high on the medicinal weed Aunt Elise gets for her glaucoma. Some days it was both. The worse the glaucoma got, the higher they got, and the performances were always gems, in a 'did she really just sing what I think she just sang?' kind of way. They don't sing anymore now, but the archives of those early podcasts are still popular.

The Warbling Wrens were a hit, but my subscriber list didn't grow into triple digits until Uncle Julius, the family's token Viet Nam vet, caught wind of the attention his sisters-in-law were getting and suggested I interview him about some of his conspiracy theories. From Marilyn Monroe's murder by Abbot and Costello to Elvis' reincarnation as a humming llama in Decatur, IL, he was privy to them all and more than happy to disseminate them to the world at large.

Then one day he shocked the shit out of me with his completely unexpected 'on air' description of the time he spent with a French-Canadian psychic while they were POWs in 'Nam. How could I do anything but let the 'tape' roll and then dedicate an entire podcast to the stunning tale? In a matter of hours my subscribership set sail into the sea of high five-digits, with fans writing in from McMurdo Station in Antarctica to Nassau to Beijing. Julius was an almost instant hit and the Warbling Wrens were forgotten, which is probably good because one died and two are in rehab.

As much fun as Julius and I were having, the ride wasn't expected to last, however, because like everything else he ever got involved in, I figured my uncle would quickly get bored and find something shining to draw his attention away. Not a fricking chance! There was no way in Hell that Uncle Julius was walking away when he finally had an audience who wanted to hear everything he said, no matter how outrageous it originally sounded when he lobbed the idea onto the table during a family dinner like a conversational grenade.

He got so caught up in the whole podcast process that after only three scintillating episodes of **Tales of Telekinesis from the Hanoi Hilton** he brought in his own intro music, to 'spice up' my humble little narrow-cast. Then, holy crap of craps, once he found out that he could actually subscribe to the podcast and download the whole thing to an MP3 player so he could listen to it all again and again, he had my mother drive him into town to get an iPod!

Uncle Julius was actually the first member of his generation in town to get an iPod, and after only an hour of his showing it off to the Thursday Morning Coffee & Scotch crowd down at Legion #1, the local Circuit City was inundated with walker-supported, curse-muttering, half-informed seniors joining the 21st century with 'one of them there I-music-pod-people thingies'. When Circuit City ran out of stock, the Crestline minibus from the Eleanor Roosevelt Retirement Centre was quickly commandeered for an impromptu road trip to Wal-Mart's Electronics Department. There was even a little side-trip to the in-store McDonald's wedged between the Portrait Studio and the Crafts Department, because nothing says "I'm on the cutting edge of technology" like fumbling with a too-damned small-to-read instruction manual over regular fries and a deep-fried Filet-o-Fish sandwich that sticks to your dentures.

All was goofy but pretty quiet on the podcast front for a while when all of a sudden one afternoon Uncle Julius made the seemingly harmless offer to actually channel some of his psychic energy through the podcast, to share his 'gift' with the masses as it were. Oh, it didn't matter that I explained fairly patiently to him that the show wasn't live, that it was all pre-recorded and then uploaded—he wanted what he wanted, and why on earth would his favourite nephew deny him that bit of joy? So I didn't. I suppose part of the reason I went along with the idea was that Julius had laid claim to special powers for almost as long as I'd known him, and I figured at worst, it would make an interesting episode for his growing 'fanhood' but at best, he would actually succeed and we'd both become famous.

My memory is a bit spotty when it comes to anything before the age of five, but since I was one of those kids always hitting my head on things when trying a stupid stunt while my big brother egged me on, I'm hardly surprised. My first memory of Uncle Julius' 'strange and wonderful gift' was when he used it to stop me from running away from home on my brother Lucas' bike. It was my fifth summer and I was one pissed-off little brat.

I went tearing past him on the old lane out back of the barn with my school bag stuffed with my favourite G.I. Joe, my entire Hot Wheels collection, fresh underwear and a stale bag of Hostess Salt & Vinegar Potato Chips bouncing on my back. The fact that I wasn't stopping to pick up the Hot Wheels as they tumbled out of the hastily closed bag and onto the dusty lane told my uncle something was seriously wrong—my Hot Wheels were my life! He shouted four or five times for me to hold up and he even made an attempt to chase me on foot, but I was peddling like all four school bullies were on my tail and stopping meant being beaten to death. The stupid thing is that I was running away because Mom wouldn't let me eat a third post-school, pre-chore chocolate chip cookie, having already consumed my standard-issue allotment of two. Like I said, I was a brat.

The way my brother—the ever-reliable prosecution's witness against me—tells the story, Uncle Julius stopped shouting, dropped to one knee, put his hands to his temples and fixed his Stare of Power at the receding bike. Lucas said that our uncle willed the bike to stop and it did, 'dead' in its tracks. I, on the other hand, flew more than a little awkwardly over the handlebars and landed on my unhelmeted head. When my senses finally cleared, I swore up and down that my tumble was because the front tire had slammed into a fist-sized rock, but the rock was nowhere to be seen, so maybe it was Julius. Even now I suspect that I probably hit the damned thing hard enough to knock it over into the weeds, but good old Uncle Julius claimed it was his psychic powers that had stopped me and who was I to argue? I was only a cookie-deprived five-year-old fugitive escaping from the drudgery of helping Mom hang the wash out to dry.

That's my first memory of the strange and wonderful world of Uncle Julius and his 'powers'. Unable to work due to a shrapnel-shredded shoulder from his second tour in 'Nam, Julius had all the time in the world to dedicate to strengthening his mental powers. From that day on, Julius spent one-hundred-and-forty-four minutes each day working to refine his gift. He said that one-hundred-and-forty-four was a number of power. He'd read it somewhere—probably in the back of one of the comic books he loved to pour over while sitting in the barber's chair every third Tuesday—and he accepted the fact without question. So it was one-hundred-and-forty-four minutes each day, day in and day out without fail for the rest of his life. Julius was nothing if not persistent.

This 'working to refine his power' took a number of forms over time. In the first two years all he really did was sit in front of the old, over-heating, static-spouting G.E. radio he kept out in the barn and concentrate on adjusting the volume with only the powers of his mind. This was back in the days before cable television took away humanity's imagination and from what I remember of that damned radio, when it did actually pick up a broadcast, the volume was known to vary all on its lonesome, with or without Uncle Julius and his 'powers'.

Then the G.E. blew a tube and nearly burned down the barn. Mom was a whole lot less than impressed and said her brother-in-law was putting crazy ideas in her sons' heads so it had to stop. Julius took that as the challenge it was not meant to be and now that he was satisfied that he had some measure of control over his powers he graduated himself to tougher tasks.

One Saturday in my sixth summer he finally made the leap in faith to try influencing a living creature. Bicycles and radios were one thing, but God's creatures would really test his power. Uncle Julius was up at sunrise that day and spent the first two hours staring at the swallows that swooped and dived from their nests in the barn to the fallow field and back. When I noticed his focus I asked, in all childhood innocence, if stopping a flying bird would make it drop like a stone to the ground where it could be hurt, or worse. Well, that ended the experiment with the swallows. Julius wasn't a cruel man; sometimes he just needed someone to point out the flaw in his methodology.

He thanked me for the insight and assured me that, if they could, the birds would thank me, too—and I was still young enough to believe him. He then took my tiny, six-year-old hand in his dry, oversized paw and led me around to the side of the house where Mom had her vegetable garden.

"Lad, there's a rabbit hereabouts whose bin eatin' your mother's carrots'n tomatoes. She wants me to set up a snare to kill him but I think I have a better way, and it starts with becomin' invisible."

By "invisible", Julius meant the very mundane method of using a blind, like Dad did when he went duck hunting every fall; but this kid was still excited to be included in such serious adult goings on so off we went to find the necessary materials to our becoming invisible. We built our blind out of some of Mom's lesser bed sheets and planted ourselves in the wicker chairs carried over from the porch so we could watch through the spaces between the sheets in comfort. I really didn't expect to see the rabbit because I'd seen him out there earlier; getting his fill while Uncle Julius was staring at the swallows. Mom said I was to throw rocks at the rabbit if I ever saw it, but it wasn't growing carrots and it didn't make me eat carrots. It ate the carrots I hated so so much and that, in my books, made Little Bunny Froo Froo my friend, and I don't throw rocks at friends.

Now, Uncle Julius may have had some strange ideas, but, except for last weeks' freight train incident, he had the most incredible luck of anyone I've ever met. If a flipped coin landed heads five out of ten times for me, for Julius it would land tails eight times. At the time, like him, I believed it was his powers, but when the rabbit hopped out of the bushes only five minutes into our vigil, even my uncle said "Well, ain't that lucky." Then he leaned in, hands raised, palms forward, closed one eye and stared kind of lopsided at the bunny; and this six-year-old blood kin who hoped some of the power could rub off, leaned forward, raised my hands, closed one eye and stared, too.

In my experience, rabbits, when not being chased, are cautious little critters. Even at six I knew that. To this day I've never seen one hop more than a couple feet without stopping to listen and sniff, and that little carrot-eater way back then didn't disappoint me. He took two hops and froze. After a second or so he moved again only to stop again after two more hops. It was typical cottontail behaviour, but the barefooted six-year-old in dungarees and his thirtyish uncle in his dusty cammo combat pants, drab olive t-shirt and floppy G.I.-issue jungle hat swore that every stop that rabbit made was caused by nothing less than the powers held in our brains. I started that simple little vigil just wanting to keep my offbeat uncle company on a sunny Saturday, but I finished it a firm believer in the extraordinary powers of certain human minds.

I became a true convert that day and, as is typical in rural communities, word spread faster than a ticked-off bumblebee. Pretty soon some of the more superstitious farmers came by to ask the psychic if he could heal or predict. Well, if he couldn't before, Julius certainly found that he could now. Never as popular a man as my hard-working father, his brother, Julius now had visitors on a regular basis, and he loved it. They'd come to him for bunions, breaks, sprains, gout and one daring old gent brought his piles, but Julius was wise enough to refer him to the herbalist down the road.

Let me point out something before I go on: Julius Flack may have been shell-shocked and gullible enough to believe himself a psychic, but he was a thinking man. As my mother never failed to point out, Julius always had an answer for everything.

"Why don't you make it rain an' save the crops, Julius?" a neighbour asked.

"If'n I make it rain now, Jonathan, we'll have a colder winter due to the variation in pressure caused by the unexpected cloud cover and the new level of humidity during this new moon."

"Why cain't you heal my leg faster, Mr. Flack?"

"If'n it heals too quickly, Bobby, the break will take calcites from the rest of the bone and weaken it, an' then your limp'll be worse than before."

"Julius, if you kin make a hoppity rabbit stand still, why not make my chickens lay twice as many eggs?"

"Chickens only got so many eggs in them, Mr. Wilkins, an' if you force them to give them to you all at once it'll kill them an' then all you'll have is one good roast, a handful of feathers, a bunch of eggs and an empty spot in your coop."

Even my brother took a shot at him. "Uncle Julius, kin you use yer powers t' make the girls at school like me?"

"Lucas, lad, I'm a psychic, not a miracle worker."

He didn't always make sense, but he did have a sense of humour. If he got a dilly of a question, though, he simply countered with "That's more a question for the good Lord in church on Sunday" and that shut up the lot of them. They were willing to believe a psychic healer walked among them but they were also good Episcopalians and some questions threatened to lead them onto sacrilegious ground where the devil sows his wicked ideas.

It may not sound like it, but every once in a while Uncle Julius had a flash of common sense and it was usually when was at his healing. While he was concentrating his power on a back injury he would knead the muscle with his hands. He said it was to help the transfer of power but I know now that a good circulation-aiding muscle rub has been known to do wonders for an injury.

Another time, I sprained my left ankle while playing with Dad's snowshoes and Julius applied his power while my foot was propped up in a snow bank. Whether I now credit the snow's cold or my uncle's powers, the swelling did go down with uncanny speed.

Did Julius notice any of the coincidences? He never said, one way or another. And Dad? Well, Julius was his little brother, and it never hurt business having a healer in the family—someone who drove from two counties away to see that same healer could quite often be convinced to take home a bushel of fresh corn or apples, for a small price.

Then, as I said, one day my somewhat mixed up, but harmless 'telepathetic' uncle (as Lucas used to call him at school to keep from being pummelled when the others mocked Julius behind his back) offered to share his healing power with the subscribers of my podcast and took his game to a whole new level. Before we knew it, what seemed like half the world was coming along for the ride. I guess people will believe just about anything if it'll make them feel special and less alone in a continually more disconnected and lonely world, so them wanting to develop their psychic abilities through a pre-recorded podcast shouldn't have surprised me as much as it did.

In two blinks of an eye Uncle Julius went from being a self-proclaimed psychic war vet trying to predict the upcoming seasons better than The Farmers' Almanac, to being the talk of the internet, the prince of the podosphere and the lord of every general store front porch and Wal-Mart checkout-line in the great state of Kansas and well beyond. And then he went and got himself hit by a train.

Being hit by a train has that effect on a person's reputation, psychic or not, and before I set about putting together a podcast tribute for a man twice the age of the average pod-monkey, I'd better tell you about the end.

Two weeks ago Julius returned from one of his forays into the city, walking on a cloud of sheer enthusiastic joy. It was the 8th, a fact I remember because it was Lucas' son's birthday and we were all getting ready for the party. Mom, ever the practical one, asked her brother-in-law if he'd found a job. He was seventy-two but she never gave up hope.

"A job? No. A calling? Yes ma'am."

And that's all he said until dinner, when the whole family was gathered around the table while young Lucas Jr. blew out candles and talked about his first year of college. I, myself, was flashing back to my childhood, making a mountain and lake of my mashed potatoes and gravy and most everyone else was eating as much of Mom's incredible home-cooked feast as, they could. Mom still cooked for growing sons, even though we're now well into our forties, and these family events were a welcomed chance to purge the fast food crap that was clogging up our intestines. As a matter of fact, Luke did happen to grow up to be a giant of a man a full head taller than my own five-nine, and I swear it was because of Mom's cooking. Since he gladly took over the farm when Dad retired in '99, I guess it was a good thing he was the size of a reliable Clydesdale. But back to my uncle.

Julius told the story all at once, in an uncharacteristic blurt. "I stopped a streetcar today. It came to a complete stop. They tried to say it was a power surge on the 3rd Street line, but they just can't admit the truth. It was me."

Mom stayed quiet, Dad looked up and made some weak agreement, my sister-in-law Lisa just nodded, her pretty little mouth full of fresh biscuit, and my brother paid no attention whatsoever, intent as he was on his roast beast. Only Lucas Jr. and I showed any real enthusiasm, and it was me that didn't get the brain into gear before releasing the brake on my mouth, again.

"A streetcar, Uncle Julius?! That's better than a rabbit or a bike by far. Next thing you know you'll be stopping a freight train." Shit. I'd said it. I couldn't take it back even if I'd known what idea I'd just put into the head of my well-meaning fool of an uncle. 20/20 hindsight isn't much of a gift, people.

"A freight train..." He just locked his gaze on the centrepiece candle for a moment and his smile grew from a single seed to a whole crop in a handful of blinks. This time no one but me noticed, most of them having found that hot sweet potatoes are infinitely more interesting than yet another story from Julius. Needless to say, my own family weren't subscribers of my podcast.

For a week things went on as usual with folks still dropping by to visit with Uncle Julius, ask for his help and maybe even buy some corn or a handful or two of carrots from Mom's smaller-than-it-used-to-be vegetable garden. Two nights later, on Tuesday, the moon was full ripe and the night felt thick with energy. It might be that's what inspired Julius because he sat on the porch until 2 a.m., leaning forward, arms up, palms forward and one eye closed, staring at the moon's disk as if he could soak up all its mystical powers to augment his own.

Maybe my uncle really did stop that rickety old streetcar, and maybe, after more practice, a small, empty freight train could have been within his reach, but at 11:55 the next morning, the fully-laden, three engine, Wichita-bound Kansas Central ran over the kindest soul to ever come back mixed up from a war that should never have been. They said his end was quick, but I wonder if he even saw it coming, what with his hands up in front of him and his good eye closed as he focussed his power on the not-so-simple task at hand.

oOo

# From Anna to Yousef

**First Published:**
*Podthology: The Pod Complex*. Dragon Moon Press, 2009.

This story was originally written for an online course with the International Correspondence Schools. When I was editing the anthology *Podthology: The Pod Complex*, I needed stories about podcasting, to go with the stories which had actually been podcast, so I took the original story and tweaked it to fit the theme. It was the first of my stories about a Russian character, and also my first in which Death played a role as something more than an abstract.

~~~

## From Anna to Yousef

Alexander T. Crisp, American Image Press. May 29th, 2009.

On October 30th, 2008, Londonderry massage therapist Zeke Boggs, 28, uploaded his weekly podcast, **Zen of Zeke**, to his server and went about planning next week's show.

An hour later there were sixty-two emails in his inbox regarding the poor quality of the audio. Boggs investigated and determined that an unintelligible audio track had been overlaid during or after the upload. He deleted the corrupted file and uploaded the podcast again. This time it went up clean and stayed that way.

Twelve days later, on November 11th, at 1900hrs GMT, Allyson St. James, 31, of Dubai, opened her Gmail account to find 497 emails complaining about the 'mixed up' audio of her erotica podcast. St. James looked into the problem, confirmed the poor quality, and redid the upload, just as Boggs had before her. Problem solved.

According to PodioAudio Tracking and Review, the audio problem occurred another one-hundred-and-forty-two times in the podosphere over the next forty-eight hours.

Occurrence eighty-one was on the philosophically-inclined podcast of Toronto sound engineer, Seth Waisglass, 26. But, rather than simply deleting the offending file and performing the upload a second time, Waisglass posted a note on the 'wall' of his Facebook group asking if anyone else had experienced the same thing. The response was almost instantaneous: twenty-three of his four-hundred-and-ninety-four Facebook 'friends' confirmed similar corruptions. Waisglass listened to the clip again, then, acting on a hunch, he separated out the offending audio track, played it back-to-front and got one step closer to explaining the strange phenomenon.

Although he couldn't understand all of the re-engineered audio, Waisglass recognized enough to know that he needed the help of his maternal grandmother, Ruth Wahlmstein of Rochester, NY. Formerly of Ekaterinburg in the U.S.S.R, it took Mrs. Wahlmstein only two hours to translate the clip from its original Russian into English. What follows is the translated transcript of the message, which somehow found its way onto one-hundred-and-forty-four apparently random podcasts between October 30th, 2008 and March 13th, 2009.

***

*"Dearest Yousef, my rebel brother, it's me, Anna.*

*Surprised to hear from me? I know, I know. It's been a long while but I'm here at the cabin, curled up in Opa's wicker rocker, and thought that this would be a good time for you to get a letter from your little sister.*

*I've been up here for a couple days now, waiting for an old friend of mine. He didn't say exactly when he'd arrive but I have a feeling he'll be here soon. As it happens, I have time to kill and this place reminds me so much of you, therefore I'm writing.*

*From my vantage point, wrapped in the old quilt in the rocker, I can see the stuffed fish on the wall. Remember it? Not much bigger than my hand, now, but back then it was your pride and joy. You must have taken half the morning to reel it in. Even at eight years old you had that determination to succeed. Next to it on the mantle is that cracker-dry sparrow's nest I found under the cedar hedge. Mother called me a "little Cossack" that day when I spent more time examining the dead fledgling than caring for the living one. I didn't know then what she meant by that comment I was only five but I'd heard the tone many times before, and was to hear it for many years after.*

*There's a question I've always wanted to ask you, Yousef, and this is a good time, I think. Do you believe Mother ever forgave me for living while Marina died? I don't. I've always believed she hated me more every day. She almost died giving birth to Marina and me, did she ever tell you that? If we both had died early in the pregnancy she maybe could have tried again for healthy babies, but the midwife saved me and that destroyed Mother's chances for more babies.*

*She was ashamed of herself, I think. She believed that God had judged her and cursed her with one dead baby, one crippled baby and no more hope. It didn't take long for me to start wishing I'd died with Marina.*

*I'm getting morbid, again, sorry. You had enough of that when we were growing up. No point in wondering about Mother she's as dead as your fish, now.*

*Oh, the rain is starting up again. It rained all last night and it lulled me to sleep. I love rainy in the night. Everything so dark and damp with nature's rhythm tapped out on the shingle roof and on the hearth when the wind is soft and the drops make it down the chimney. I left the kettle on the hook this morning and now the rain is playing a copper drum song. If I close my eyes and concentrate I hear the marches they used to play for us in school. I missed many things, having a twisted leg, but not marching like a good little communist didn't break* my heart.

So, how have you been, Yousef? Your own children growing tall and strong? Did Karl ever get through that book I sent him last birthday? I was afraid he might find a collection of folk tales too old fashioned.

I only have the one oil lamp burning, now, so that I might see the lightning while still writing this. There's a current in the air tonight, the light hairs on my arms are standing up and the wolf skin rug under my foot is charged with power. My friend is coming. I'm using the stove for heat tonight because there are always fewer stray embers that way. The scent of the burning cedar is an opiate to me, lifting me to planes of existence my leg has kept me from reaching.

Do you ever talk to your dead wife, Olga? I talk to Marina, sometimes. I did it a lot when I was young and recently have started again. She doesn't answer me, of course, but sometimes it helps just to talk to her. I wonder if she forgives me.

Oh my, that lightning flash lit up the whole world, I think. The shadows all came to life and started to dance. When my friend arrives we'll dance, I think. He doesn't mind my leg. We've been close a long time, he and I, and now that the time is nigh (I read that in a book, once: "The time is nigh, and I must fly" and have always wanted to use it. Doesn't sound like something I'd say, does it?) Where was I? Oh yes, now that the time is... here, I'm looking forward to the dance.

I heard from Konrad last week, or maybe it was the week before. He thinks I should get out of research and back into teaching. He just doesn't seem to listen when I say that doing research is much more interesting than sitting in a classroom guiding narrow minds down old roads. He says that I spend more time with dead historians than living friends. Sometimes he's so touchy sensitive --- he should be an artist, not a government clerk.

The rain is heavier now. The drum beat is more of a loud thrumming, and I had to stir out of my warm chair to move the kettle --- I was afraid the little thing was going to be beaten into slag by the rain and hail coming down the chimney. The *old cast iron pot can catch it all now. The lightning is more frequent now and the thunder is shaking the place like the echoes of the footsteps of a colossus or two trampling Oma's long dead cabbage patch. Maybe they're doing the dance, too, and are waiting for me to go out and partner up. I'll wait, thank you.*

*Have you ever danced in the wan moon light, Yousef? I don't think there'll be moonlight getting through the cloud to fall on the cabin tonight, though. I hope he's happy with just the light from one oily lamp, but, then, I don't suppose it matters much to him.*

*It's been almost too long since he last came around. I think Papa's funeral was the last time. He's been busy, of course, but when you get used to someone looking over your shoulder for most of your life, well, you miss him when he's off doing what he does.*

*Ah, the old cuckoo clock Papa smuggled up from Bern is sounding eleven o'clock. I suppose it would be too Chekhovian of me to expect him to arrive at the stroke of twelve. His schedule is his own secret and while in my heart I know he'll be here tonight, he never actually promised me. When it's time it's time, he once said. That answer will just have to keep me happy and, to tell you the truth of it, it does. Not knowing exactly when adds an edge to life, believe it or not. Mmm... there is a current in the air that has nothing to do with the storm pounding the cabin.*

*Yousef, I wish you could be here with me to see that I am happy, and not crazy at all. You're not ready to dance, though. You have too many things left to do. I just thought... oh, my. I think the clock has stopped. Has it ever done that before? Probably once or twice, I'm sure.*

*The air is so charged, now. I can almost see sparks. The rain has stopped, too. Oh! Yousef! I see moonlight! Pale and beautiful and casting more dancing shadows! Wait. One shadow is separating from the others! He's here and it's my turn to dance. God bless, Yousef! I'll*

***

None of the support staff at the dozens of affected servers were able to offer an explanation. Apparently there are no trails to follow, no e-files to open, no digital viruses or worms to quarantine --- just the audio itself.

Yousef, if you read this article, please contact me through this publication's offices.

oOo

# The Farm

**Not Previously Published.**

The Farm is a real place, just as I've described it in the story. It was one of my favourite places in the world. This story is a tribute to The Farm, which has since been sold by my cousin. I just checked it out on Google Maps and it looks like the old place is gone. Even the tennis court looks to be overgrown. But it still lives here, and in my heart.

~~~

# The Farm

Hopes and dreams are for suckers. Suicide is a viable alternative.

"Hey Joe."

"Hey Rose. Been a long time."

Three tail-chasing barn swallows caught my eye.

"Twenty years."

My slightly stoned, somewhat drunk attention wandered back. Ex-girlfriends popping up out of nowhere have that effect on me. "Whatcha been up to, girl?"

Industrious bees hovered, buzzed and airlifted to and from the patch of clover to my right, and two sprites played dodge-ball with a severed yellow dandelion head near the daisy-filled, quarter-barrel planter, behind Rose's back.

"A couple of marriages, a couple of sons, and a career."

"Dancer?" It was always her dream.

"Nurse."

"Good choice." I sat on the wrought-iron-and-wood bench on the one-step-up stoop of my cousin Rob's farm, though it's not really a farm. It's more of a cottage, nestled on the side of a well-kept gravel road with no exit, overlooking a man-made pond with a mock island and a duck blind. It's been called The Farm since Rob's parents built it, long before I was born. I know it was before my time because my parents spent their honeymoon here forty-two years ago.

"How about yourself? Married? Kids? Pulitzer Prize or two?"

I spun the wedding ring on my finger, not wanting to think about it. "No Pulitzer, no kids. Widowed."

A small, five-room cottage—not including the screened-in sun-room—with a field-stone fireplace topped with a ten-point buck's glassy-eyed stare.

"Oh no! I'm sorry. What happened."

"Drunk driver. Four killed, one injured."

"Did she suffer?"

"Nope. Like I said, she was drunk." I sipped my rye.

"Oh, shit."

"Yah." It was a gentleman's farm, with no animals other than the ones supplied by nature, including Canada Geese, leopard frogs, barn swallows, little bluetail damselflies, and a few dozen medium-sized rainbow trout. Actually, the trout were brought in and tossed into the pond for a little fishing from the squarish turquoise rowboat. There were the sprites, too, but they certainly couldn't be politely counted amongst the animals.

"So, what brings you out this way?"

"I think I'm lost. This looked like a good place to get directions."

"It's just a glorified driveway, kiddo. It doesn't go anywhere but around the end of the pond and up the hill to the Robertson place. Three properties here, that's it. Where are you trying to get to?"

"I guess I'm not lost, then. I'm staying with the Robertsons for the weekend."

I pointed left, unnecessarily. "Follow the road along past the tennis court, the faerie ring, and up the hill. I'd tell you that Doc Robertson's house is the one with the pool, but it's the only thing up there except the barn, so you'll find it okay."

"Then I suppose I will. Thanks. I gotta go check in with them and then I'll come back and we'll catch up. Twenty-years-worth."

I smiled and meant it. "Sounds good."

She got back in her little blue Subaru and drove off while I left the sprites to their stupid games and went back inside to sit at the pine dining room table, continue sipping neat rye, and stare at my blank notebook. I'd driven up from Toronto this morning and haven't written a damned word since I arrived. Or doodled a sketch or even hummed a song. Not a damned thing creative. My brief conversation with Rose was the most creative part of the day. Hell, it was the most creative thing I've done in two long, goddamned years, which is why I was up at the Farm in the first place. The emptiness in my soul needed to be dealt with.

I spent a lot of weekends up here as a kid, losing hooks and worms, and at least one Mepps 3 Spinner to underwater snags in the pond; playing crib with Dad, Snakes and Ladders with the whole family, and the wooden Danish lap-labyrinth by myself—and no, that's not a euphemism for enjoying Scandinavian porn. I've always found the place to be something of a sanctuary, warm and comforting, though when they honoured me with an appearance, the sprites were more entertainment than comfort.

I wrote a word—"BLANK"—on the page, in blocky uppercase letters, pretty close to the middle, top-to-bottom, left-to-right. I'm not OCD, but I like things balanced, which is why I had called Rob on Sunday evening and asked if I could borrow the place for a few days. He and Sharon were taking the girls off to Montreal for the weekend so I could actually have the place for almost two weeks if I wanted it. I didn't. A couple of days would be plenty.

I stared at the freshly violated page and...*nothing*. Not a damned thing. No second word, not even a stupid smiley face. Creative genius is all bullshit anyway. Produce on a regular basis and you're accused of being a 'pop whore', selling to the marketplace. Produce sporadically and you starve. The whole 'starving artist' thing is bullshit, too, but for a different reason. The women who are attracted to starving artists drift away as soon as the ramen noodles in a battered yard-sale pot on a one-element hotplate becomes ravioli Bolognese with a carafe of pleasant Chianti at The Olde Spaghetti Factory. They feed off the starving-chic thing like soul vampires; tossing the drained husks aside once prosperity shows up. Bitches. I've been called a 'pop whore', I've been abandoned at The Olde Spaghetti Factory, and I've been left for dead on the dark side of a dark highway on the darkest night of the year.

I came up here to die. Not at the Farm, specifically, because I couldn't do that to Rob and Sharon, or any of the other family members who had pleasant memories of the place. I may be a self-centred asshole but I'm not evil. No, my plan was to hang out here for a few days, say goodbye to my ghosts, then go find a giant oak next to the nearby Bruce Trail and slip a shiv up under my ribcage and into my heart. Hopefully quick, most likely painful, definitely final. Either the creative juices had to flow or the blood did. I was beyond caring which at this point.

Maybe I'm being dramatic, should suck it up, and push past the block, but dammit I was once a golden boy in the world of Canadian Literature. I won the Great Canadian Fable Contest with my tale of how some stupid beluga whale lost his colour and my name was in every Arts Section of every major paper in the country, thanks to the wire service that picked up the story. Leading into a radio interview I was even introduced as "Canada's Modern-day Aesop". A national television network's mid day news show called and wanted to send a crew out to interview me. I was on a roll. Solid gold.

Then Palestine heated up, the Federal Budget came down, and too bad, so sad, the news crews were suddenly needed elsewhere. My moment in the sun was done. Five minutes of fame gone in a puff of smoke. The ghost of Andy Warhol owed me ten fucking minutes.

Since then I've written and written and written. I did some Three-Day Novel Contest where you write a novel over the Labour Day long weekend. One-hundred-and-eighteen pages... of crap. Then I wrote some short stories—all crap. I started a 'distinctly Canadian' sci-fi novel and... pedestrian crap, in space.

All crap. So I pulled out my camera, took a few thousand scenic shots and sold a few for postcards, calendars and books. Even sold one to National Geographic for a calendar. After that, a few weddings and then... crap. Less than crap—nothing. Which was fine, no problem because I had another back-up plan. I started painting, teaching myself how to work with acrylics. Still-lifes, abstracts, photo-realism and stuff somewhere in the middle. I sold two pieces. The rest has been shoved into an armoire and is... everyone together now... crap. I think that's the one that hurts the most, because painters run in the family. My grandmother Katie was a friend and contemporary of Georgia O'Keefe, and Katie's daughter, my Aunt Jane, was best known for her murals of Disney characters in space suits in the surgery recovery areas of the local Children's Hospital. I can draw, I can paint, but without inspiration... crap.

Then marriage, alcohol, accident, and the biggest crap of all.

I shoved the notebook away from me and it bumped into the ceramic mallard duck saltshaker, which jostled the peppershaker mallard next to it. They looked like they were waddling on the table top and I smiled for the second time that day—a rare thing. As a little kid I used to sit at this table and have conversations with these two shakers.

I looked around at the place and there seemed to be an otherworldly atmosphere that wasn't there a couple minutes ago. The Farm has always had an incredible, warm light, but right at that moment the air seemed oxygen-richer and the pine seemed to have a little extra inner glow, and there was a shit-load of pine. The antique spinning wheel was pine, the expandable dining table and the spindle chairs were pine. The frame of the dining room window overlooking the patch of lawn where my mother once saw a garter snake while hanging laundry on the line and screamed like a forty-foot tarantula had crested the hill and was bearing down on her—pine. The book shelves, the kitchen cabinets, the lathe-turned lamps... pine. The place was all blonde pine, wool blankets and homemade quilts. The Farm was the real deal that L.L. Bean shoppers spent small fortunes trying to emulate.

Leaving the S & P Mallards to ponder the lone word inscribed on the page, I picked up my double-shot of Crown Royal and drifted over to the pine rocker waiting in front of the fireplace like the set of The Friendly Giant kids' show.

Rye and a rocking chair—so apropos for someone feeling so much older than forty. All I needed was one of my late Uncle Roger's prized hunting Labrador retrievers at my feet and his well-worn pipe in my hand and the picture would be complete. The tobacco would be sweet and the lab would be curled up on the oval rug that looked like it was made of braids of cotton fabric wound in a tight spiral and stitched together. I'm sure there's a proper name for the technique but right now I don't give a shit.

I leaned back in the chair, heartened by the wood-on-wood creaking as my weight shifted in it. Man, I was exhausted. Not long-weekend-bouncing-in-the-sack exhausted, but a bone-weary, soul-drained, end-of-the-road exhausted. I revelled in the smoothness of the rye and remembered my one and only trip to the Seagram's Distillery in Waterloo where they make the elixir. I'd gone to hear W.O. Mitchell read from his novel, Roses Are Difficult Here because studying his Jake and the Kid in Grade Ten was what made me want to be a writer. I told Mr. Mitchell as much when I met him after his reading. When I asked him to sign my copy of Jake and the Kid he wrote "To Joe. Don't ever quit. Bill." Don't ever quit. A lot easier to say than do some days, someday being today. They said it would get easier. They said I would learn to cope. They are idiots.

Gravel crunched under tires as a car passed by, going from the Robertson place out toward the main road. I looked up, sort of hoping the driver would stop, but they didn't. My eyes settled on a brightly-toned oil painting of the pond and the jetty. I could see the signature from the rocker and it was one of my grandmother's oils. She'd painted up here, then. On the opposite wall was one of my Aunt Jane's paintings, this one of the Farm nestled in the red maples of fall so characteristic of an Ontario autumn. Inspiration and creation, perception and interpretation, here in the spritely woods, between Something Mills and Whatchamacallit Landing—and me coming up bone-ugly dry. I took another sip and got nothing. The glass was dry, too. I was thirsty so I abandoned the rocker and escorted the tumbler back to the kitchen. The car drove past again, going the other way, back towards the pool. Someone had probably just gone down to the main road to check the mail.

Despite my wishes, the glass didn't magically refill itself so I did it manually, tossing in a couple cubes from the old aluminum tray in the freezer. A long sip of the Crown Royal and my cockles warmed with a jolt. I returned to the table, as much for the silent company of the Mallard boys, Drake and Donald, than for access to the pad and pen.

The two five-inch-tall shakers waited expectantly, Drake sitting up tall and proud and Donald leaning forward, neck stretched out as if he were looking at the pad. Their colours were vibrant and the high-gloss finishing glaze reflected the soft north light coming through the window. A small, indistinct, shadow flashed across the window but by the time I looked up, whatever it was had passed by. Probably a sprite. Or a red-winged blackbird headed for the bulrushes ringing the pond. It was definitely not that world-devouring garter snake.

I'm easily distracted at the best of times and with fuzzy Crown-Royal-and-pot-edges my attention was bouncing all over the place. A light 'clinking' of ceramic on ceramic drew me back to the table. Donald Mallard was still pointing bill-down at the paper but now even Drake seemed to be glaring at it. Had I reached for the tumbler and nudged the peppershaker instead? Did it matter? Not a whit.

Just to make the two of them happy, though, I picked up the pen, took a sip of quickly-chilling amber fire and... nothing. Not a goddamned thing. I spun the gold band on my finger. Through the open window I could hear the sprites' giggling nearby and a pair of frogs down by the pond loudly discussing the situation in the Middle East, but that's it. Except for the tires approaching on gravel again. I leaned to the right and glimpsed a flash of blue as the Subaru drove past.

"Rose", I said. Then I wrote it. I crossed out the smart-ass "BLANK" and drew a circle around "Rose". Then I wrote "dark blonde", "fit" and "thirtyish" in a list to the right of "Rose". My hand tingled, my buzz faded, and my focus tightened. I circled the list and joined it to the first circle with a single line. Wow. Words. It felt great! "borrowed Blue Subaru", "deep blue eyes" and "blue lady lost", each within their own circles, joined back to the first one. Then "angry husband", "running away" and "Robertsons". Good! My imagination was getting into the game. The Robertsons had lost a son when the Twin Towers went down so "9/11" got its own little spot off to the side, leaving room for expansion.

It went on like that for an hour, though I slowed periodically to manifest a link rather than just scribble spontaneously. The page wasn't quite full when I grabbed a clean sheet and started the story. The pen squiggled and squirmed and even fought me once or twice, but three hours later I wrapped up a good solid first draft before taking a break. I needed to crack my knuckles, stretch my back and empty my bladder. Thirsty as hell, I picked up the barely touched tumbler but halfway up I caught a whiff and gagged. The rye hadn't changed, just my need for it. On the way to the bathroom I dumped the glass out in the kitchen sink—a hanging offence in my family—and pulled my steak out of the fridge. I'd planned to barbeque it up as a last meal, but now it seemed better suited to a celebration.

*** 

That steak... how can I describe a steak that tastes like life? How can a slab of dead cow rump taste like a spiritual cleansing? What the hell does a spiritual cleansing taste like? I suppose it wasn't really the steak, or sobering up, or even the long, steady piss that preceded both the steak and the sobering up, that rewired whatever synapses had been misfiring in my head for at least the last two years. Whatever it was, I felt like most of the crap had been purged, like an intellectual high colonic enema. I flipped through the eighteen pages of the Rose story, squared them up by tapping the bottom of the stack on the table, and then I set the tale down in front of the Mallard Brothers.

"Read it or don't read it, boys—either way, it's written, and that's what counts. I'm going out to have a nap in the sun-room." And I did, curled up on the wicker sofa, embraced by the flowered cushions, lulled by the buzz of insect wings on the breeze, frog croaks at the pond, sprite laughter in the grass, and soft duck chatter from the top of the dining room table.

***

When I woke up, the sun was hanging just above the hills to the west, waiting for its cue to drop out of sight and give the moon its moments to shine. The sprites would be back at the circle now, settled down for the night. At first I thought it was a woodpecker knocking away on a sappy pine that woke me, but the sound wasn't quite right. There was a domestic hollowness to it and after another ten seconds or so I clued in that someone was politely knuckle-rapping on the wooden screen door. Without sun, the sunroom was seriously chilly so it took no effort at all for me to get my ass off the sofa and to the door.

"Hey Rose."

"Do bitter scribes drink beer, or is that redundant, pretty much part of the definition?" She held up a cold, sweaty five-of-six-pack of cans all linked together by a plastic ring thingy.

"No, some of us actually drink rye."

37

"Ah, you take being bitter seriously."

I motioned to one of the two wicker chairs on the one-step-up porch and plunked my ass down in the other one. She sat, twisted a can of Molson Export out of its ring and held out the conjoined remaining four. I waved them off and shook my head. "I did. Past tense."

"My oh my. Sounds like you've turned a corner."

The nap had finished sobering me up and it felt pretty good. "Nothing lasts forever, even bad habits."

She smiled. Her nose crinkled and her bright eyes squinted just a little, which seemed to make them sparkle in the dusk. A soft, miniature quack came from inside, through the screen door. Rose didn't seem to notice but I sure as hell wondered what was going on in there.

"Didn't you used to say that there's no Hobbit like a bad Hobbit, Joe."

I laughed, partly because of the memory of my goofy youth but more to cover a longer series of tiny quacks. "You have a great memory."

Quack. Shit! I'm entertaining the woman I once thought was my soul mate outside while inside two ceramic ducks are quacking at me. I jumped to my feet. "Give me a second to turn off the TV and you can tell me all about it." I darted back into the house and charged straight for the table where the Mallard Boys stared up at me. I was about to whisper at them to shut up when I noticed that Drake was standing on my sketchpad. What the hell?! I'd left it in my bag, next to my camera. Donald stood next to a pencil—the Staedtler Mars one that had been in the side pocket of the bag.

"You two are seriously screwing with my head," I whispered. "Knock it off!" They stared up, all peppery innocence and salty charm. Then I understood, and my hand twitched. I picked up the pencil and grabbed the pad with the other hand. Unbidden, my mind's eye suddenly saw a future sketch of Rose, sitting on the porch with her feet tucked up under her and the beer can balanced on her knee.

I took the pad and pencil back out to the one-step-up stoop. Rose was gone. So was the little blue Subaru, the tire ruts in the gravel semi-circular drive, and even the severed dandelion head. I laughed, long and hard, there in front of the Farm as dusk became night. Then I turned back to the two culprits on the pine table and I asked what I couldn't not ask. "So, what's real and what's not?"

"All of it and none of it. Does it matter? You're a writer. Use it all." Muses. It turns out I have two of them and they're ceramic ducks who live in a gentleman's farm, guarded by sprites.

oOo

# The Mighty Inuksuk

**Not Previously Published:**

I wanted to write a unique Canadian superhero story that didn't involve hockey, donuts, or maple syrup, with a hero whose power was cool to others, but not cool enough for him.

~~~

## The Mighty Inuksuk

David was sure he was going to die. His nose was clogging from the dust on the dirty rag stuffed in his mouth, through which he desperately sucked in air. He was going to suffocate in the stinky-ass trunk of some pervert's car just because he didn't hear the guy sneak up on him. As he panicked, his mind jumped through random thoughts, none of which might help him escape; that they'd find his mutilated body in Lake Ontario, that he'd worn his new suit before his *seudat mitzvah* and it would be ruined, and that when they found him covered in shit and blood his mother would be disappointed that he hadn't the sense to die with dignity.

He twisted his head from side to side, trying to shake the rag out, but it wouldn't budge. He tried spitting it out, but it was in too deep. He was getting woozy, blacking out, dying. He kicked the lid of the huge trunk, wishing he had superpowers he could call on to just boot the damned thing open. He kicked and kicked, but he was running out of air and his kicks were pretty feeble. The car jerked as it came to a stop and the trunk popped open. One of the doors opened and slammed, but before he could make a break for it in his wobbly condition, the trunk lid was yanked up and a burly silhouette blocked his way.

"Oh no! You're turning blue!"

The rag was pulled out of his mouth and he gulped in air as fast as he could. Thank God he wasn't going to die in that stink-ass trunk. Then the silhouette pulled his fist back and punched David so hard that the whole world went black.

\*\*\*

*Five Years Later:*

David and Scotty hadn't seen Adam in days, which meant that they hadn't eaten in that long, either. He was famished, but David could still think clearly. He grabbed the chain that ran from Scotty's ankle manacle, through the ring on his manacle, and into the hole in the wall. He pulled hard, and the fire-bell-like alarm bell sounded immediately. Scotty jumped up, furious.

"What the hell are you doing?! Father is going to beat us!"

"He's *not* our father, and we haven't seen him in three days. If he's gone away, then this is our chance." A faint white glow appeared around the hole where the chain disappeared into the wall. David blinked, thinking that it was sunlight being reflected off something else in the barn.

"Davey, it could be a trick. Maybe Father just wants to see what we'll do if he leaves us alone. I don't want to disappoint him."

For a kid twice his size, David thought, Scotty was such a big coward. He always seemed to be more concerned about their captor's feelings than with escaping. "In five years Adam has never gone more than a day without checking on us. I've survived every beating so far and I'm willing to risk it. This may be our *only* chance, ever." He tugged on the chain but the alarm continued to sound.

"Your family has forgotten you! After five years they

think you're dead, dumped in Algonquin Park probably. That's what my mother thinks. I know it. Father is all we have now."

"My family would never give up. I'm going home. I *need* to get home." He tugged on the chain and the light around the hole grew brighter. He braced his feet and put his meager weight into it. He'd always been a scrawny kid, but there was no damned way he was going to let that stop him. It's now or never. He walked the chain toward the hole, gathering up the slack. It went taut on the other end, where it was locked to the ring on Scotty's manacle. "Are you going to help?"

"No. I want you to stay." The alarm bell continued to clang away.

"Stay? Are you nuts?"

"Stay, Davey. Father will come back. I need you to *stay*."

Suddenly David *did* want to stay. There was something in Scotty's voice that reassured him and made him simply wanted to sit and wait for Adam. For *Father*. The scar on his back itched. Father had carved an 'A', like a brand, shortly after he dragged him from the trunk of the Lincoln. The scar didn't usually bother him, but suddenly it felt freshly carved. He fought back a scream.

Then the white light pulsed blindingly bright on the chain, right where his hands were. The burning pain of the brand and thoughts of staying on the farm became dust and blew away. "Fine." He said through clenched teeth. "Stay." He grabbed tight to the chain and ran away from the hole. When he got to the end of the slack he was jerked up and off his feet. The chain held strong. The light pulsed around the hole. David got up, shook it off, walked in more slack, tightened his grip until his knuckles turned white, and ran. He sprinted like the Devil himself was coming for him.

The chain tightened and jerked him off his feet, but this time something in the hole gave way and as he crashed to the floor of the barn, the end of the chain popped out of the hole, and clanked onto the floor beside him. Incredulous, he sat up and pulled the chain through the ring on his manacle until he was free. He stood, his legs weak, his hands trembling. After five years of being chained up, forced to do chores during the day and kept like an animal in the barn at night, they were free.

Sunlight streamed through the east window, an invitation to go outside. The white light that had illuminated the chain now shone like a path in front of him, leading to the side door. He followed it. The manacle on his ankle, above his shoe, clanked. He barely noticed it.

"Davey, don't leave me!"

"You're free, Scotty," he called over his shoulder. "Go home."

"This *is* home. *Our* home."

"Hardly." He followed the path of light outside, squinting to see it in the bright sun. It grew even brighter, as if it knew he needed it to.

"DAVEY!"

David kept walking. There was something dark and dangerous in Scotty's voice, and something warm and trustworthy about his newfound path. He lifted his chin, clenched his fists in determination, and marched. He followed the path of light east, into the orchard. It veered right, then back left. He followed it exactly. Then he saw the almost hidden steel teeth of the leg trap, waiting. He knew there were dozens of them around the property, but Adam had always led the two of them safely around the traps. Now his light did that. He followed it, through the orchard and eventually out onto the road. His path led to the left, so he followed it until he came to a sign. "Chalk River 2km. Atomic Energy of Canada Ltd." The lighted path pulsed for his attention and led down the road. David walked.

\*\*\*

*Another Two Years Later:*

The mirror stared back, accusingly. David started his

speech again. "In 2008, fifty-six Canadian children were abducted by people they didn't know. I was one of them. My name is David, and today your principal, Mrs. Juno, has asked me to come talk to you about this great new project to keep you safe on the sheets of... the *streets* of Toronto... Holy shit this speech sucks." He balled up the printout and dropped it into the wastebasket next to the toilet.

"Kids, I wasn't 'abducted', I was *grabbed* from the streets by a complete stranger, torn from my home and family, and *kept chained in a barn saturated with nuclear spill groundwater* for five years. I only escaped because, according to the police who went back there to investigate, my abductor, Adam, died of a heart attack in the comfort of his farmhouse while Scotty and I were chained together in the barn. I broke free and ran. I got away and back to my family.

"When the police questioned Scotty, it turned out he really was Adam's son. It was his home, and since he was over eighteen, they couldn't make him leave. How that sick bastard Adam could chain up his own son is beyond me. Scotty calls me every couple of months, but I haven't seen him in person since I escaped."

Frustrated, he splashed cold water on his face, rubbed his closed eyes vigorously, then shuffled into the small bedroom, where he grabbed the phone and punched in the only number he'd never forget. Thankfully, after five rings he only got the voicemail.

"Mom, it's David. About that presentation we're making to the school kids next week. I'm sorry, but I can't read that speech you wrote. I'll put something of my own together. Don't worry. I'll see you at *shul* on Saturday. Give Dad a hug for me." He hung up and tossed the phone onto the bed. "Dammit." He started for the living room, but a full-body shiver shook him hard and threatened to knock him down. His superstitious mother would say that someone had just walked across his grave, but *he* knew that someone was lost and in danger. He knew it with absolute certainty, because *that* was his freaking nuclear waste-caused 'super' power, to sense their danger, their *need*, and be sucked out of his body and to wherever it was they were, to guide them to safety, by following the same light that had helped him escape the farm.

He could fight it and not go, but he was The Mighty Inuksuk, guiding people to safety like a man-shaped pile of rocks on a Canadian Arctic horizon. The name was Uncle Murray's idea when he told him about the path of light and everything, after his first out-of-body 'rescue' where he'd guided a little girl to help after she survived a plane crash that killed the rest of her family. "Super Dave and Captain Canuck are both taken, kiddo, and you gotta pick something. Inuksuk is original, and as Canadian as it gets."

"HELP! GRAMPAPA! MAMA! HELLLLP!"

The cry for help sounded so close, but he knew it was his power, magnifying the urgency. David stumbled into the living room, pulled his hood up, and dropped onto the old couch. A second later he was out of his body and on his way.

\*\*\*

Rahim Naji knew he was going to get smacked when he got back to the motorhome. First, he went off without telling anyone, and then he spent the last of his holiday money on admission down to the beach to see the giant 'Flower Pot Rocks' Grampapa Ahmad had been on and on about the whole trip. Rahim was almost eight, and smart enough to know how to use his sister's iPhone to look up the Bay of Fundy and get directions from the campground to the beach on the shore of the Atlantic.

Rahim just wanted a quick look. It was a beach, how dangerous could it be? But now the water was starting to rise. Some of the fastest rising tides in the world, the website said. The water wasn't deep yet so Rahim ran for the stairs that led up to the top, except that there were no stairs, at least not where he was looking. The water rose fast, sloshing over his Reeboks, and now almost to his knees. He felt the current pulling at him, threatening to pull him out into the ocean to the sharks and squids. He turned and slogged slowly back the way he came. "HELP! GRAMPAPA! MAMA! HELLLLLPP!"

"This way, Rahim!"

\*\*\*

Rahim spun around. "Grampapa?" He couldn't see anyone in the bright sunlight.

"No Rahim." David concentrated and felt his presence grow stronger on the New Brunswick beach. "I'm *here.*"

"Mighty Inuksuk?!" Rahim laughed, whipped out his phone and snapped a picture. "You saved me, Hero Inuksuk!"

"Not yet, buddy. You need to hurry. Run as fast as you can, that way!" David could clearly see on the surface of the water the white path Rahim had to follow, but it was flickering in and out. The tide was rolling in too damned fast. "Rahim, run!" The boy looked confused, clearly not understanding that David couldn't simply fly him to safety. "Rahim, follow me now or die!" In his mind, David ran as fast as he could along the flickering white path. A quick glance over his shoulder showed Rahim hesitate, and then wade after him as fast as he could manage. The bright path went dark for a moment and then appeared again, and David realized that he had to try something else.

"Keep running Rahim! Don't stop for anything! I'm going to get help! Okay?"

The boy nodded and David left the beach. He willed his mind to find the cliff top, the top of the stairs. He found himself in the middle of the parking lot, surrounded by people sauntering to their various vehicles. "Help! Somebody!"

Heads turned. One dude about his own age, with dreads and a nose ring was having a smoke next to an SUV with a pair of sea kayaks strapped to the top. "Inuksuk?! Cool! What's up, man?"

David was sure they would be too late. "There's a boy, Rahim, on the beach, caught by the tide. He's going to die. I'll guide him as close to the stairs as I can get him. Quick!" He willed himself back to Rahim.

At first David couldn't see the boy, but then he heard a sputtered cough and found Rahim clinging to the rocks. The tide sloshed at him, shoving his tiny frame against the reddish bluff. David was too late.

"Mighty Inuksuk!" Rahim smiled. He trusted the not-so-super hero to save him and there wasn't a damned thing David could do but watch him die.

"Hey, buddy. How you doing?"

"The water is cold."

"Yah, I'll bet it is."

"So, where is the white walkway?"

"The what?"

"The way you're going to take me to safety. What I read about on the internet."

"Oh, the path." He looked around but there was just ocean and rock and a boy filled with faith that his wannabe rescuer didn't share. "Um, it's..." Then he saw it. It was spotted, on the rock face. He could see shallow handgrips for Rahim. "It's right there, buddy! Turn around and face the rock. You gotta climb, and I'll tell you where to put your hands."

"Climb?"

"Up! Out of the water! Quick. Right hand up, a few inches further, more to the right. There! Grab hold! Good! Left hand up past your right, now a little to your left. Five more inches... there! Grab!" For the next minute David guided Rahim slowly up the rock while the tide bounced off the boy and tried to drag him away. David started to believe Rahim was going to be okay when suddenly the white-illuminated handholds stopped. They were nowhere near the top but David couldn't see Rahim's path to safety any more. So close! He could see that Rahim was exhausted. He was only a kid after all, and David was trying to get him to climb a goddamned cliff! He closed his eyes and tried to imagine his projected hands getting solid enough to lift David, but no such luck.

"I FOUND THEM! Hang on kid, I'm right here! Right behind you, Inuksuk!"

David opened his spectral eyes as the smiling dude from the parking lot paddled up in his kayak and grabbed Rahim right off the rock. There was a moment when David was sure the awkward weight would roll the craft, or the tide would slam the two of them into the rock, but the dude had some mad skills, and got pushed off and out into open water. He smiled at David.

"Can you make sure there's someone at the stairs to give me a hand? Meet you there in a couple." He paddled off with Rahim laughing and splashing and enjoying himself way too much for someone who'd just been facing death.

David went to the top of the stairs and found a human chain of rescuers waiting for the dude to return. "He got him." The waiting throng turned to him. "They're safe and should be here any minute now."

"Thank God you were here, man!"

A camera clicked, and then another. Raised phones snapped his photo repeatedly. He smiled shyly and pulled his hood lower over his face. "Glad to help, folks."

Just then the kayaker arrived with Rahim, and everyone forgot David, which was just fine with him. Once he was sure everyone was going to be safe, his awareness was yanked back to his body in Toronto, where he immediately fell into a deep sleep.

*** 

"So, where were you *this* time?"

"Uhn? What?"

"Where... were... you... this... time... *hero boy*?"

David pulled his hood back, shook off his disorientation, and looked around. He was at home, in his dingy apartment. That was his signed and framed Captain Canuck poster, that was his cheap-ass retro lava lamp, and that was Sondra, leaning back against the kitchen counter with her arms folded and her emotional armour welded shut.

"New Brunswick. The Bay of Fundy." He picked up a

mug from the second-hand coffee table and checked the contents—water. He drank it all, not caring that it was room temperature.

"What was it this time? A busload of seniors in a wreck? A Mormon family stuck in a well?"

Sondra's sarcasm wasn't lost on David but he chose to ignore it, as always. "A boy stuck on the beach as the tide was rising."

"Ooh, I'm all a-tingle. Must have been the rescue of the century."

"Why are you here, Sondra?" He tried to push himself up off the couch but was still too weak. He flopped back down. "You said you were leaving me."

"I am. But I wanted to make sure you know I'm taking the cat, just so you don't think he got out and do something stupid like try to find him with your stupor-power." She held out an envelope, obviously torn open. "And I wanted to give this to you in person." She tossed the envelope at him and it fluttered to the floor, short of the mark. "Your grant has been cancelled. Time to go get a real job."

"What?!" David retrieved the envelope, yanked out the letter, and read it. "Dammit."

"Oh, and I took a phone message for you. You know, it wouldn't kill you to get voicemail or at least Call Display so I don't have to waste my time answering calls that aren't for me."

"You took a message?"

"Yah. The landlord called to say that your rent cheque bounced. Second time this year. You've got two days to get him cash or you're going to be Inuksuck of the Streets."

A deep breath helped David from taking the bait and letting Sondra drag him down into her world of cynicism and negativity.

"Now, if you'll excuse me, Less-than-Mighty Inuk*suck*, I have a life to get back to while you astrally project your stupid ass everywhere but here, where it was needed most." She picked up the cat kennel and left.

Smoothing out the envelope, David barely heard her

slam the door on her way out.

\*\*\*

Twenty minutes later David was still on the couch, staring at the envelope. Between being beaten up by Sondra's anger and exhausted from saving Rahim, there was no way he could handle arguing with some civil servant about money he really didn't deserve anyway. The phone rang somewhere in the apartment, startling him. "Shit!"

He found the phone on the third ring. "H...h...hi. Um, hello."

"David? It's Peter Dutton from the Times. I just got an email from a hiker you guided to safety in the Blue Ridge Mountains a few days ago. He didn't know how to reach you so he emailed me at the paper, figuring that if I wrote that article about you last week then I'd know where you were."

"You didn't tell him..." David didn't want anyone seeing the crappy digs he lived in.

"No way. Your real identity is still safe with me. I'm Skyping him tomorrow. You're welcome to join in or, if not, how about a statement for the article?"

"A statement?" He looked at the crunched-up envelope. "Tell everyone to buy a GPS because The Mighty Inuksuk is done showing them the way to safety."

"What? You've lost your powers?"

"No. Worse. My funding. My grant was cancelled, thanks to the current Canadian government's disdain for the Arts."

"Oh shit."

"Yah. And I had to find out from my now-ex-girlfriend, just before she walked out the door with the cat."

"That's harsh."

"What can I say? She's a bitch."

"So you're quitting?"

"I don't have much choice. I have to pay the rent and I'm not sure if radioactive mutants qualify for Welfare."

"Shit."

"You said that." He stifled a yawn. "Anyway, Inuksuk had a tough one today and I need to get some food and some sleep. When you Skype Eduardo, please tell him that I'm glad he got home to his family okay."

"Of course, David."

"Thanks." He hung up and drifted into the kitchen to see if Sondra had left him anything to eat.

***

Two fish sticks and some instant rice later, David was ready for another nap. He stretched out on the couch. "Ginsberg! Come here, crazy cat." Then he remembered that Sondra had taken Ginsberg with her. "Shit." He closed his eyes and concentrated on the sound of traffic rolling past. A scooter horn honked pathetically, and someone yelled 'asshole'. "Ah, Toronto the Good." A second later he was sound asleep.

***

He drifted awake just before noon, with the phone ringing. "Hello."

"David. Peter Dutton again. I'd hoped for another exclusive interview with you but I see you've been hard at it and couldn't wait for me to talk to Eduardo." David was still half asleep and the reporter wasn't making sense.

"Not at all. I can wait."

"A little too late for that, my friend. The Mighty Inuksuk has gone viral."

"What?"

"Young Rahim's rescue is all over YouTube, Facebook, Twitter, and Flickr. Between you and Billy with the kayak, there are at least two hundred thousand hits on YouTube alone. You're a hero, David, and the world needs heroes. It always has—even an astral-projecting, English Lit Major."

"Yah, I suppose. But I have to pay the bills."

"You're sure about quitting?"

"Yes sir. I have to get a real job. Even my therapist suggested it last week." There was a firm knock at the apartment door. "I've got company, Mr. Dutton. Can we talk about this later?"

"Sure thing."

"Thanks." He hung up. With the phone still in his hand he leaned in to look through the peephole, but a path of light suddenly appeared at his feet, leading away from the door, toward the kitchen.

"What the...?"

"Davey, aren't you going to let me in?" Even through the thick door, David recognized Scotty's voice. This time, though, it sounded fuller, different from the phone calls. He reached for the deadbolt to unlock it and let Scotty in, but a blinding light flashed just before he touched the lock, stunning him. The lock was now cast in shadow, while the light at his feet pulsed even brighter, almost frantically.

"C'mon, Davey. Offer me a coffee."

David wanted to open the door. He *needed* to open the door...but the light couldn't be ignored. He needed his feet to move and was trying to move them, but some external force was fighting him and it felt like he was dragging his feet in mud.

"You can't run, Inuksuk. Right about now you're discovering my super power. People come to me whether they want to or not. Just call me the Pied Piper. I've come to take you back to the farm, and one of your neighbours has even agreed to join us. "

Eventually David's feet *did* move. He put his left one on the light, and then pulled the right one up and over and down. Soon he was following it through the kitchen, straight to the pantry. The path flashed faster and brighter so David ducked into the small pantry and quietly closed the narrow door. The moment the latched clicked, the path became a circle around his feet indicating that he should stay put. Not a heartbeat later, there was a loud thump of a heavy weight being thrown against the front door, followed by a horrific crash as the deadbolt gave way and the door smashed open.

"Davey, I'm here!" Scotty then lowered his voice, but David could make out most of it. "What a shit hole. I'd rather live in a barn. Stay here, kid." He heard Scotty clomping about, from room to room, then the circle of light under his feet shifted to the door and flashed madly. David exited the little pantry as quickly and as quietly as he could, following the path back through the kitchen and out to the remains of the front door. Next to the wreckage was twelve-year-old Jakob from across the hall, just standing there, looking dazed. He grabbed Jake by the sleeve and dragged him out into the corridor. The path flashed so quickly that they had to run to keep up.

David followed his path of light to the stairwell as fast as he could, without question. Once on the dimly lit stairs, he led Jake down the path of light, to the second floor, along the hallway, into the north stairwell, down to the sidewalk, and around back of a UPS truck parked at the curb. The path became a disk and David nervously stepped onto it and waited, holding tight to Jake. He heard the hissing airbrakes of an approaching city bus and nearly bolted from cover to catch it, but for the briefest moment his saving light flashed red. He froze.

"Davey, come out and play..."

Scotty had already figured out where they were. Damn.

"Come here, boys."

David felt an invisible tug, a strange desire to turn around and go to Scotty, to see what he wanted. Jakob pulled at him, trying to return to the Pied Piper. David's light disk flashed red again then returned to a slow, pulsing white. He heard a boot scuff on the sidewalk. Scotty was really close. The red and white bus drove past, that opportunity now lost. He sighed, and almost didn't hear the second boot scuff, or see the path take off and lead him around the courier truck and into traffic.

"Davey! I see you both! C'mon back, Mighty Inuksuk!"

The path flashed fast and tight beside the brown-on-brown truck, so David scuttled along with Jake, following it while traffic flowed past what seemed like only inches away.

"Davey!!"

David risked a glance back over his shoulder. Scotty was just edging around the front of the truck, a foot-long Bowie knife in his hand. David had seen that knife before. It had carved the 'A' in his back. He didn't doubt Jake would get a brand, too, if he let him get taken.

His path flashed hard and fast in a straight line for twenty feet, so David ran with Jake in tow, expecting the light to take him back to the sidewalk. Scotty was close behind, but David couldn't afford to look back again. He had to trust his radiation-mutated power. They got to the end of the flashing strip and it just ended in another circle. They had to wait?! He could practically feel the steel of the hunting knife between his shoulder blades. The path flashed red, then suddenly darted out into traffic. He followed, terrified, ready to piss his pants with fear. What he needed most, right now, was for the two of them to *just not be there.*

His saving light vanished. Right in the middle of traffic, it was gone. He looked around, frantic. It couldn't have just abandoned him! Then he saw it—a manically flashing disc alternating red and white, red and white, on the sidewalk on the south side of the street. A truck horn blasted at him, almost in his ear, and in that single moment he wanted nothing more than for him and Jake to be standing on that disk of light. That's *all* he wanted. To be safe.

And then they were. Instantly. One second they were about to die in traffic, and the next he *teleported* himself out of danger. "What the fuck did I just do?!" Behind him there was a screech of brakes, more horns, and a loud metal-on-metal crash and crunch. He spun around just in time to see Scotty step up onto the far sidewalk, where he threw David a crisp salute.

"You can't save them all, Inuksuk!" The Pied Piper disappeared into the gathering crowd, and Jake finally stopped resisting David's hold on him.

"Dammit. I should have known quitting the super hero biz wouldn't be so easy. Let's get you home to your mom, Jake."

oOo

# Blue-Black Night

**First Published:**
*Danse Macabre: Close Encounters with the Reaper.* Edge Science Fiction & Fantasy Publishing. 2012.

Written specifically for this anthology, the first draft of **"Blue-Black Night"** was written in ninety minutes during a break at work. Because most stories I've ever read or seen about Death are dark stories about the cloaked incarnation shuffling along with a scythe held tight in a skeletal hand, I wanted to write something different, so it is about music and the human heart. Yes, it's a love story.

The story was inspired by the Harry Chapin song, "I Want to Learn a Love Song", which is about how he met his wife, Sandy. It's also set in one of my favourite places in the USA—Southern Utah.

~~~

## Blue-Black Night

It was a cool Southern Utah evening and I was sitting on the front stoop of my rented trailer, strumming on my battered flat-top. I say 'battered', but even with worn strings, a missing pick guard and through-and-through bullet holes that have matching ones in the case from a long night in Buffalo, it was in a sight better shape than me. Granted, I have no bullet holes, but who needs them when you've got cancer?

"I want to learn a love song, Mark."

I looked up from the barre chord I was working on and nearly crapped my drawers. "Are you shi—kidding me?!" I was raised to not curse in front of a lady, especially a full-on beautiful one; even if that lady is Death. Yah, that's what I said. Death is a woman, and she wanted to me to teach her a love song.

"I'll pay you." She sat down next to me and vanilla drifted over to tickle my nose and tease me.

"No disrespect, miss, but money's not much use to me this late on." She knew what I meant. None of my friends or family would have had a clue because none of them knew the cancer was back. Matter of fact, none of them had seen me in at least six months; not since I stood up at Easter dinner and told them I was heading out the next day to tour with a buddy and his band. I was to be the show's MC, throwing out a little stand-up, a few song parodies, and keeping the boys out of all the small town jails waiting for 21st-century troubadours like us.

Of course there was no tour. There wasn't even a band. There was just my own Yamaha guitar, the Chevy and the wide-open state of Utah. And my tent, at least until I decided a few weeks ago to make my way to St. George and spend what time I had left with a roof over my head.

So, like I said, Death is a woman, at least to me. She's a pretty, pony-tailed brunette with dark-green eyes and a little gap between her front teeth. She wears a well-loved, baggy, soft denim shirt with just enough buttons undone that her cleavage taunts me. Her jeans are tight enough so as to not hide her cute little butt and loose enough that she could spend three days in them on a saddled chestnut mare following trails wherever they lead without chaffing or burning. And she's wearing sneakers. Simple, no-logo, timeless, white sneakers.

"What payment would you accept? I can't cure you, though I can help a little with the pain."

"I can't."

"Can't what? Teach me a love song?"

"No, I can't take payment."

"I insist."

She was a stubborn one, Death was, but I was no rookie

either. "You're hardly in a position to insist on anything."

"You do know who I am, don't you? The power I have?"

"I know exactly who you are. You've been standing just off to the side since I was a kid. With any face, in any shape, I'd know you."

"So then —"

"But I'm not taking payment. If you pay me, all you'll get is a song about love. If you just sit back and let me give you this one thing, then you'll get a love song, a song from my heart to yours."

She got real quiet for a moment, caught off guard most likely. It's nice to know that even Death can still be surprised.

"How do you know I've got a heart? I'm not exactly mortal, with blood coursing through my veins."

"A heart isn't about being a blood pump, and it doesn't matter whether you have one or not, because I do."

"Yes, you most certainly do." She gently placed her palm on my chest, over my heart. While she felt the rhythm of my life still beating, I noticed her long, slender fingers, her nails short, clean, and simple. She had good picker's hands, as my teacher used to say. Chord shapes would come easily to those fingers and picking would be sure and quick with practise.

"So, do you want to learn a song about love or do you want to learn a love song?"

"You'll teach me a love song?"

"I've been playing love songs for you for the past ten years or so, so I suppose it's time I teach you to play one yourself." I traverse-picked a simple G-C-D progression to punctuate my point, but she put a hand on the strings to still them.

"Back up a minute there. What do you mean, you've been playing love songs for me?"

"Just what I said. What's so tough to understand?"

"You're saying you love me?"

"Love you, in love with you—yes'm."

"You love Death?"

"Ever since the car accident. I saw you smile down at

me lying on the shoulder of the I-65 and when you shook your head to say 'not yet', I was hooked."

"But--"

"You're in my dreams, waking and sleeping. You're first in my thoughts in the morning and last in them at night. Everywhere I go, every happy laugh I hear, every taste that touches my tongue, every sunset I watch, you're with me. Every perfect moment I want to share with you and every imperfect, painful moment I lean on the knowledge that you aren't far away."

"You're just in love with this form, this face."

"Is it your form? Your face?"

"One of the many."

"Then that's part of it. But there's your essence, what makes you unique. Your light."

"I'm Death, Mark. My essence is death. My light is darkness."

"Not to me."

She wasn't getting it. She didn't know that love sees none of those things.

"You're not afraid?" she asked.

"Of what? Dying? I'm fifty-one. I've had more time than many and less than others. Now, do you want to learn a love song or not?"

"There's nothing I would rather do more. What did you have in mind?"

I have over a hundred songs in my repertoire, and probably a third are love songs of one sort or another. Croce's *Time in a Bottle*? Chapin's *Taxi*? Or The King's *Fools Rush In*. "One of my own, " I said. "One I wrote for you when I was finishing up chemo the last time."

"*Blue-Black Night?!*"

If I thought she'd lit up when she was feeling my heartbeat, then finding out I'd written Blue-Black Night for her made her go supernova. She glowed like there was no darkness left in the world, let alone the darkness that she carried with her.

"None other. Or would you prefer something more

popular? Some Michael Bublé?"

"Your song, please."

"Yes, ma'am."

"Call me...Jill."

What? No, I sure as Hell didn't see that coming. "Jill?"

"It's a twist on Giltinė, one of my many names."

After all these years I now had a name to go with the face. "Thanks."

I shifted my butt back to make room for her and patted the wood between my legs. Yah, I know how rude that sounds, but it's what I did, literally. "Sit here, please." I swung the guitar out of the way so she could sit but she just looked over at me and raised one eyebrow.

"Are you sure? I can see just fine from here."

"If we had two guitars a side-by-side might do, though I'd go for a face-to-face, but this old Yammy is all we've got so this is how it has to be."

She didn't move.

"Look, Jill, you're the one who wants to learn a love song. You opened that can of worms that is my heart so let's get past it."

"But--"

"Are you afraid I'm going to try and take advantage of you? Just because my heart's full of you doesn't mean I'm going to be anything less than a gentleman."

"I don't feel fear, Mark." She scooted herself up and over my left leg until she was sitting on the wood stoop in the V between my open legs. She leaned left and spoke at me over her right shoulder. She kept leaning forward so only her thighs touched mine. "It's just that this wasn't what I had in mind when I asked you to teach me. To be honest, I was really just hoping you'd play one for me. I really needed to hear you play."

Damn. "Had a long day and you needed a break so you thought you'd come taunt the dying folkie?"

"No! That's not it at all! Well, yes it's been a long day, but that's the nature of what I do. No, I was at the Long Island Expressway yesterday and was just thinking about a musician I had to take a few years back."

"Harry."

"Harry. And thinking about him made me think of you and then I realized that what I needed was to hear a love song, maybe even learn to play one."

"So no one is dying right now because you're here for a guitar lesson? Wow."

"Not quite." She looked out into the yard and I followed where she was looking. There was a sleeping hound, a prowling tabby and two sparrows. The tabby was stopped in mid-step and the sparrows frozen in mid-air.

"Wow. You stopped time?"

"Something like that." She leaned back into me, slowly, but trusting me now, for some reason.

"How long have we got?"

"As long as it takes to teach me, Mark."

She twisted around and kissed me on my unshaven cheek. Her lips were cool, but not cold. It was nicer than it shoulda been. I swung the guitar around in front of her and she placed her hands where they were supposed to be. "We'll keep it pretty simple. Start with the easiest chords that'll get the job done and go from there." I put three finger tips down on the strings and strummed her a G chord. "This here's a G and pretty much the underlying chord to the whole song. Give it a try."

I shifted my fingers up a fret but kept the chord shape and pretty little Death copied my finger position almost exactly. I lifted my fingers and strummed her chord. It was a bit off. I adjusted her fingers a tad to get them back from the brass fret then pressed them down a bit harder. I strummed it again and it sounded a whole lot better. "You've got the perfect fingers for this."

Then she leaned back into me and we fit together like it was pre-ordained or destined or something like that. My heart pounded, my head swam and I was thinking that I'd just died and gone to Heaven. That wasn't the case, though. The birds were still frozen in the air and Death-who-was-also-Jill still sat in my arms, learning to play a love song. My love song to her. I took a deep breath and got back to the task at hand. I'd been waiting for Death's arrival for a long time but now that she was here, I wasn't ready to stop or give up. There was at least time for one more song.

"The chorus is the easiest part so let me just sing it for you. You watch my left hand so you can start associating chord changes with the lyrics."

"Okay." She whispered it like she was afraid to break the moment, so I stopped talking and started singing, softly, in her ear, like I'd imagined ever since I wrote the song for her.

*It was a car wreck on the I-65,*
*that made me stick around.*
*It was the blue-black night and the light from her smile,*
*That kept my feet from touching the ground.*
*In the pouring rain, with the thunder growls*
*I walked on into Huntsville.*
*It was the blue-black night and the light from her smile*
*That lights my way and always will.*

I let the last chord fade away. She took my picking hand in hers and kissed it.

"Thank you, Mark."

"It's just an old-fashioned love song."

"But you wrote it for me. I can honestly say that it's a first."

"Not true. There are plenty of songs about you, about Death."

"They're usually about obsession with Death or fear of Death or taunting Death with the immortality of Youth. Never a love song."

"Then I suppose it behooves me to teach it to you."

"That would be the highlight of my eon."

\*\*\*

I can honestly say that I have no idea whatsoever how long we sat on that stoop like lovers, close and intimate, teaching and learning and making the stolen time our own. I felt more alive than I had in a long, long time. I suppose that's why I considered writing it all down in the old leather-bound journal I picked up in Sedona my last time through. Why? Beats me. Some nod to the immortality I didn't think I cared about? I've got a few other more personal thoughts in there, mostly about the cancer stuff that I just can't talk about to anybody. Some day someone'll read it, or it'll end up in a box, ignored. Either way, I won't care 'cause I'll be gone. Immortality is for, well, Immortals.

Jill stood, stretched the kinks out of her back, then turned and kissed me firmly on the lips.

"Time to go ?" I knew it was, but I had to ask.

She took my hands and pulled me to my feet. "Shall we sing while we walk?"

"Whatever your little heart desires, missy."

Then Death linked her arm through mine and we sang our love song as we strolled off into the blue-black night.

oOo

# Credibility

**Not Previously Published.**

Some stories just come out of nowhere, and Flash Fiction (usually no more than 1000 words) is especially susceptible to that tendency. I wanted to put as much about two people's relationship and personalities into a single, very short conversation as I could, and **"Credibility"** is the result.

~~~

## Credibility

"I want a divorce." Remo added another tablespoon of raw sugar to his steaming mug.

"But we're not married." Dana looked up from her laptop, raised one greying eyebrow above her reading glasses.

"Fine. Let's get married and THEN get divorced."

"What the hell are you talking about?" She leaned back, curious but doubtful. Remo was full of strange ideas, though few of them were ever thought through from beginning to end.

"Nobody takes single people seriously. If you haven't got at least one divorce under your belt then they completely discount your opinion on everything from politics to religion to grocery shopping."

She was wrong. He was being a moron again. "I'm not marrying you so you can divorce me and get some stupid cred in some stupid social standing that doesn't even matter."

"Excellent. Irreconcilable differences. Perfect grounds."

"Perfect grounds for *nothing*. We have to be married

before we get divorced and I'm not marrying your stupid ass if all you want to do is get divorced. You're a *retard*."

"Mental anguish, then. I know I drive you crazy day after day."

"No crazier than my kids do, and I'm not divorcing them."

"Sure you are. They've all moved out. Trial separation. One's already come home once and tried to reconcile."

"Get stuffed. Kids are supposed to grow up and move out."

"So are adults."

"What?! How much sugar have you had?"

"No, no, listen to me—I'm right. The leading cause of divorce is marriage. Most divorced couples would have stayed together if they'd never gotten married in the first place. *Marriage* broke them up."

"You are seriously screwed in the head. You were single far too long to have a clue what you're talking about."

"Exactly! But if I'm divorced, then people will nod and agree and think I was wise, because I'd already been through 'that hell'.

"If you want to go through hell, then keep up with the stupid conversations. I can guarantee you hell."

"Perfect! Abuse. Excellent grounds, too. Come on, we can come up with more if we try."

"How about if we get married and I become a widow?" She turned her attention back to her laptop and the blog post she'd been working on.

"No, it wouldn't work. People just feel sorry for widows, they don't really listen to them."

"Are you even listening to *yourself?* In order for me to become a widow, *you* would have to die. If you're dead, your cred will be worthless."

"Not if I weren't really dead. I could fake my own death. You'd still get to be the widow."

"And you would still have to leave town because you're supposed to be dead but you're not. I'm sure there's a felony being committed in there somewhere. So, the cred you got because you were dead would be useless because you couldn't be around the people you have the cred with." She gave up on the blog and closed the computer.

"I could email them."

"From beyond the grave?"

"Oh. Good point. Wanna shag, then?"

"Yah, sure. Works for me." *Occasionally* he had a good idea.

oOo

# Goodnight, Barstow! I Love You!

**Not Previously Published.**

Originally written for submission to an anthology about menopause (& rejected), this is my male attempt to give a character a place to vent.

~~~

## Goodnight, Barstow! I Love You!

Winnie leaned over the toilet in the bar bathroom and threw up. Again. She was terrified, but she'd faced fear before. Duke once said he faced fear every night. Her late husband of twenty years, Duke, had been a mediocre stand-up comic who eked out a meager living making fun of his—of their—life. For three of the last four years, he'd cracked wise about living with a 'menopausal demon'. Sometimes, Duke was a real asshole. From small town bars to corporate gigs, he went on and on about her getting hot flashes and giving him the cold shoulder, his drunk sweats versus her cold sweats, and mood swings like something out of The Exorcist. When he passed back through Barstow, she often sat in the audience and took his shit in silence, but that didn't mean she didn't want to go all 'praying mantis' on him and rip his head off. She moved to the sink to clean up.

She'd loved him once-upon-a-time, but the week she cleared her last hormonal hurdle was the same week she'd had to send him bail money up in Sacramento for another solicitation charge. She filed for divorce the next morning. Two days later, Duke died in a rollover on the Pacific Coast Highway, racing back to talk her out of it. Her period of mourning extended for exactly three days after the funeral. Considering his verbal abuse both on and off stage for the past ten years, three days was two more than he deserved.

That was a month ago. Tonight she was stretching her own wings and taking no prisoners, or would be as soon as she stopped throwing up. She'd seen Duke do it so often, she figured it couldn't be all that hard, and her priest told her that maybe it would be good therapy. Over the years, she'd thought that Duke was the weak one, and she was the strong one. She knew now that what she really was, was wrong. Terror twisted her gut.

The door to bathroom opened up a crack. "You're up, rookie." It was the headliner, the Seattle comedian two-dozen people had come to see on a rainy Wednesday.

"Got it. On my way. Thanks, Freddy." She stuck her mouth under the spigot, gulped in a mouthful of tepid tap water, swirled and spit, then did the same with her vodka cooler. Out in the bar, she heard the MC introducing her up on stage. She rushed out, weaved through the half-empty bar, and snatched the proffered microphone just as the MC told the audience to 'give it up for Winsome Kowalski'.

"Hello, Barstow!"

"You suck!" A young jerk from somewhere in the back.

She ignored the heckling, but felt the bile threatening to rise again. She refused to puke while she was facing a room full of complete strangers, dammit! "I just got back from an Assholes Anonymous Meeting. It turns out that I've been addicted to jerks for my entire adult life. It's a great group. They helped me lose 185 pounds of 'ugly weight'. Yup, they found me a divorce lawyer and now I'm single again." A lie, but Duke said most comedy was.

Some of the men groaned good-naturedly and most of the women laughed politely, but the older, chain-smoking server shouted out "Right on, sister!"

Winnie laughed and her confidence got the boost she needed. "Speaking of lawyers, what do you call a divorce lawyer on the bottom of the ocean?" She waited the obligatory beat, then tossed out "A good start."

The laughter was still sporadic, but the gaps were starting to fill in. The stoned MC had introduced her as a 'comedy virgin dying to pop her chuckle-cherry', and it was only five minutes of an open mic night, but she thought that she could get used to this. She was beginning to understand why Duke kept at this even when the gigs were few and only her chiropractic practice paid the bills. A long sip of her vodka cooler gave her a moment to refocus. "My ex husband was a comic. He used to bring our daughter to his shows for support. Well, she wasn't our daughter, she was our step-daughter." Quick sip. "No, that's not quite true. She was a hooker he paid $200 to call him 'Daddy' for the night."

The small crowd howled. One old boy at a scarred table near the stage spit out his mouthful of beer and slapped his knee. She had them right where she wanted them. It was time to ramp it up. "So, I'm officially post-menopausal, which, for you men, means that I'm done with the crazy years and you're safe...just so long as you don't make eye contact, and bring chocolate as an offering. To tell you the truth, that's how you should approach all women."

The server agreed. "Fuckin' A! You heard her, boys!"

"Thanks, honey." Always be nice to the wait staff, Duke had said. "I had the migraines, the mood swings, and this thing called 'formication', when it feels like your skin is crawling in ants. At least I thought I had it. Turns out Mr. Funnyman brought home a full family of crabs from one of his 'daughters'." Only a few laughs and a lot of groans. Oops.

"Too much information? You mean you don't want to hear about watery discharge, or decreased libido, boys? But I'll bet you'd love to hear how my tits swelled."

Laughs and one "Yah, baby!" from the buck in back.

"So I guess this officially makes me a cougar. Or does being post-menopausal make me a sabre tooth?" A light flashed at her twice from the back of the bar. She had one minute to wrap up her virgin set. "Although I don't do drugs, because I was married for over twenty years to Mr. Funnyman I do have something in common with Bob Marley..." She wasn't sure they were going to get her final joke here in the backwater of Barstow, but she was committed to it now. "We've both blown a little dope." Silence. "That's my—" The room erupted with laughter. It took a second, but they got it. "Goodnight, Barstow! I love you!"

Winnie sat in her condo's living room, picking through her Menopause Journal and still riding the adrenalin high from her clunky set. She'd started the journal as a resource for her blog, but now was finding unexpected material for the next time she got up on stage. Chiropractor by day, Comedy Queen by night; or at least every other Wednesday on Amateur Night.

She survived Duke. She got through menopause. Show business should be a breeze.

oOo

# Hanako's Life in a Tray

**Not Previously Published.**

A call in the local writing community went out for stories about The Green Man of legend and myth. Wanting to do something a little different about the caretaker of the forests, I tapped into my interest in bonsai trees and set this story in modern-day Japan. It was turned down by the editors because it didn't quite fit with the direction the anthology was going, but that's okay because it's still one of my favourite stories, and not just because I wrote the opening haiku when I was ten.

~~~

## Hanako's Life in a Tray

*"A fallen raindrop,*
*Ensnared by a spider,*
*Window on summer.*

"Very pretty, don't you think, Fuyuki-sensei?" Hanako refreshed her professor's cooling tea, steam pirouetting up from his cup to dissipate in the delicate, earthy air of Hanako's tiny Ichikawa City apartment.

"It is simplistic, without grace. Crass English haiku—a pale imitation of the true Japanese form. I had thought you could do better, Hanako-san."

'Hanako-san', not 'Hanako' or even 'Hanako-kohai'. A stiff honorific for this student from her professor. She hardly expected familiarity, even though Fuyuki had still been in the grad school when she started, but his chilly, superior tone rankled nonetheless. Hanako knew Fuyuki's faculty position at Wayo University elevated him above her station, not least in his own mind. The rising boy-genius of the department was her adviser, though, and she knew that getting through her master's program in Human Ecology would be a much easier task if she indulged his need to play his little power games. Her undergrad years had never seemed this silly. Well, almost never.

"It was a gift from my ten-year-old cousin in Chiba. Aoki wants to be a writer."

"He has a gift for scribbling cartoons, at best." He grabbed a leaf of one of Hanako's half-dozen lovingly tended bonsai trees, twisting it as if it were artificial and flexible. There was a little 'pop' and the miniature leaf of the Japanese red maple came off in his hand. "Or maybe he could tend tiny, stupid trees for stupid people with no lives." He dropped the leaf on the mat beside him.

Hanako fought the urge to shower Fuyuki Shinobu with very hot green tea. With great effort, she placed the teapot back on the tray and took a deep breath, forcing a smile. "Aoki would be happy to hear your praise. Getting famous from Manga would be a dream come true for him." For the tenth time in as many minutes, Hanako wondered if inviting her adviser to her home had been a bad idea. Her mother would say that it was improper for a young woman to invite a man home with no chaperone, but her mother was still very much a traditionalist with a few strange ideas of her own thrown in. Hanako's father, on the other hand, would have trusted his only daughter's instincts while still insisting on standing sentinel outside in the corridor to ensure that her honour was in no way at risk. The thought of her father with his arms folded, nodding seriously at her neighbours as they shuffled past her guarded door, brought a genuine smile to Hanako's lips. She promised herself that she would send her father a Happy-Saturday text after Fuyuki went back to his mirror and his life of self-grooming, or whatever it was he did with his spare time.

Inspiration struck! What this social disaster needed was cookies—she was sure of it. "Excuse me a moment, please, Fuyuki-sensei. I forgot the cookies. They are fresh-made... yesterday." She hopped up from the mat and slipped into the tiny kitchen, watching her guest out of the corner of her eye. She'd not even opened the cupboard for a plate when Fuyuki had his phone out and was texting something to someone. Probably something trite to someone equally banal, she thought darkly to herself. Oh well, a few more minutes of this social silliness and she would propose the change to her thesis, get Fuyuki's approval, and thank him for gracing her home with his presence.

As she arranged eight matcha-flavoured cookies on a plate she caught a glimpse of Fuyuki dumping his tea over the roots of the bonsai, the perfectly aerated soil quickly absorbing the hot liquid. She could almost hear the roots of the maple screaming in pain. This was enough silliness. Her thesis could wait until Monday. She nearly dropped the plate of cookies in her haste. "Fuyuki-sensei. Thank you so kindly for honouring my humble home with your visit. I don't want to take up any more of your valuable time."

The pompous ass looked up from his texting. "I thought you asked me here to discuss your thesis."

Hanako nearly slammed Fuyuki's now-empty cup on the enamelled tray and scooped the entire tea service up and away from the low table, ending the mini social moment. "Really, there is nothing that cannot wait until Monday during your office hours, Fuyuki-sensei. It was rude of me to impose on you like this." She retrieved his jacket from the coat tree and held it out to him.

*** 

Hanako poured another shot of Jack Daniels into her tea to give it a bit more oomph—a trick she'd learned from her father—and settled back in her beanbag chair.

"I thought your nephew's poem was beautiful." The voice was tiny and quite close by.

Hanako tried to spin around in the giant beanbag to

find the invader but got stuck. She plunked the cup of spiked tea on the floor, sloshing it on the grass mat, then levered herself up and around with both hands. "Who?"

"Up here, with Momiji-chan."

She looked around, panicked, but she was alone. Speakerphone?

"Over here, Hanako-san. I have to work quickly to help poor Momiji-chan."

Momiji? She could see her phone on the kitchen counter, but the voice came from the direction of the red maple tree.

"Down here, Hanako-san."

She squinted, and there it—he—was, standing ankle deep in the soil of the bonsai's tray. A little green man? It was miniature topiary, six inches tall, seemingly made of leaves and vines... until it moved and waved up at her. "Konnichiwa, Hanako-san!"

"Um, konnichiwa. Who? Uh, what?"

"Tomoki. Caretaker of bonsai. We have very little time. May I bother you for a pot of lukewarm water, please? I will answer all of your questions shortly." He reached out and placed a tiny, leafy hand on the trunk of the miniature, wind-swept red maple. "Patience, Momiji-chan, patience."

Hanako stumbled into the kitchen, filled a pot, felt the water, deemed it too cold, added a bit more hot, tested it again, and rushed it back to the little green man talking to one of her cherished bonsai trees.

"Put it here, please, Hanako-san, as close to the tray as you can." He pointed at the tabletop.

Hanako did as asked, afraid to speak, to break the spell, and find that it was really the whiskey talking to her. Tomoki sat down on the bonsai's soil, swung his leafy legs over the edge of the two-quart pot and into the water, and then dove both hands back and into the soil, as if reaching down to the roots. He leaned back and closed his eyes, much like Hanako had only a minute before on the beanbag chair, but he looked far more pained than she had. Hanako watched, fascinated. The little Japanese red maple had already started to droop from the effects of Fuyuki's hot tea, and when Hanako thought of the hours she had spent gently growing and grooming and shaping her beautiful miniature maple, it broke her heart.

She dragged her beanbag chair over to the table and sat, dazed and confused. Tomoki kicked his feet slowly forward and back in the pot of water, almost like he was enjoying himself. Then Hanako noticed that the water was changing colour. Clear when she put the pot down for the bonsai man, it was now turning the colour of tea. She leaned over, squinting, wanting to fetch her glasses but not daring to leave to find them. Swirls of tea came from Tomoki's feet. If she had to explain what she was seeing, she would have to sayTomoki was using his own body to draw the tea from the soil and into the water. Like a syphon. Or a leech, maybe. She was both disturbed and fascinated; and she couldn't take her eyes off of the spectacle.

After a few minutes, Tomoki pulled his hands from the soil and stood up. "Thank you, Hanako-san. I suggest you pour that water away and boil some fresh to sterilize your pot. Momiji-chan was poisoned not just by the tea, but also by that awful man's presence in your home. She says you should keep him away, and don't let your branches intermingle with his any more than you have to."

Hanako placed the pot in the sink, retrieved her own tea, and returned to the chair. "What are you, Tomoki-sama?"

The caretaker of bonsai hopped over to the shelf unit where the rest of Hanako's cultivated trees lived, inspecting them as he spoke back over his shoulder. "I am the Green Man, a guardian of the forest. I followed you around the Rose Garden in the Nature Park after I saw how you gathered small amounts of soil from different spots and spirited them away in your lunch box. I had no idea what you were doing until I saw one of Momiji-chan's tiny little red leaves clinging to your stocking. At once I knew you for a lover of bonsai, a kindred soul."

"You live in the Rose Garden?"

"I did, for a time. Before that I spent many, many

summers in the Imperial Palace in Tokyo, working amongst many friends and family. Excuse me a moment, I think Miye-chan here needs some help." He leaned over and opened his mouth. At first Hanako couldn't see what he was doing, but after a moment she saw leaves and vines spewing out of his mouth, covering the soil, and working their way up the tree's little trunk.

Tomoki continued. "I cared for the half-millennium-old, five-needle pine, Sandai-Shogunno Matsu, alongside venerable Shogun Tokugawa Iemitsu. Before Tokugawa-dono passed on, I promised him I would continue his work with his treasured pine, as well as the rest of the Imperial collection. For five hundred summers I kept that promise. Then, two summers ago I finally decided I was in dire need of a—what do you call it? A 'vacation'? Yes, a vacation. So I wandered from garden to garden, bonsai to bonsai, until I ended up in the Rose Garden."

"And now you are here, in my home."

"That I am, Hanako-san. You have done such beautiful work, caring for this little family. If you will permit it, I would like to do my part to help."

"I hope you don't want me to take them out and plant them in a park where they can grow properly and not in a tray?"

"Not at all. They are quite happy here. Miye-chan says you have a lovely singing voice, and they all prefer the scent of your cooking to the fumes of the world outside. My larger green brothers and sisters have no small task caring for the wood lots and parks and forests of the world, where the air and soil are full of such deadly toxins."

"I do what I can. I'm just one person."

"But you are a person who cares, and that is what matters most. Also, I think you have your own toxins to deal with. Maybe I can teach you a little something about the art of purity."

"You want me to be pure? I don't want to die of boredom, Tomoki-sama."

The Green Man roared out a tiny laugh. "That would

not do at all, Hanako-san. I meant the art of giving your soul to the light of the universe, so that what comes out of it is pure and worthy of growth."

She smiled at her new roommate. "Now that I can live with."

o0o

# Dragons in Suburbia

**First Published:**
*Mytherium: Tales of Mythical and Magical Creatures.* Indigo Mosaic. 2012.

I'm a grandfather, and this story came about when I asked myself about family structure in other 'cultures'. It was also inspired by a pothole, which was nearly a sinkhole, on a suburban Calgary street.

**"Dragons in Suburbia"** was an Honourable Mention in *Imaginarium 2013: The Best Canadian Speculative Writing*, from ChiZine Publications.

~~~

## Dragons in Suburbia

Old Newt shuffled along the sidewalk in the moonlight with his grandchildren, Harper and Sarah, leading the way. "There be dragons about, little ones." He sniffed the air loudly, for dramatic effect. He relished the times he spent with the little ones and always tried to make the most of it.

"Dragons?" Harper challenged him but little Sarah just gawked at Grampa Newt.

"Aye."

"Here? In the neighborhoodaburbia?"

"In suburbia."

"That's what I just said."

"Yes."

"Prove it." Harper had no problem calling this old-timer's bluff but Sarah looked both awed that her Grampa knew such an amazing fact and terrified that he might be telling the truth. Of course, she was still too young to think that a grown-up would be fibbing to them, telling a story just to entertain them.

"Fine." Newt pointed at the ten-by-ten, foot-deep, depression in the road. "See that sinkhole?"

Harper-the-skeptic nodded. "Yah."

"'Yah'?"

"Yes sir. I see it."

"Much better, lad." He turned his attention back to the sinkhole and lowered his voice to his Whisper of Secrets. "That was made by a dragon."

"By a dragon? Underground? Under the road? Gramps, what do you smoke when I'm not around?"

Newt looked at his adolescent grandson in a new light, but what Newt put in his pipe when he was alone wasn't the point. The point was the sinkhole and he pointed at it again. "Dirt dragons."

"Dirt dragons? Grampa, you are so full of—"

"Don't you dare say it, young fella. Show some respect."

"Sorry, sir. But dirt dragons?"

"It's true." He hesitated, wondering how much of the tale he wanted to tell, now that he'd started it. Too late to stop now, he supposed. "Your grandmother even killed one once."

"Grandma? Itsy, bitsy, half-Sarah's-size Grandma? Killed a dragon?"

"Just a dirt dragon, but it was with her bare hands."

Harper stopped abruptly where he was and sat down on the stone wall in front of number 5, three doors down from their own home at number 2. As usual, little Sarah sat beside him, silent. "I won't say it Gramps, but you know I'm thinking it, so sit your big, hairy butt down and tell us all about it."

Newt put his meaty hands on his hips and cocked his one good eye at the two doubters. Harper sighed loudly and patted the stone beside him. "Please oh please, Grampa Newt, tell us the story of how Grandma killed a dirt dragon with her bare hands."

Newt rubbed the patch of wiry grey hair on the top of his leathery head then plunked his old bones down next to his sarcasm-spewing grandson. "Mock me all you want, lad, but if you're up for a tale, then well and good because I'm in no hurry to get back to your mother and her list of chores made to keep idle hands busy." He shifted around on the stone until he found a comfortable position and farted.

"Your mother was about Sarah's age when this happened. She and your grandmother had spent the afternoon baking when the attack came."

"The attack?"

"The dirt dragon. In Latin, Draconus Subterraneous."

"That is not Latin."

"Now you're a linguist?"

"No, but I know that much. So... this 'attack'?" Even with only one good eye, Newt could see that Harper was hooked, but running out of patience.

"The attack came up through the kitchen floor. That dirter musta caught the scent of your... of the... baking crumbs. I kept telling Hilly—your grandma—something like this would happen but she and your mom were just having too much fun and got carried away, forgetting to keep the floor crumb-free and safe." He scratched his belly through his leather shirt and farted again. Harper and Sarah either didn't notice or didn't care. "Crumbs'll attract pixies, rats and relatives, but mostly... dirt dragons."

"And Grandma killed one? Barehanded?"

"Don't underestimate your grandmother, Harp. She's always been a lot more hunter than gatherer. She may not be as big-boned as her sisters but what she lacks in size she makes up for in patience and tenacity. As a matter of fact, when we first met she was at that old bridge over the Thames, the stone span north of town. Patience? When I ducked up underneath the bridge to shelter for the day she'd already been sitting three days in the cold, thumping-down rain without a bite to eat, waiting. Then we sat and talked for another day-and-a-half before I finally wandered off to scare her up a meal. In that day-and-a-bit of chatting and bantering and verbal jousting, we fell warts over scabs for each other."

"Gramps... what about the attack?"

"It was... the crumbs."

Harper sighed, again. "You said that."

"And I'm saying it again." He slowed his cadence down, slipping into a this-is-important-so-listen-up rhythm. "There were a couple handfuls of crumbs and a small blood spill in the middle of the floor, right next to the table, and it was the bloody crumbs that it was after. It was downright tiny for an aerial dragon but mighty big for a dirter. I think it measured out to four-and-a-half yards, from underbite to triple tail spikes.

He lowered his voice to just above a whisper and the youngsters leaned in, hanging on every word. "I felt the spine-shivering approach-rumble two rooms away and next thing I know... there was a Humungous, blasting, crash!" he boomed. The two youngsters fell backwards off the low wall as if to avoid the attack. "Your grandmother's favourite oak-stump table and a days-worth of baking got flipped right over, end-over-end, ass-over-tea-kettle, onto the floor. I bolted up out of my chair fast as a gnome and was halfway through the doorway and into the kitchen when your mother came flying across the room, bounced twice, and came to an abrupt stop up against my toes. Found out after it was all over that your Grandma had kicked her to safety, nearly ricocheting her off the wall."

"Are you sure she didn't? That would explain a lot, especially when it comes to curfews in our house."

"I'm quite sure, Harp. And you need to be lookin' at your own reflection if you want to know why your mother sets curfews, young master."

"Whatever. So this dragon comes roaring up out of the floor and attacks Grandma in a fire-breathing rage..."

"Hardly. It burst through the floor like it was soft, fresh peat instead of hard-pack, but the wyrm was deadly silent, cuz that's how dirters work. They just sneak up on you and before you know it, it's all over."

"Then what, Grampa?"

81

"Then what, Sarah?" Maybe he could still steer them away from the truth his tongue was determined to spill. "Then, little one, your baking is all gone! Scooped up by their four rows of teeth and swallowed down in a blink-and-three-quarters. Every elf cookie, every dwarf biscuit... every hobgoblin cupcake."

"Is that why Grandma killed it?"

"Um, of course it was. It's The Law. You see, this big dirter was already tagged, which meant that this wasn't its first time. They get one free shot and that's it. Um, the first time they get caught and tagged and relocated far away from civilization and sweets. But if they don't toe the line, if they go and get caught again, then they're deemed beyond saving and killed."

Harper turned to stare at Newt. "That's the law?"

"A Royal Decree, actually, lad."

"The King said that, decided that?"

Newt wondered briefly how a fantabulous tale of a sinkhole had wandered down this dark path. "It wasn't exactly the King, but the people who speak for him."

"And that's why we kill dirt dragons?"

"Sure. Just the unredeemables, though. The hopeless cases that we can't save." He hadn't had to lie this fast since Hilly's mother had caught them skinny-dipping before the wedding.

"What did the dragons say?"

"The dragons? I have absolutely no idea. I'll have to ask the Dragon Queen when I see her next."

Sarah whispered softly. "You know the Dragon Queen?"

"Of course, silly kobold. Since I was your age, in fact."

Harper laughed cruelly. "Bull!"

"Not bull. I met her in the woods one day when she was just a princess. Before she learned to fly."

"And I know the way to Rivendell." Newt smiled. Harper was getting bored with the tale meant more for little ones like Sarah than smart lads like himself.

"There's no such thing as Rivendell, Harp."

"And you don't know the Dragon Queen, Grandma

never killed a dirt dragon, and there's no Royal Decree letting us kill dragons who steal sweets!"

Newt took a long minute to think over his next words very carefully. He could spin the tale further making it up as he went along, or just tell the truth. He sighed. Why hadn't he seen the direction this would go before he started telling it? Hilly was going to flay him alive and stake him out in the sun when she caught wind of it. "Okay, I lied."

Sarah gasped in shock.

"The law clearly states that when a dragon kills one of us it's deemed a violation of the Treaty of Compton Down and the offender can be dealt with appropriately. With the Greater Dragons, the civilized ones, there has to be a trial, but with the Lesser Dragons—dirters, moat-floaters and the like—in the face of overwhelming evidence, execution can be carried out immediately."

"What do you mean, 'kills one of us'? I thought you said it ate sweet crumbs."

Newt wondered why the truth hurt so bloody much? "Not for eating crumbs. It... the dragon...that vicious little dirter, killed my baby son, your uncle, Dub."

Sarah sobbed, "The dirter killed a baby?!"

Harper was shocked. "I have an uncle? Mom has a brother?"

"Had." Newt hung his head. After all these years it still hurt like the dickens to remember. No one else ever wanted to talk about it so no one ever did, but losing a child wasn't easily shoved under the blankets and forgotten about. It was time the kids knew the truth. "Dub was just a wee thing, sitting on the floor, playing with the crumbs when the dirter came. He didn't have a chance. Grandma barely saved your mom." The youngsters were stunned into silence.

"It was a nasty, knock-down-drag-out battle. At first when she grabbed hold, your grandma was just trying to get the dragon to spit your Uncle Dub out, but once she was sure it was a lost cause, she tightened her grip around its neck and squeezed. It snapped and thrashed and pretty much destroyed what was left of the kitchen. I charged in and tackled the spiked tail as best as I could..." He lifted his heavy shirt to show a mess of deep, thick scars. "...and got these." Sarah reached out and gently caressed the old wounds as if she could heal her grandfather's hurt with love. He kissed the top of her head and lowered his shirt.

"Hilly never let go, not even for a second. Not until the dirter was choked-out-dead, with its tongue lolling out and both eyes burst from the pressure. I had to punch her in the head twice to get her to release her hold cuz I was sure she was going to pop a blood vessel and die right there, wrapped around the dirt dragon that killed our baby." A tear rolled down his craggy face.

"I guess the dragon was hungry, too, Grampa."

"Hungry? For a baby?" Newt wondered how many times Sarah had been dropped on her head in her few years.

"Well, we eat lambs and calves. Aren't they babies, too?"

It wasn't the same, he raged in his heart, but he did his best to keep his voice calm. "They're only animals, Sarah."

Harper shook his head, contradicting Newt. "That's what they say about us, Grampa."

"Who says?"

"Humans."

"Yes, well, they kill their own over a difference of ideas so don't get your shorts in a knot over what humans call us Trolls."

"Grampa?"

"Yes, Sarah-sweets?"

"Can we go home now so I can give Grandma a hug?"

"You know, little one, that might just be the best idea we've had all day." He picked his granddaughter up and ruffled her wild red hair. "I don't suppose I could get you both to pretend you never heard that story, eh?"

Harper put his fist to his chin and squinted, considering the request. "Nope. Not a chance."

"Didn't think so. Had to ask, though." He put Sarah down on the sidewalk. "Shall we go give your grandma those hugs and see if she needs help cleaning up the kitchen?"

Harper nodded. "We don't want the crumbs to bring another dirter, do we Grampa?"

"No lad, we sure don't. Never again." Newt held out his massive, scarred hands and his grandchildren each took one and led his old bones home.

o0o

# Hawkwood's Folly

**First Published:**
*20,001: A Steampunk Odyssey*. Kindling Press. 2010.

When I wrote **"Hawkwood's Folly"**, steampunk was a new thing to me. The editors were looking for Jules Verne-ish undersea stories with a steampunk twist. I wrote this in a week, had it critiqued, rewritten, and submitted by Saturday. It was accepted on Sunday and I had the contract received, signed and returned by Sunday night. This is unusual speed.

**"Hawkwood's Folly"**, was also selected as one of Canada's best speculative writings for 2012, and reprinted in *Imaginarium 2012* from ChiZine Press. It is also the first of my stories involving the murdered Russian Royals or Rasputin. Here we meet him as a young man.

~~~

## Hawkwood's Folly

le 17e septembre, 1889.
I write this down and lock it away. Let the world know the truth—la vérité—after I am gone.

\*\*\*

There was a time, not so long ago, before they erected that iron monstrosity, the Eiffel Tower—before I lost my family's entire fortune at the bottom of the Atlantic Ocean—when I would have awakened to the rapturous perfume of warm crêpes, fresh strawberries and rich cream commingled with dark, African roast coffee and a petite portion of potatoes and scallions pan-fried in garlic butter and dill. In through the double doors out over the Champs Élysées I would have been serenaded by the pleasant jingle of harness, clop of hoof and clatter of carriage as all of Paris seemed to pass beneath my balcony. Not very exciting, I agree, but certainly a more delicious start to the day than a trio of pistol shots, a garbled shout in Russian, heavy metal clanging rhythmically on the cobbles beneath my window, and frantic, clumsy, human footsteps racing up two flights of stairs, ending in a life-or-death iron pounding on the cheap fabricated door of my rented room.

With this rude awakening, gone were the crêpes, the dark roast, the dill, and the balcony overlooking the Champs Élysées. I stumbled from the lopsided cot, lit the lamp and tore open the door, fully prepared to give a sound beating to the offender, only to be met by Grigori. A tall, lanky, boy of twenty, he was soaking wet in a torn waistcoat and stinking foully of la rivier Seine. He sported a bleeding wound to his left temple and was holding a smoking pistol up to pound its butt on my portal once again.

Gone, too, was Grigori, meek bo's'n's mate who never looked comfortable amongst his social betters, a group I once proudly counted myself a member of. Scruffy and bearded, he tripped past me and into my squalid room. His wide-eyed, terrified gaze searched the nine-yard-square space for any threat greater than the empty bottle of cheap Bordeaux and the chamber pot much in need of emptying. There was no threat here. I, Georges DeBlois, surgeon, entrepreneur and multiple patent-holder, was not at my best.

"Bolt the door! Quick! Do you have a pistol, docteur?!" Grigori had been a rough-edged Russian peasant at the best of times so I was only slightly put off by his brusque entrance and complete lack of civil greeting.

"A pistol? Do you have one? I have only one bullet remaining!"

"A pistol?" The loud crash of the destruction of the front door of the building froze us both where we stood, but

Grigori recovered soonest.

"Too late!" He shoved a small, surprisingly heavy, burlap sac into my hands and grabbed my old walking stick leaning against the bed. With the pistol in one hand and the stick in the other, he backed toward the open window. "Flee with me or die my brother mariner! We are betrayed!"

"But I cannot simply—" a high-pitched hiss of steam whistled from the stairwell followed by the grinding of small mechanical gears and pistons, whining and struggling. I knew those sounds only too well. "An automaton, boy? You flee an automaton?! Impossible!" I knew only too well that this was not just any man-mocking, mechanical, side-show puppet, but one of Lord Mordecai Hawkwood's custom designed, steam-driven men of metal. Terror twisted my intestines and inspiration struck—I glanced in the sac. I wanted so badly to be wrong but fear I was not. The sac contained the head of another such mechanical man. "Mon dieu! You stupid boy!! What have you done?!"

Slower on foot than a man of flesh and bone, the contraption ascending toward us possessed the strength of five men and through wireless signals could communicate with others of its ilk. If a living, breathing man were at the other end of the transmission doing the thinking and decision-making then it would be an unstoppable force.

I clutched the burlapped mechanical skull and followed the terrified Grigori over the sill and onto the fire escape. Having fallen so far from grace I no longer had a carriage at my disposal nor the funds with which to hire one so this would be a footrace. As I backed myself out into the cool, damp air, the papier-thin barricade masquerading as a door erupted inward. Shards of cheap board and veneer flew every which way as one of Hawkwood's humanistic contraptions crashed through. I saw my money belt on the night stand at the same moment the metal menace sighted me. That belt contained all I had left in the world and so I hesitated. That moment of indecision was all that the automaton needed. Despite the poor light I saw the dart leave the end of the index finger of its right hand a moment before I felt its sting. I slumped forward over the sill, wondering with my last conscious thought how it had come to pass that the dart was used against my self rather than a denizen of the deep.

\*\*\*

When consciousness tracked me down I was back in my own bed, which is to say that I lay between fine Egyptian cotton sheets under a goose-down duvet a hundred yards beneath the surface of the Atlantic Ocean off the coast of North Africa. I was once again in Hawkwood's Haven, which meant that I was dreaming with great lucidity or that the explosion of the volcanic hydrothermal vent and the resultant collapse of the supporting rock face didn't do nearly the degrees of damage to the Haven as I had assumed when I was retreating back to the surface in the self-contained escape pod six months before.

As curiously divine as the flea-free bedding was, it was the scent of strawberries, cream and dark roast which brought me to full, though confused, wakefulness. I sat bolt upright and paid the price with a rush of nausea my own patients regularly complained of on the other side of a heavy dose of sodium bromide. I leaned over the edge of the bed and vomited what little my stomach contained. It was only then, in that less-than-flattering position that I took notice of the lack of a rug of any sort and, despite the domed ceiling and rounded walls, was now quite certain that I was not in my former suite at all but a former storage closet.

With my stomach emptied of its pitiful contents I laid my throbbing head back on the stately pillow and immediately succumbed to sleep, the breakfast forgotten.

\*\*\*

When at last I awoke with a steady head, the food, the vomir and the throbbing were gone. In their places were a jug of water, a crystal water goblet, a clear head, and a handwritten note in a choppy, unsure version of Hawkwood's own hand. My own hand was now much steadier as I retrieved the note and read it aloud, to no one in particular.

"Georges—my friend -- please excuse the rough handling which brought you back here to the Haven. I have answers to all of your questions but one I will answer here and now. You are here because I am alive. Please come to the infirmary as soon as you are able. Your fellow submariner and friend, Hawkwood." And so I drank a goodly amount of water, splashed a dab more on my face to bring a bit of wakefulness and left the closet behind. Once in the corridor I was met by one of the cursed automatons. Yes, cursed. Though I once believed them mechanical marvels, since being darted, drugged and abducted, I was less enthused of Hawkwood's brilliance.

But I had returned to the Haven and there were questions I needed answered so I set forth for the infirmary as requested, with the metal menace two steps behind me. There was no sign of Grigori about so I suspect that his boyish reflexes had aided his escape where mine had failed.

It took a moment to get myself reoriented, especially since the floor canted somewhat to the left. An arrow accompanied by a red cross painted on the wall told me exactly where I was in the complex and with one hand on the downhill wall for support I stumbled on. I may have soured on the presence of the automatons, but as I made my way through the complex I was still quite proud of our little project. Between Hawkwood's structural engineering genius and my respirator design modified to scrub and revitalize our air, we had done the impossible and established a ten-edifice complex on the ocean floor! We had powered it off the hydrothermal vents and, judging by the flickering electric light illuminating our way and the clean crispness of the cool air, the generators worked still. More and more I marveled at how much had survived the sub-marine landslide.

We came to a junction and I turned left, following the arrow and the red cross, but the way was blocked by a wall of collapsed rock. Closer inspection showed fresh repairs and a petite puddle of seawater at the base of the rubble-cum-wall so I turned and followed the corridor the long way around. My silent companion – Delta by the insignia on his scratched and dented chest plate—clanked and whirred along behind me.

Two turns later I was reminded why I fell in love with Hawkwood's proposal in that salon in Marseille three years before. The corridor lighting was greatly reduced, but that was by design, so that the view through the massive bubbled window was as clear as could be. I stopped, as I had every other time I passed this look-out, this sub-oceanic observatory.

The hydrothermic vents powering our little habitat provided heat and chemistry unavailable elsewhere and despite the rift in the vent which had caused the structural collapse behind us, life continued in abundance there, on the other side of the glass. A lethargic, white zoarcid fish snapped at an orange tube worm but missed, and the yard-long worm retracted at lightning speed back into its hard, protective chitin tube. I saw a modest tentacle reach out from behind a mass of tubes and our petite, resident octopus plucked a white Galatheid crab from his own meal on the mussel bed. Life went on here and not one of them cared that I watched in wonder.

Delta waited patiently whilst I let myself be lulled by the gentle waving to-and-fro of the two-foot-long sea worms in the current. I regarded my escort, wondering.

"Do you see what I see, metal man?" I placed my palm affectionately on the glass, still surprised at the warmth this far below the surface. "Do you understand the marvel that we created here or do you simply follow your wireless commands and complete your tasks? Does the tableau magnifique before us stir you in any way? Does it make your clockworks speed up at all, or even slow, as it matches the marine rhythm?" It turned its head toward me but remained

91

silent.

"You and your three fellows were the brawn to our brain and did the heavy, tedious work we were incapable of at this depth, but did you understand then or even now what was being constructed? What a marvel this was—is?" It blinked twice at me, but whether it was programming or a sign of understanding I know not. I returned to watching our maritime neighbours, observing features and behaviours no man had seen before, certainly no man of science.

After a moment Delta did acknowledge my presence by gently taking my elbow in its steel grip and turning me firmly back on track. We were expected in the Infirmary and I suspect he just received a command to see that we arrived post haste. With a last look out at the magnificent seabed within arm's reach, I shook free of the hand and marched on.

Three more piles of rubble in collapsed and blocked passages told me that the sea cliff's collapse had indeed destroyed much of our mariners' residence, including the dormitories carved out of the cliff itself. We continued on, once or twice taking a longer route to avoid what I guessed were impassable areas. I could see that Hawkwood's three remaining automatons had been busy, with pathways cleared through rubble and in some cases the rubble cleaned up entirely and probably taken elsewhere to shore up a failing dam to the sea water yearning to burst through.

A quiescent bilge pump sat next to one such dam and I realized then how truly precarious the situation was. When the domed buildings were intact and firmly seated on the sea floor, the habitat was safe and secure, but now, with the breaches so evident and the automatons struggling to keep the sea at bay, we were in danger and the novelty of it all left me cold and un peu claustrophobic. Even the biologist in me wanted no more of it. Exploration by bathysphere would be more than sufficient.

I hurried my step and with little further guidance from Delta, soon found myself sitting at the bedside of the man I had, until recently, presumed dead.

"Do I terrify you, Georges?"

"I am a man of medicine—there is nothing of the human condition which terrifies me." I had seen leprosy, pox, syphilis, but nothing like this. Rien. Nothing.

"Yes, you've seen much, ol' chap, but I would wager that this is new."

I looked at a mechanical eye, a skull more metal plate and bolt than bone. The left arm above the sheet was mechanical contrivance from the elbow down to a steel-cable and lubricated-piston hand whilst beneath the sheet the right was machine from the shoulder down. The angry violet redness of an infection radiated from the shoulder socket across his once strong pectoral toward his heart. I suspected he had little time remaining.

"Nouveau? Bien sûr. Certainly."

"Also both inner ears, one lung and both legs below the knee."

"How...?"

"They found me after the cave-in, trapped in an air pocket inside the Refectory." He took a long, rasping breath and coughed sputum into that mechanized hand. Very human bloody spittle flecked his full Victorian whiskers and I saw sadness in his still human eye.

"The Refectory. We were three men and four automatons—what did we need with a full-sized refectory. A simple dining room would have sufficed."

"Maybe in the beginning, but our plans were to expand." I reassured him. "To bring selected men and women here to live and work. Your mining operation and my marine-farm."

"Were we out of our minds? Did we throw good money after bad and dream beyond reality?"

I rested my hand on his good shoulder and squeezed gently. "Greatness is only achieved when honest men take risks, mon ami." But silently, to myself, I now agree that we had over-reached here.

"Were we honest, Georges? To ourselves? To each other?" He coughed and I went to a small cabinet behind what had once been my desk. There I found a small satchel of personal 'elixirs of medicinal nature', as my grandmama was want to call such things.

"Honest? I would suppose that we were as honest as business partners can be, although our motives may have differed somewhat when we built our misguided sub-maritime paradise." I administered to him a good-sized dose of my narcotic blend and Mordecai, Lord Hawkwood, smiled lopsidedly.

"We did do it, though, did we not? We carved a settlement beneath the sea and powered it all from the adjacent steam vents..."

"Oui, mon ami, we did indeed. In one year we constructed what no man had ever dared and for six months we lived in it, aided by your 'marvellous' creations. We had big dreams, Mordecai."

"Yet, have I wasted the talents of a brilliant surgeon? Kept him from the greatness he deserves?" More coughing, though not as heavily as before.

"Save both your strength and your kind words of praise. I am a simple country chirurgien who has allowed this failed venture to keep me down in a morass of self-pity. I have been living as one lost in les catacombes beneath Paris where we first tested your theories; but seeing you here, not willing to fold your hand and lay your cards down has renewed my vigour for life."

"Excellent, excellent."

"May I ask how you found me? Out of shame, I have not been living under my own name for some months now."

From deep within, Hawkwood seemed to find joy at his inventiveness and allowed it to bubble up into a smile worthy of the dreamer who had sold me on his great scheme in the first place. "Grigori. Between his mystical visions he found time and means to launch a small salvage operation."

"Grigori?" I was doubtful.

"Our young Russian returned to our Moroccan warehouse in Agadir and cobbled together enough equipment to make his way back down. That impetuous boy learned more from both of us than we could have imagined."

He coughed, shuddered and his eye drifted in the orbit for a moment, appearing untethered. He regained control and once more focused on my face, though with some difficulty.

"He found me here, just after the surgery. I was in much better condition than what you are witnessing now and so, once we were both satisfied that neither was here to kill the other, we chatted at some length. He had believed he was the only survivor of the Haven, since he was topside checking the buoys when the vent ruptured.

We talked some more and eventually I sent him with poor Gamma's skull to find you, knowing that you would better believe his story of my survival with the head as proof. I sent him merely to extend an invitation to return, unfortunately my condition worsened after he departed and with no way to get a message to him to change the degree of urgency, I was left with no choice but to send Alpha out into the world to fetch you."

"But how?"

"He followed the homing signal still active in Gamma's cerebrum. I should have known that Grigori would react the way he did when Alpha caught up to him—he never really trusted the mechanicals. Of course, when Grigori shot at him, Alpha reacted as he was trained and it all tumbled downhill from there, starting with gunfire in the streets of Paris and ending in your subsequent drugged abduction."

"I would have come willingly. I never had a chance to get your message from Grigori, nor to ponder the contents of the sac for long."

"I know, I know. My sincerest apologies, ol' chap. The single-mindedness of task completion in the automatons is one of the issues I wish to address on the cognitive level."

I looked again at the infected shoulder and his grey pallor, listened to his belabored breathing, and doubted he had time enough to address anything, though I kept that thought very much to myself as well.

"Before he departed to find you, Grigori squared up and told me that, thinking us all dead, he had returned for the gold. Once I knew that I gave him a handful of doblón as partial advance payment for the delivery of the message. Since he did not return with you and Alpha I must assume he is still running and will eventually make his way back home to Russia where he will marry Praskovia and try to forget the sea and the gold owed to him."

"Gold?" I knew of no gold here.

"The doblón we recovered that very morning. I was on my way to show you the amazing samples when all bloody hell broke loose. Although the cliff collapsed on this wing, the domed structure which allows Haven to resist the pressure of the sea saved her from the rock above."

I was shocked. "Mordecai, when the silt settled and my sealed-off laboratory was all that remained, I despaired. Like Grigori, I thought myself the only survivor. I waited three days but when my air-revitalizer failed I had no choice but to gather my journal and a bottle of port and trigger the emergency surfacer. My heart broke, sir, when I rose up from and above the ruin of our dreams and—less importantly— our fortunes. Gold, you say?"

"Doblón. Eighteenth Century Spanish coins. We managed to save one chest before the cave-in buried the lion's share. Your half is in that small box behind you, against the wall."

I turned and spotted the boite immediately. Making a poor attempt to appear less eager than I felt, I opened it and my heart nearly stopped. It was no Blackbeard's treasure, but it was gold and it was easily twice what I had invested in Hawkwood's Haven. I looked back over my shoulder to my dying partner. "You are certain of this?"

"It is the least I owe you for your faith in this madman's dream. I have but one last favour to ask of you, as a doctor. The doblón are yours whether you accept or refuse so feel no obligation from that quarter."

"A medicant to aid your final release? Something to ease your pain as you move on?" He would not live long in his bastardized mélange of a shell, which was probably best. I saw less of mon ami in that face than I did a mechanical contrivance.

He laughed. "Not at all, my friend. My automatons are most capable in that field, should it become necessary. In fact, they are so capable that they have one final surgery to perform."

"*Surgery*? You have an infection. Poisoned blood. No surgeries will repair that."

"None but one, my skeptical Frenchman. Or it may not. But should it succeed... should it be done with any degree of success, I would have you by my side through it all to oversee the work and to revel in the greatness of my new reality."

\*\*\*

And so, not two hours later, Mordecai, Lord Hawkwood, had his mad, dying brain transplanted from his failing hybrid of flesh and machine into a fully mechanical host designed in part by myself a year previous, although at the drawing board I had believed it was to be a somewhat more conventional life-support system. The procedure took a bit more than eight hours and throughout it all I could only stare dumbstruck as Mordecai's remaining three mechanicals worked with a surgical speed and precision far beyond that of any human surgeons I had ever worked with or even heard mention of.

I will admit that more than once during the long night I nearly ripped the human brain from the metal pan and dashed it to the floor to keep this horror from continuing, but I was rooted in place, simultaneously fascinated and repulsed. I was at both a God-fearing man and a scientist, an innovator. Their achievement was sheer brilliance, but also an abomination. Oui, they transplanted his brain, his own thinking, reasoning machine, but what of his soul? What of his essence?

My hands quivered and shook even after I stuffed them down into my pockets but when I saw that Epsilon—the mechanical taking the lead—was referring to my own notes on Medical Field Improvisation, Amputation, and Surgical

Procedure I wept silently at the inhumanity of it all. I had not even known they could read!

What had we created down here in Poseidon's domain?! At least young Mary Shelley's fictional monster was cobbled together from human parts. This machine—this clockwork caricature—being given life before my eyes was both so much more and so much less than a man.

But, alas, at heart I a cowardly doctor. Other than increasing the dosage of the bromide cocktail being used as a sedative and anti-convulsant, I kept out of their way and let them work.

\*\*\*

Twenty hours after Mordecai's yellowed, bloodshot human eye closed for the last time, two new, brass-and-glass optical receptors spun open and the 'reinvented' man performed a miracle—he spoke. He spoke in a voice resonating of light machine oil and a miniature metal orchestra, yet he spoke, and I nearly fell off the cot where I had been grasping at fitful sleep. His words at first were soft and quite raspy, yet as he learned the ways of his new apparatus there grew strength and purpose.

"This... is... a... most interesting experience. I can detect my mechanical brethren in way quite similar to how I am hearing my own voice. We are... as a small, four-unit hive, yet I retain my individuality... Ah, I see now that they are distinct individuals, though not yet as well-defined as I am." A hive? Mon dieu!

He paused, most probably listening to a voice broadcast between himself and his new kin. His piston and cable fingers twitched and he cocked his clockwork head like a dog attempting to hear better.

"The surfacer is ready and the hydro-boat awaits topside." It was Mordecai's voice, but at the same time it wasn't and it jarred my nerves quite harshly. I realized at that moment that as dearly as I wanted to stay and participate in this incredible breakthrough in medical and engineering science, I found I no longer had either taste or tolerance for life on the ocean floor. The offer to return me topside was perfection.

"How will you fare, mon ami?"

"I will fare well and not want for activity, ol' chap. We have a great deal of work to complete here before it is a sustainable environ once again." He gestured sloppily with his new arms and I believe that a hinge lifted on his speaking aperture, affecting a smile. "At least now I will have the opportunity. Some day, when your mind is still sharp but your body begins to fail, I hope then you will consider joining me on this adventure, my friend. As marvelous as this new body of mine is, over time it will appear crude and primitive as we modify and improve the designs."

I shivered at the thought of trading a flesh body for mechanical self and prayed that I managed to return to the world of humanity before these creations learned to read minds and could see the dark intent forming in my heart. I am no zealot, but I do so believe that beyond this world there is a paradise waiting and I will face my earthly end here with Gallic pride and stubborn faith. At least that is my hope. I see now in Hawkwood's actions and words that it is très possible that he will not stop until all mankind joins his new hive, his dark collective.

***

And so, I returned to the surface world, the world of sunlight and rain and humanity, taking with me both the Spanish gold I was given and a fresh insight into what dreams may come to. Here, outside Paris, I am well satisfied to invest in dry land and in the new industrial automation growing in London and America. I rebuild what I gambled away on Hawkwood's Haven and mayhap someday will confess to our local Monsignor why I spent a month in that warehouse in Agadir erasing all signs of my involvement in a bizarre project somewhere off the coast.

Perhaps, too, the monsignor will understand why I converted a goodly portion of those Spanish coins to simple francs and then quietly used the francs for a shipment of explosives in waterproof crates sent down from Stockholm.

I like to believe that some day the world will be ready for a genius the likes of Lord Mordecai Hawkwood, inventor, noble, and steam-driven mechanical dreamer. Mais il ne sera pas aujourd'hui. But it will not be today.

oOo

# Picking a Professor

**Not Previously Published.**

This is the original story, written for a Sherlock Holmes tribute. I tried to tweak it for a Professor Challenger tribute anthology, but I never got the story quite right. I've always been fond of the little original, so here it is.

Believe it or not, I actually have a display case of all of the watches described here in the story.

~~~

## Picking a Professor

Allyson could hear the professor half a block away, his deep-chested voice booming not only above the mixed group of detractors and sycophants, but also over an exhaust-spewing Humber chugging past Royal Albert Hall.

"You're hardly worthy of my time, even for a dram at The Queens Arms, lad, but your question during that mockery of a Royal Society academic dissertation was well considered and has earned you my company for forty minutes."

"Thank you, Professor Challenger. I appreciate the opportunity to discuss your findings further."

"Oh, there'll be no discussion, lad. I will disseminate all I know on the topic — which is everything worth knowing — you will be awed and we will part company much later than I would like just so you can all rush to gatherings of fellow lesser minds whom will attempt to assist you in understanding all I have pronounced to be true and inviolable."

Allyson smiled behind her dove-grey, satin glove and adjusted the angle of her large, feathered hat. Her pulse raced in the anticipation of the game afoot. Professor George Edward Challenger and hangers-on fussed a moment longer, then top-hat-crowned Challenger himself led the procession off to The Queens Arms, which would bring them right past her hired carriage. Her timing had to be perfect but she knew it would be, because she was no neophyte at this tedium-busting game.

She tapped knuckles twice on the carriage roof and in a moment the driver was down and opening the door. He held a white-gloved hand up for her to take and Allyson slowed her exit just a trifle so that she might observe out of the corner of her eye Challenger's pointed-toe step, dancer-like in its odd gracefulness. She counted his strides and measured his gait in the space of a few seconds. When, the moonlight glinted off the links of the immaculately polished gold chain looping from his one waistcoat pocket to the other, she finally committed herself to her plan. She stepped down and crossed to the doorway of Number 26 and as Challenger et al passed behind her she turned suddenly as if she had forgotten something in the cab. Her turn and step took her directly into Challenger's path and if not for his pugilist's reflexes and bullish strength catching her, Allyson would have been knocked to the stones. The professor and his entire following skidded to a halt.

Trained by the best fine wirer pickpocket in London, who now happened to be a coachman for her brother, Allyson uttered a startled yelp for added misdirection then she pressed, dipped, slipped and eventually concealed away in the folds of her cape the chain, the fob, and the pocket watch on the other end.

"M'lady! What mean you, changing direction so suddenly and catching this bear unawares?" Challenger gently guided Allyson by the elbow to one side. "You are, I pray, unhurt."

"Merely ruffled, sir."

"Which is better than most get when they choose

physicality with G.E.C. Now be a good little Miss and decide which direction you are going so that we may pass and these insufferable mental flyweights might follow me to the pub where they will spend no more than forty minutes haranguing me with dullards queries."

"Pardon, me, sir. I just wished to have a last word with the driver." She backstepped out of Challenger's way, favouring him with the dimpled smile stronger men than he had fallen prey to. He puffed up his chest, straightened his huge black beard, returned her smile, and steered around her, the moment probably forgotten almost as quickly as it happened. Allyson waited until the pack of intellectuals disappeared around the corner to the right then she accepted the cabbie's assistance to mount the four-wheeled growler. A moment later they were off with the snap of the whip, Number 26 left behind.

***

Charlotte drew the heavy curtains then helped Lady Allyson out of her cape and hat.

"Thank you, Charlotte. You can turn in for the night. I'll finish up myself."

"But your corset, Miss."

"Ah, true enough. What would I do without you, Charlotte?"

"Probably sprain your shoulder trying to loosen the lacing, Miss."

"Most likely, yes." Allyson turned around to let Charlotte reach the heavy laces, which the young woman's nimble, practised fingers made quick work of. As Allyson stepped out of the stiff-boned garment she wondered if maybe Charlotte had some pocket-picking skills of her own.

"Thank you Charlotte. Now go and get some rest for pity's sake. You've had a long day and I've kept you up much too late waiting for me to find my way home."

"I don't mind, Miss."

"I insist, Charlotte. Get along, please."

Charlotte curtseyed and left her mistress alone. As soon as the latch clicked, Allyson whipped out her prize and held it up to the light. It would sparkle in daylight but even now in the dim electric light she could make out the fine gold filigree on the face and the floral case back. The timepiece was stunning. Challenger — or more likely his wife — had excellent taste.

"You will be the crowning glory of my collection. I have a place for you right next to Professor Breul's simple, functional Swiss piece. Or should you go next to the Aronnax piece, to contrast the silver with your gold? Oh, decisions, decisions. An even dozen and professors one and all."

Lady Allyson gently laid Challenger's pilfered property on her duvet and retrieved a foot-square, locked mahogany case from beneath her huge, regal four-poster bed. With a key from a ribbon around her neck she opened the case and admired her growing collection. With great care she nestled the watch into the little indent above the hand-written

"CHALLENGER" label she had made up in anticipation of the evening's success.

"Oh, Allyson, you've been a naughty girl, again."

"That, young lady, is an understatement."

She spun at the sound of the voice, but she didn't scream, so overconfident was she that she could handle any and all trouble. "Professor, what on earth...? How did you get in here? How did you get past the palace guards?"

"The same way you lifted my watch, young lady — with misdirection and skill. I'll be taking my property back now, thank you." And with the speed of a snake he had a gold cord from the bed's canopy around her neck and drawn tight before she could scream.

***

Scoble woke to the pounding of a fist on his door. He took only a moment to run his hand through his thinning hair before replying to the interruption of his slumber. He reached for his robe as he spoke through the closed door.

"Who is it?!"

"Constable Doyle, sir. There's been a murder."

"There's always a murder, Doyle — this is London."

"It's up at the Palace, Inspector, sir."

"Murder at Buckingham Palace?" He threw the bolt back and whipped open the door to surprise the fidgety constable. The man recovered quickly and straightened up.

"No sir. *Kensington Palace.* Lord Cambrian's sister, Allyson."

"Someone broke into Kensington Palace?"

"We're not sure how 'e got in, sir, or out."

"Anything missing? Anyone else hurt? Any witnesses?"

"No one saw or heard a peep, and so far as the staff can tell, the only thing missing is a pocket watch."

"Lady..."

"Allyson."

"Lady Allyson owned a pocket watch?"

"Not exactly, sir. She had what appears to be an 'illicitly-gained' collection of gentlemen's pocket watches."

"Illicitly gained?" The inspector stepped into his bedroom and dressed while calling back out to the constable.

"Pilfered, sir. Picked, lifted, and stolen. She's got them labelled like a butterfly collection and there's even one marked 'Challenger'."

"Challenger? The professor?"

"None other than. He reported his timepiece stolen 'round about nine bells last evening and it looks to be we've recovered it."

"Could he have done this? Murdered Lady Allyson? I've dealt with him on a few occasions and that pompous braggart has a temper on him and the strength of three men."

"From what we gather, he's vouched for until this morning."

"I'll be the judge of that, Doyle. What was the missing watch labelled?"

"'Moriarty', sir."

Scoble dropped the cufflink he was fumbling with. "Bloody hell! Moriarty?" He snatched the cufflink off the rug and jammed it into place. "Go get Mrs. Williams to put a pot on while I get dressed. Can't very well charge into a storm at the Yard without my morning cup, now can I?"

"No sir. Of course not, sir."

oOo

# Lyoshka and the Steam Butterfly

**First Published:**
*In Place Between: The Robyn Herrington Memorial Short Story Contest.* IFWA. 2012.

Cruising along with my obsession with the Russian Royal family, this story was originally written for an Asian steampunk anthology, but it was rejected for not being Asian enough. No worries. I then submitted it to a local short story contest where it made it into the top eight and was published in their limited-run anthology.

~~~

## Lyoshka and the Steam Butterfly

It started with a little brass ball and a pot of steaming water when Alexei Nicolaevich Romanov, Tsarevich of Russia was twelve and people close to him still called him by his nickname.

"Lyoshka, I have a gift for you." Grigori Rasputin was hated by many but none could deny his deep affection for the boy.

"But Christmas is still two weeks away."

"This cannot wait, little one. If ever you must flee Mother Russia, this 'dragon whistle' will bring aid. It is not a bell you ring and expect faithful soldiers at your door in a moment. You sound it once and then, twenty-four hours later, sound it once more. The second sounding must be made in an open area so that your rescuers can reach you and—."

The lad examined the brass ball, trying to find a way through the seams, past the intricate Chinese figures. "How do I...?"

"Listen, boy!" The healer rolled the ball over and indicated a small button in a depression on the surface of the device. "This is the trigger." He spent half-an-hour explaining how to use it, then Alexei placed the small brass ball in his trousers pocket, and there it remained.

Rasputin was murdered days later. He was the first of them to die.

\*\*\*

Two-and-a-half years later Alexei's family, their staff, and Anastasia's dog, were all dragged into the basement of a house in Yekaterinburg and butchered by the Bolshevik secret police. Alexei was sorely wounded, assumed dead, but in the confusion of bodies being loaded into a truck he was spirited away by a man loyal to his father, the Tsar.

Alexei was kept safe but his bleeding didn't stop and on the third night, weaker than ever, he sounded the whistle for the first time. They were in danger of being discovered so it took little to convince his rescuer to get him out of the city. The next night they arrived at the farm of the man's mother. As loyal to the Tsar as her son, Olga didn't question Alexei when he boiled up the whistle and asked her strongest grandson, Yuri, to carry him, his crutch, a shuttered lamp, and the pot to the middle of their fallow field. Once there, Alexei ordered Yuri to leave.

"Babushka will kill me if I do not stay, your Highness. You cannot *stand*."

As helpless as he was, as afraid as he was, Alexei knew he had to follow Rasputin's instructions to the letter and be alone when he sounded the whistle the second time. "Go, Yuri. I command it." It saddened Alexei to treat a good man harshly but the loyal peasant knew his place and dared not disobey.

Yuri left and Alexei sounded the little steam-driven whistle and waited. He listened for the sound of hooves and a wagon, either of the enemy or of his rescuers he didn't know. But the roads remained silent and the whistle steamed and bounced around inside the pot as the pressure was released through three small holes, sending out the call far beyond his hearing.

Wolves heard it, though. He heard them howling to each other and prayed they would stay away. With one final clank and thump, the whistle ran dry and, he assumed, stopped sending out the call. His bandages were soaked with blood. The pack grew braver and soon he could hear their snuffling as they followed his bloody metallic scent on the breeze. He pulled the lamp close and kept his fingers near the closed shutter.

As one huge beast made his silent way across the ploughed ruts in the starlight they were both startled by the chugging hiss of what sounded like a small locomotive. The pack leader froze mid-step and listened. Alexei knew they were miles from the nearest rail line but steam puffed, gears turned and metal strained in a slow rhythm, getting closer. Finally the wolf fled and Alexei unshuttered the lamp.

It was by the light of that tiny lamp that he saw the magnificent metal dragon descend from the night sky and set down only yards away, steam puffing from its flared, brass nostrils.

An order was shouted that he couldn't understand and suddenly a masked, black-garbed man appeared, scooped up the whistle and the lad and ran for the dragon. He stared at the incredible, golden, bat-winged machine. It was Chinese in the style of its sinewy, metal body but he didn't think Chinese dragons had massive wings like these. He was quickly handed up to a pair of strong arms and wrapped in fur, and then there was a clank, a piercing hiss, and the release of a large spring somewhere within the dragon beneath them. With three great, clanking steps they were airborne. Bleeding and near death, Alexei was full of wonder and marvel in that moment before he lost consciousness.

***

He awoke in darkness, in a hammock, still wrapped in heavy furs. Thin, crisp air reached into his lungs and he coughed weakly. A flint struck steel and then there was light. He was in a room, not on a dragon. Judging by the sway of the hammock he assumed they were at sea.

"You are awake. Excellent."

He tried to twist around to see the speaker but she was just out of sight. To his practiced ear she sounded young and she spoke the Queen's English with what his mother had once referred to as a 'Chinese colonial accent'.

"My apologies, sir. A moment, please, and I will come around." She fiddled with something metallic and something else of leather, and then a face appeared at his side. When Alexei first saw his rescuer he was suddenly too smitten by her beauty to notice any of the little facets that were the parts of the whole gem—her slender, feminine form, dark Asian eyes, tanned skin and silky, braided, black hair tied back with a sky-blue ribbon were all details he wouldn't notice until much later.

"Drink this tea, please." She blew on the steaming porcelain cup to cool the brew then held it to his lips. He sipped slowly and discovered that it wasn't nearly as hot as he feared. He reached up and lifted her hand to tilt the cup for more but an electric shock knocked his hand away and the young woman frowned.

"I am so sorry, sir. One moment please." She reached behind to her belt and he heard a heavy click. It was only then that he realized there had been a humming like electric lights, underlying all of the muted noise of that odd ship. The hum was silenced with the click then she reached out and took his hand. He flinched but held steady. There was no shock this time.

"It is a small current which dances across my skin and gives me an advantage in close combat." Her half-smile completed the apology but she didn't release her gentle grip on his hand. He drank the tea in silence, feeling some little bit of strength return as the honey-flavoured brew slid down his throat. With difficulty he held the cup to his lips and drained it. When he was done she took the cup and placed it down beside the bed.

"Thank you, miss."

"I am Fenghuang, sir. We are attempting to get you to medical assistance as quickly as possible, though we are fighting a headwind and doing our best to avoid a quartet of Russian Red Army aeroplanes. We don't believe they spotted us but we found cover in the clouds nonetheless."

"Clouds?! Are we in the dragon?"

"No, silly. This is a dirigible. My steam dragon is harnessed below. Now sleep, please. We have changed your bandages but cannot stop the bleeding completely. Slumber is your friend now, until my father can reach into your Qi and find a way to halt the flow."

"I'm afraid of sleep. What if I don't wake?" But he felt sleep creeping up behind him.

"You will. You have my word."

Despite her being a complete stranger, Alexei was reassured and drifted off to sleep.

***

He dreamed of deafening gunfire, splattering blood, and his sisters' screams. Then the choking stench of gunpowder became the comforting scent of cedar smoke and Alexei woke, thoroughly confused. Weak and sweat-soaked, he marshaled the strength to sit up. By the light of a small sconce on the wall he could see that he was no longer in the airship and was now on solid ground in a stone structure. Large, woven tapestries covered much of the stone walls and a small fire burned in an iron stove near his low pallet. There was a well-used rocking chair in one corner and heavy fur rugs covering the floor. It was all very comforting, especially after the horrific nightmare, and he drifted back to sleep.

***

Voices slipped into Alexei's sleep. First Fenghuang spoke a language he'd never heard before and then a man answered in English. "He's awake. Speak English, please. Or French, at least. His Highness is fluent in both." Alexei opened his eyes and Fenghuang's smile was the first thing he saw, to one side and back a step.

"How are you feeling, sir?" The man's voice came from the other side and with difficulty Alexei dragged himself away from Fenghuang's smile. He thought the man was old, maybe as old as forty, the same as his father.

"I am Keung, sire. Welcome to our humble little settlement. We are merely eight, including our cook, Kamala, and her children, but it is home."

"Where are we?"

"Tibet. Specifically, a monastery in the Col of Clouds—a saddle high up on the southeast slope of Noijin Kangsang."

"The soldiers... they will find us. Those Bolsheviks will never give up. You're not safe as long as you're hiding me."

"Four rickety aeroplanes will hardly be a match for one steam dragon, wouldn't you agree?" He sat on a short stool beside the pallet. "But that is not what has me concerned. We have cleaned and closed your wounds and applied poultices here and there where necessary, but much more drastic action needs to be taken."

"Nothing could be more drastic than what has already been done to me in the name of healing. I have hemophilia and have spent years being poked and prodded and drained and poulticed and bandaged and anything else they could think of to stop the bleeding and make me strong. I never want to see another leech as long as I live, sir."

"We can stop the bleeding now, but as for healing your illness, we cannot be sure the treatment will work. But I *will* promise you no leeches. That would only make matters worse. What I have in mind will not be a one-time cure, young sire. It will require periodic application for there to be a chance of success. And it may be somewhat unpleasant."

"I'll do anything you ask. I should be dead now, Mr. Keung. I owe you my life and the best way for me to repay that debt is to keep living so that I might be of service in some small way."

"You are wise for such a young man. You have been through much, seen much death. A child should be allowed his childhood."

"Dying is far too easy. The true hardship is in living well. I am only fourteen and would dearly like more hardship, please."

"As you wish, Your High—"

"*Lyoshka*. Please call me Lyoshka. That other self is now dead. He *must* be, for everyone's safety. No one can know who or what I am or you'll all be in danger." He was still weak and the room swayed a bit.

Fenghuang stepped forward, placed her right fist over her left breast and looked him solemnly in the eyes. "You will be safe, Lyoshka. I swear it."

The young Russian smiled and reached for Fenghuang's other hand but the room went dark.

***

He first noticed the warmth of the room.

"Please do not move, Lyoshka." In truth, he could *not* move, even had he wanted to disobey Master Keung. Neither straps nor hands held him, but nonetheless he was completely immobilized.

"We will be finished in a moment and then I will release you and you will understand."

He could feel his limbs, but had no more control over them than he did the ceiling above him. He tried to speak, but couldn't. He could hear at least two people moving about with sliding steps in soft slippers. Although his eyelids had opened, his head would not turn, nor his neck lift. He breathed in and out and the warm, dry air felt good. His heart beat steadily in his chest and there was strength in it where

113

very little had been before. He was giddy and light-headed, though from blood-loss or excitement he couldn't say.

There was a mechanical click and the whirring of dynamos as someone hand-cranked a device to his left. A second click was followed by a familiar hum that was magnified in the room. There were murmured words off to the side and then Fenghuang's face appeared above his own.

"Hello. You had me—us—worried, Lyoshka. We have had to keep you unconscious for nearly two days as we did what we could to treat your still-bleeding wounds through surgery and various herbs." That sweet accent of hers electrified his soul and he barely heard her words. "But there is no more my father can do for you using traditional healing. It is now time for the unconventional. I will explain, quickly."

She held her hands up and he could see the tiny hairs on her arm standing on end. He could hear the hum of the generator at her back and in that dim lamplight he was certain he could see the electrical current crisscrossing her body. She pointed at his chest. "You cannot see them, but all across your body, touching on every meridian both medical and mystical, are tiny, thin, steel needles, thin as hairs. I am going to take hold of your feet with my hands and my current will flow into you to the needles. It may hurt, but if movement returns, you *must* remain still. Please."

He struggled to speak but couldn't. His eyes widened with alarm until she reached down to his throat and plucked one of the needles out. "On one... condition," he finally gasped.

"A *condition*?"

"Smile for me. Please. I'm scared, but if you can find a smile for me, then I will be as brave as you need me to be."

Fenghuang skillfully placed the needle back into Lyoshka's throat and smiled. She smiled big and wide and with her heart. The smile sparkled and outshone the sun, Lyoshka was sure of it. Then, while he was in thrall, she stepped out of sight, grabbed hold of both of his feet and sent the current lancing through his body.

Though his body arched itself in reflex, he felt no actual

pain. He felt mild stinging in the souls of his feet and in each of what must have been scores of warming needles across his body, but no pain. After ten seconds of the current coursing through him, Fenghuang released his feet and his body sagged back down. His nerves tingled all over and he thought it was marvelous. He felt incredible.

Five minutes later all but one of the needles had been retrieved. He couldn't see it and couldn't sense exactly where it was, but it kept him pinned down. Fenghuang came back to lean over him.

"One more, then you can move again, though it's best if you remain abed while your body adjusts." Then, without preamble or warning, she bent down and kissed him quickly on the lips. "My apologies. I couldn't resist." She smiled all over.

Master Keung appeared at her shoulder and frowned. "And *my* apologies for my impetuous daughter." He looked at her with mock disapproval and Lyoshka could now see the family resemblance in their cheekbones, narrow noses and the set of their eyes. "Fenghuang, I am certain that if you had waited one moment and simply *asked* Lyoshka for the kiss, you would have been rewarded twice over." He reached to the top of his patient's head and hesitated. "Lad, as silly as my daughter is, she was quite correct. Please do your best to lie still and allow your body to recover. I will be taking her with me in order to remove the temptation for you to sit up too soon for a second kiss. Before we go, how are you feeling?"

"Very much alive, thank you, sir. I feel... normal. *Healthy.*"

"Excellent." The master indicated neatly folded garments on the rocking chair.

"We will give you a moment to dress and then we shall eat. If you need assistance, I can stay while my Little Warrior of Mischief fetches the meal."

Lyoshka shook his head kindly. "Thank you, but it has been so long since I was able to dress myself that I would truly like to do this on my own."

The master nodded. "The things we all take for granted are often those which are the most important. We will be back shortly." They left without another word, although Fenghuang did manage to toss a smile back over her shoulder.

While they were gone Lyoshka dressed in loose, black, lined garments and a pair of sheepskin-lined, leather-soled, knitted boots identical to the ones Fenghuang and her father wore.

\*\*\*

By the time they returned as promised, Lyoshka was sitting in the rocker, gently nudging it back and forth with one toasty warm foot. Master Keung and Fenghuang each carried a tray laden with steaming dishes and a step behind them followed two solemn men, one bearing four sturdy stools and the other a stack of bowls and a handful of chopsticks. Master Keung put his tray on the bed and turned to face his guest.

"Lyoshka, may I present Brothers Anil and Xiao, the best archers in all of Tibet and the other two Cloud Warriors." The two men bowed so Lyoshka gingerly levered himself up from the rocking chair and returned the greeting.

With the formalities done, the five of them dined on spiced rice and buttery chicken in contented silence. When they were done eating, Lyoshka stood again and, in reverent, heart-felt silence, he embraced each of his saviors. He felt reborn and told them so.

Master Keung nodded. "Then there remains just one thing, and it is the most important. Will you remain here on Noijin Kangsang and continue treatments, perhaps becoming a Cloud Warrior and learning all that we have to teach you? Your hands and mind will not be idle, *that* I promise. Of course you can take short forays down off the mountain to breathe the air of civilization. Everyone should visit Lhasa at least once in their lifetime."

"Will...does...um..." Lyoshka couldn't articulate what his heart so very much needed to ask, but Master Keung understood.

"Yes, my little Steam Butterfly will be here. She is a Cloud Warrior, Rider of the Steam Dragon and this is her home—"

From somewhere outside a deep-toned gong interrupted Master Keung as someone repeatedly slammed a mallet against the gong's boss. The master was on his feet in a blur giving urgent orders in what Lyoshka assumed was Tibetan. Fenghuang and Anil were out the door and gone without a word. The master turned to Lyoshka before following his daughter.

"Brother Xiao will remain to protect you, your High... *Lyoshka.* Please remain here, out of sight." Before Lyoshka could reply, he was alone with Brother Xiao, who was busy snuffing the two lamps.

*** 

The gong continued for a few more minutes and then it stopped suddenly. Lyoshka could think of nothing except the safety of beautiful Fenghuang and managed two awkward steps toward the door before his monk guard blocked his way. Xiao shook his head and spoke with a heavy accent. "Please, no. Stay."

"But Fenghuang...!"

"Fenghuang is warrior. Lyoshka not. Keung say stay."

"But—"

Lyoshka's protest was cut off by the sound of gunfire, shouts in Russian muffled by the thick door, and a woman's piercing scream. Xiao himself moved for the door but stopped. He looked at the closed door and then back at his royal charge. Lyoshka could see that the man was torn. Xiao was a warrior and was needed outside, not hiding in the shadows with a boy he'd just met.

"Go Xiao! Fight!" Lyoshka hunkered down between the

pallet and the stone wall. "I will hide!"

Xiao hesitated a moment longer but two more rifle shots sounded and he slipped out, closing the door firmly behind him. Lyoshka stayed hidden for a few seconds and then made his way to the heavy door where he placed his ear hard against it. He heard a woman shout in alarm and then an order barked loud and clear in Russian.

"Kill them all! Find the royal brat!"

These good people were going to die just to protect him while he hid! If she were still alive, he was certain his sister Anastasia would have grabbed a rifle and waded into the battle in a ball gown if she had to. He didn't have a rifle but he had his crutch and he was *not* going to let lives be lost for him. Lyoshka grabbed the crutch that leaned against the wall, and dragged open the heavy wooden door to face whatever battle was beyond, armed only with the stick and the determination that he would die fighting like the man he had not yet become.

Fear coursed through his veins at that moment, but terrified or not, he couldn't help but grin when he looked down onto the courtyard surrounded by dawn-lit, snow-capped mountains and saw that magnificent mechanical dragon swoop down, pick up an invader in its claws, and drop the man over a precipice like a child drops an unwanted toy. The enemy soldier's collapsed parachute trailed off behind him, as useless as his scream.

With great sweeps of its brass and steel wings, the steam dragon swung gracefully back around and Lyoshka could now see Fenghuang high atop the back, controlling the monstrous mechanism with incredible skill. One-handed, she held her place on the dragon's long saddle while the other hand reached behind her and unsheathed a sword. Sparks appeared to dance along the steel. She banked the steam dragon hard, landed it in the cobbled courtyard and before it skidded and clanked to a complete stop she was out of the saddle, running along the lowering, scaled neck. She planted her petite feet on the dragon's metal-horned head and somersaulted onto the back of a leather-geared Red Army soldier aiming his pistol at a prone woman—most likely Kamala the cook, Lyoshka guessed.

Despite her small stature, Fenghuang managed to knock the soldier away and to the ground, but he came up with his pistol still in hand. As he swung around to acquire his target Fenghuang ducked, rolled and popped up behind him. Her steel flashed in and out twice then she spun and kicked him in the back. The soldier stumbled forward two steps, folded, and stayed down.

With her foe beaten, Fenghuang grabbed Kamala by her collar and ran, dragging her like she was a twenty-pound bag of potatoes, not a full-grown woman. Fenghuang pelted across the courtyard and into one of the other two low buildings seemingly carved right out of the mountains.

Only a moment passed before she was back out into the courtyard and scaling the building like a spider. She flipped up onto the roof, sprinted across the peak of the steep slope, reached the end of the tiles, and then leaped out and up. Alexei was sure the distance was at least thirty feet, but when Fenghuang landed neatly on the next roof and darted back into the shadows, he knew he must have been wrong. It had to have been a trick of distance, thin air and his weakened condition.

Another of the enemy burst out of the building beneath Fenghuang, kicking the door open so that his rifle could sweep the courtyard before him. He scanned left and right, obviously searching for something or someone. When he didn't find it in the courtyard his eyes scanned up the slope to the building Lyoshka stood in and at the same moment the enemy spotted him, the young, crippled Russian wished he had stayed inside, out of sight. But it was too late now. The damage was done.

The man managed two running steps in Lyoshka's direction before Fenghuang launched herself off the roof, at the soldier's back. A sound behind him or maybe a seasoned soldier's sixth sense made the man twist and duck at the last second and Fenghuang soared over his hunched back and landed with a slight stumble on the cobblestones beyond her target. Twice her size, he brought his rifle around to cut her in half with the bayonet but with a ballerina's grace and fluidity she parried the heavy blow easily and danced back, out of reach.

He recovered quickly and instead of wasting time with the bayonet again, he simply swung the rifle back around and pulled the trigger. The crack of the shot echoed off the buildings, back and forth across the courtyard, and Fenghuang collapsed on the stones. Her blood flowed slowly away and Lyoshka wanted to scream but the air had been sucked right out of his lungs as if he'd been punched. He wavered, leaning hard on the crutch, helpless and lost.

A scream of rage cut through all other sounds in the monastery and Master Keung flew in a blur to stand over his daughter, sword in hand. The soldier jabbed forward with his rifle while reloading but Master Keung parried the thrust easily, spun in place and beheaded his daughter's killer with ease. The soldier's body stayed upright for a moment longer, though the head had already tumbled off and rolled away.

Watching in shock while the master of the Cloud Warriors dropped to his knees and cradled his little Steam Butterfly's body, Lyoshka was startled by the sounds of a nearby boot scuff, a rifle bolt sliding, and a cartridge being chambered. He leaned out of the doorway and came face-to-back with a Russian Red Army soldier raising his own bayonet-equipped rifle to his shoulder, taking aim at the back of the grieving father.

Mustering all the strength he had, the slender Tsarevich swung his crutch as hard as he could in a grief-fuelled backhand that caught the traitor in the shoulder and knocked his shot off-target. The broad-shouldered, thick-necked man spun around to face his attacker, expertly sliding the bolt and chambering the next cartridge from the clip even as his bayonet came up a foot away from Lyoshka's belly.

"You Royal—!"

The soldier failed to finish whatever he was saying because a long arrow suddenly sprouted from his throat. He tottered on his feet long enough to take two more arrows in the back of his heavy, sheep-skin-collared jacket before toppling forward. Although Lyoshka did his best to twist out of the way, the bayonet pierced his heavy shirt and slipped between the last two ribs on his left side. The pain was unbelievable but he had little time to think about it because the full weight of his attacker slammed into him and they both went down, hard.

***

Two days later they cremated Fenghuang and wept while the wind took her ashes up into the clouds. The Steam Butterfly took to the air for one final flight and her father rang a small, brass prayer bell three times to signify the beginning of the mourning period. He then knelt by the stretcher on which Lyoshka lay covered in furs and checked the lad's bandages, but they both knew it was too late for the Tsarevich who should have inherited a nation.

Their heads bowed low, Brother Anil tapped a steady beat on his a small brass bowl with a small wooden mallet and Brother Xiao plucked a quiet melody on a seven-stringed, guitar-like instrument. Completing the circle were Kamala and her children—twin girls about six and a boy toddler. Master Keung grasped the mortally wounded Tsarevich's hands in his own and spoke softly, a verse from the Tibetan Book of the Dead.

"Now when the bardo of dying dawns upon me,
I will abandon all grasping, yearning and attachment,
Enter undistracted into a clear awareness of the teaching,
And eject my consciousness into the space of unborn awareness;
As I leave this compound body of flesh and blood
I will know it to be a transitory illusion."

He brushed the young man's cool, soft cheek with the

back of his hand and gently kissed the top of his head in farewell. "It is time for you to introduce Fenghuang to your family, my son."

Lyoshka smiled and closed his eyes.

oOo

# The Ability of Lightness

**First Published:**
*Shanghai Steam.* Absolute X-Press. 2012.

After **"Lyoshka & the Steam Butterfly"** was rejected by the editors of *Shanghai Steam*, I penned **"The Ability of Lightness"** about two Tibetan brothers and a steam-driven, brass dragon. The editors liked it much better. In another tie-in, the minor character of Master Wei is a major character in my novel, **The Broken Shield** (see excerpt later in this volume).

~~~

## The Ability of Lightness

"Watch me 'painting a rainbow', Quon!" Twelve-year-old Yu raised his arms up in curves, his hands above his shoulders, then brought his right hand over his head, turned his head to the left and brought his left arm down and out to the side, palm up. Looming above him, its neck stretched nearly up to the roof of the massive cavern, the giant brass and steel, clockwork Feilong steam-dragon watched without judgment. The mechanical flying beast's boiler was silent and its marvelous wings folded in and back, but it still dominated the cavern beneath the Galden Namgey Lahtse Monastery, waiting impassively, ready to fly at the hands of the Cloud Monks in defence of the People against the tyrants of the world.

Yu's younger brother, Quon, didn't even look up from the long wooden workbench he stood at. "Yah, yah, Yu. You're painting a fat little rainbow while I'm being a genius. Your stupid t'ai chi might make Master Wei nod and smile but when he inspects the graduates today and sees me and my steam-driven dragon-steppers display perfect Qinggong, light-stepping across the monastery rooftops, he'll accept me as his personal student and take me away to Lhasa to be the greatest Warrior Cloud Monk ever. I hope. If this thing works." He tightened the final brass nut and tugged on the thin copper pipe to test the strength of the new bracket.

"Of course it will, Quon. In only three weeks, you took all those spare dragon parts and made that machine. I just wish I was smart like you." Yu was a year older than Quon, a Rabbit to Quon's Dragon, but he was perfectly happy to follow his younger brother's lead. "You should try t'ai chi ch'uan, Quon. Come here and follow me. It's really relaxing and you really need to relax."

"I don't have time for that silliness. Master Wei only visits once every ten years and he won't be back in Tawang Town until 1899, the Year of the Pig. By then, it will be too late. It has to be today or never."

Yu leaned and pushed, moved and pivoted, 'scooping the sea'. "You haven't even tested that thing, Quon. Maybe you should." He finished by 'looking at the horizon' and stepped over to make a closer inspection of Quon's invention. "Will it really make you dragon-step? How does it work? I see an old pair of boots, some really big springs and stuff, and that looks like a tiny boiler, like the one on the horseless wood-wagon or even the dragon." He reached out to touch a polished brass strut but Quon slapped his hand away.

"No! You just break things. Go 'separate the river' or something, while I finish up. The Graduation Call-to-Arms should sound any minute."

"I thought we were going to have breakfast first. I'm starved." In spite of his hunger, though, Yu started his movement by 'raising his arms', and then followed the sequence their Cloud Monk brother, Jung, had taught him. He moved gracefully in and around the giant Feilong dragon, smiling as the flickering lamplight reflected off thousands of hand-hammered scales. As he finished up by 'balancing the chi to a close', a large-bossed gong sounded. "Perfect timing! I feel balanced and calm and even a little lighter on my feet."

"Good for you, Round Ass. You need to lose weight. Now hold the cart so I can load up my dragon-steppers. Please." Quon scrambled to shift his pair of contraptions into a handcart. "Just think, Yu, by the end of today, you will be known all across the Tawang-chu Valley as the brother of Master Wei's newest student. That should at least get you a small discount in the marketplace."

"A discount would be good, especially when I take over the farm from father." Yu kept a firm grip on the cart's handles while Quon finished loading and then draped a bright red blanket over everything.

Quon tucked in the corners of the blanket and stepped back to inspect the load. "Perfect." He led the way out and Yu followed along, faithfully using his brawn to see his brother's dream come true. "We have ten minutes to get to the kakaling entrance gate, Yu. The ceremony will be in the courtyard so I'll dragon-step from the kakaling to the library and make one magnificent leap across to the Dukhang, the assembly hall. It will be a great moment in Cloud Monk history and I want you to be there in the courtyard to make sure they all know who the steam-monk is. I'll make one final, huge, Qinggong jump down into the court to accept my place at Master Wei's side." He sighed to himself. "With luck."

Yu ignored Quon's last comment, certain his brother could do anything he set his mind to. Just before he closed the door behind him he heard Jung and the other Cloud Monks entering the cavern from the other side to prepare the steam-dragon for their daily sky patrol. He pushed the door shut as softly as he could and hurried after Quon.

*** 

The brothers arrived at the stone entrance gate just as the final gathering gong sounded. Quon gave Yu a light shove. "Go! Get to the courtyard! I can do this myself!"

"Are you sure you don't need my—"

"No! I need you in the courtyard! As soon as you get there start whispering my name. That way, when I leap over their heads, they will already be talking about me. Go! Go! Go!" Quon ripped the blanket off the cart and got to work assembling his device. Yu took off at a run just as a huge shadow passed over them. A quick glance up showed the Feilong dragon slowly gaining altitude above the monastery with Jung in the saddle.

***

Yu wound his way through the dozens of buildings until he reached the courtyard. There had to be at least a thousand people there, all dressed in their finest robes to honour both the newest Cloud Monks and Master Wei, brother of their very own Abbott, Master Keung. Yu jockeyed for a good view, working his way through the crowd, along the outside of the courtyard. He spied a nearly empty staircase and aimed for that vantage point, trying not to step on toes or knock over wobbly old-timers.

"Excuse me, pardon me, sorry." Halfway to the staircase he remembered Quon's instructions. "Where's Quon? Have you seen Quon?" he whispered loudly as he squirmed his way through the packed crowd. "I'm looking for Quon, have you seen my brother, Quon?"

An old woman jabbed an elbow in his ribs on his way past. "Shut up, boy! Master Wei is about to speak!"

"Sorry." He moved on as quickly as he could. By the time he reached the staircase and ran to the landing at the top, he was seriously short of breath. The day was hot, the crowd was massive, and the excitement was overwhelming. Yu took a deep breath to calm himself. He 'separated the clouds' and 'pushed the waves', focusing on his chi and not the buzzing crowd or the baking sun. He closed his eyes and tried to concentrate on Master Wei's voice like an island in the storm of bodies. He breathed in, and breathed out, and listened.

"Brothers and Sisters, thank you so much for your kind and generous welcome. It saddens me that my duties to the order keep me away and I can only find my way home every ten years. Much is changing in the world beyond our mountains, beyond blessed Tibet and India, so this place, this locus of peace, warms my heart greatly. Today is a very special day because it is the day we welcome new Cloud Monks to the order. My dear brother, Keung, has asked me to do the honour of introducing you to the newest warriors in the battle against oppression and slavery. But first, a prayer. O Amida, Oneness of Life and Light—"

A tremendous steam whistle, followed by a high-pitched, blood-curdling scream, interrupted the prayer. Yu opened his eyes just in time to see Quon bound, out of control, from the eastern rooftop to the western one. Quon appeared to have legs at least two feet longer than normal and when he landed on the far roof, his legs compressed and the still-building pressure shot him back up into the sky again.

Masters Wei and Keung both vaulted lightly up onto the steeply sloped tile roof of the Dukhang, running madly after the rocket boy. Without a second thought, Yu launched himself ten feet up onto the library roof, thinking only of his cousin's safety. He ran straight up to the peak, taking giant steps and doing his best not to slip. He watched as Quon rocketed past Master Keung and, although the Abbott leaped high, he was too late to reach him.

The dragon-steppers shot Quon straight down into the courtyard, forcing the crowd to run for the exits. Yu was sure that his little brother was going to hit the stones headfirst and be killed by his own invention, but at the very last moment Quon got his feet under him and the impact was absorbed. Master Wei changed directions suddenly and sprang down to the courtyard, but while the master was inbound, Quon's dragon-steppers released their pressure and blasted him sky-high like a New Year's rocket.

Yu shut down his fear, closed his mind to everything else, took a deep breath and flew straight up off the roof and into Quon's path. The young brothers crashed together and Quon's skinny little elbow slammed hard into Yu's head, but Yu held on tight. The dragon-steppers sputtered, and then ran out of steam. Yu smiled. It was over. Quon was safe. And then he looked down and saw that nearly a hundred feet above the courtyard.

He was puzzled for a moment, having no idea how on earth they got so high, but his confusion was quickly forgotten when gravity started to drag them back down. He took a deep breath, focused his chi, and tried to remember everything he was taught. Then he heard the hiss of a massive steam engine below him and saw a glint of sunlight on brass and gold wings. "Jung!" Yu shouted, and he saw Master Wei leap from roof crest to dragon wing to arrow straight toward them. "You've saved us, Master! Quon! We're saved!"

No answer. Yu felt Master Wei's arms close around them. "Quon...?"

***

Yu looked back over his shoulder at the Tawang-chu Valley and straightened his pack.

"You are homesick already, young Yu?"

"No, Master Wei, just wondering how Quon will take to farming."

"It is only until he learns some discipline and his legs are healed. If he applies himself, he should be able to apply for the academy in two years' time."

"Will his legs ever heal completely? They're really smashed up."

"Not completely. I don't think he will ever master the ability of lightness in Qinggong, but after the three of us were swept out of the sky by Jung on the Feilong dragon, I think Quon has set his sights on flying. Only time will tell, though." He took a sip from his water skin. "Now, shall we make our way to Lhasa?"

"Of course, Master. Can I ask one question, though?"

"You may ask as many questions as you wish, Yu. You are with me to learn."

"Thank you, Master. So, when do we stop for lunch?"

oOo

# Of Monsters and Men

**First Published:**
*Cavalcade of Terror.* Undead Press. 2012. No longer available.

This story is an experimental piece written in five parts, from three points-of-view, in a 3-2-1-2-3 order. It's about science and ethics, combining horror and steampunk in the tunnels beneath Paris.

~~~

## Of Monsters and Men

"Men are fat and lazy here in The City of Light. These industrial-aged men watch and listen, neither seeing my shadow nor hearing my whispers," Ezekiel said softly to the silent jumble of ancient bones beside him. "But when they do venture this far below Paris, into the catacombs beyond the light, they can feel my whispers like an ill wind, and then they flee back to their little lives of airships and clockwork servants, knowing that I have their scent and can come for them any time I please. Fear is what they deserve and it is certainly what they receive when they enter my world and I'm in a mood for food." He licked his lips and smiled.

"When I was in London ten years ago the citizens travelled in pairs or threes and started at the smallest sound, and all because of that uncouth, judgmental butcher flaying about in the Whitechapel district. Once I put an end to his clumsy antics both sides of the channel went back to their stumbling, fumbling lives. I dislike competition, especially from amateurs who don't eat what they kill, even occasionally." The skulls stared back, lulled into acquiescence by the soft sibilance of his whispers.

"I prefer it when my 'cattle' get complacent and walk around above with their heads in the clouds, thinking their grandiose thoughts and forgetting to watch the shadows like they should. Now take this German scientist and his tortured captive down that passage and around the corner. The German fears nothing and the broken man fears everything.

\*\*\*

I dreamed o' the Marseille airship dock last night. At least I'm thinkin' it was last night. For ages it's been all bloody darkness with bits o' light here an' there. It was the docks I was workin' when that bastard Hun found and took me. Slipped a mickey in the pint he bought me, I wager, then waited 'til I was laid out cold afore draggin' me off. Bastard's kept me chained in this cave like some goddamned wild animal, feedin' off me misery 'n pain most like. I can see him an' smell him, even after he's gone. Can't hear him no more. Can't talk at him neither. Went t'sleep here one night an' woke up deaf an' mute. Bastard took my tongue an' my ears, I reckon. Darkness an' silence. What would my Sally back home be thinkin' if she'd see me now? I'm no more'n a monster myself. I'll fockin' kill him if he gets close enough.

\*\*\*

**Day 63. 24th Day of May, 1899 AD. Cologne Institute Human Adaptivity Study. Notes by Dr. Gustav Cleary.**

I have recorded a 1.3% improvement in Subject Five's Zero-Lux optical receptivity, which is within acceptable parameters of natural adaptation without aural adjustments. I projected a minimum of 2% by this stage of the experiment as previous studies indicated that other senses would adapt should one be lost but those results have always been made as postscripts and noted as being secondary to the actual studies.

Unlike Subjects One through Four, Five gave us a fully-functional baseline to start with. Shortly after being transported from the dock area, surgical termination of Subject Five's auditory function was performed simultaneously with removal of the muscular hydrostat on the floor of the mouth responsible for phonetic articulation. Zero lux illumination is maintained for twenty-two hours of each twenty-four hour cycle. For the two illuminated hours, a point-zero-three lux level is maintained, which is sufficient for use of Opticular Lux-Enhancement Goggles by myself.

The grunted oral expression Human Subject Five has made post-surgery is unexpectedly less functionally articulate than that of Bonobo apes from previous studies I conducted in the Congo. Lack of audible articulation is possibly connected to loss of audio sensory capability. Will have to examine this further in a secondary study.

***

The bastard's been teachin' me to use my hands t' talk to him. Some sorta goddamned sign language. Fockin' Hun monster keeps the lights so damned low that I can barely see 'is hands. Ain't seen no one but him an' some sorta dog what follows him around. Strange dog it is, too. Even in the near-dark it looks to be made o' metal, at least in parts. Bloody horrible it is. Freak o' science I reckon, like them auto-men doin' the heaviest liftin' on the docks. Wonder if that's what the bastard's got in mind for me. Take my tongue an' my ears an' replace 'em with brass 'n copper pipes 'n wires 'n gears.

Afore 'e fed me today 'e made me learn t' make the damned finger signs that the bucket in the corner o' me cage needs emptyin'. Took bloody ages to learn what he was flashin' with his fingers in the near-dark.

After he left I could smell somethin' different. Somethin' other'n the bucket, the moist caverns around us and the dried grave-robbings shoved to the side o' me cell. There's somethin' down 'ere with us. Somethin' other than the' half-dog, I mean. I waited without movin' a muscle for what musta bin a hour after the bastard Hun left, and eventually I could see it in the shadows, watchin' and waitin'.

This thing, this demon or ghost or whatever just watches me. Its eyes've gotta be more than a mite better than mine cuz all I see is a bit o' pale skin wrapped behind dark. Once I thought I could see its mouth movin' like it was tryin' to talk with me, but deaf is deaf an' his movin' mouth is jus' so much skin flappin'. But there's evil in there, in that dark corner, or my name's not Patrick Mahoney. Makes my skin crawl like I'm covered in maggots.

\*\*\*

As a shadow, Ezekiel watched the chained man, whispering to him. The whispers were wasted on the cowering shape and the Ezekiel knew it, but he went on whispering.

"Like a cruel child jabbing a heated poker into the sides of a puppy simply to discover how it will react, this man of science has mutilated and humiliated you for the sake of his curiosity. There are many who call me 'monster'; who have hunted me without success through the centuries, but I at least have compassion. I feel. I have spared a child crying for its mother and I have even spared a mother crying for her unborn child. But not all have been spared, of course. There are limits to my compassion and I am only what I am.

"I enjoy a bit of a hunt, a bit of sport, but you are staked out like bait and your man of science is too myopic to notice life beyond his preconceived parameters. He collects his data, plays with his calculating engine, and then returns for more data. He wastes space, he wastes breath, and he wastes time. What would you do unfettered, unencumbered? I wager you'd not waste it, eh? Even mutilated as you are, you're a man of action are you not?"

133

A sound in the tunnels snapped at him, stealing his attention from his whispered, one-sided conversation. He thought for a moment then decided. "Time to see what science hath truly wrought in you." He flowed forward until he reached the heavy lock securing the manacles to the iron ring set into the floor. Clicking boot-steps and a lesser mechanical rhythm approached. He shattered the lock with a powerful twist, looked the deaf-mute captive in the eyes and nodded. The man nodded back slowly and a tear escaped down his cheek before his gaze hardened.

The living shadow withdrew up the wall to the corner furthest from the light he could now see bobbing along toward the cell. The manacled man couldn't hear the accompanying sound but Ezekiel did. Whistling echoed down the dark, dank, sub-Parisien passage and the whistler was in good spirits, judging by his choice of tune, Beethoven's Für Elise. Wrapped in his cloak, Ezekiel the shadow waited, motionless but coiled like a spring should he be discovered and need to attack. The manacled man waited, too, his chains gripped tight in his fists.

The unlocked iron gate swung open and first to enter was the mechanical creature which had once been man's best friend but now was little more than muscle and instinct in a four-legged, clockwork, piston, and steam-driven oddity. It went straight to the captive and sat beside him. The shadow saw the beaten man raise an eyebrow at the mock dog's behaviour but there was no further reaction. At least not until the scientist himself strode into the cell and sat down in the chair facing his subject.

Even though Ezekiel knew what was to come, he was both shocked and impressed at the speed with which the broken man moved. Uncoiling power like a jungle cat, the victim was off the floor and on top of his captor and torturer. There was no mercy, no hesitation, no uttered threat. He simply wrapped the chain tight around the smaller man's neck and twisted with all his strength until the neck snapped and the scientist's head lolled to one side. A sigh escaped the freed man's mangled mouth and some of the tension seemed to slough off his shoulders. Then he remembered where he was, quickly frisked the body, found the keys he sought and, fumbling with excitement, unlocked the manacles on his wrists.

With a last look up at his benefactor, the mutilated man snatched up the lantern and fled off into the tunnels. The dog-like mechanism followed after, leaving Ezekiel to drop from his shadows and stand over the broken corpse. He leaned in close and sniffed at the dead thing before him. Just like that time in Whitechapel, there was the sour stench of corruption on the meat so he slipped away to hunt elsewhere.

oOo

# Shut Up and Drive

**First Published:**
*Horrible Disasters* (anthology). HorrorAddicts.net. 2013.

This story was written for Emerian Rich's 'horror during/after a real-life natural disaster' anthology. Proceeds go to help disaster relief globally by way of the *Rescue Task Force* (www.RescueTaskForce.org).

~~~

## Shut Up and Drive

*Juan sprinted through the downpour from the hangar to the Cessna parked out on the tarmac, soaked to the skin before getting halfway to the single-engine mine-hopper. He started his flight-worthiness circle check with the starboard wing, but his ex-wife's shout from the hangar stopped him.*

*"Eh! Just get the damned umbrella and come get us!"*

*He looked to the woman with the perpetual scowl flanked by their six-year-old daughters. At that same moment lightning struck so close Juan's hair stood on end. In the brief second of stark, otherworldly illumination it seemed Consuelo and the girls were harsh, angry skeletons, judging him as inadequate. He shook his head to cast off the image and resumed his careful check of the aircraft's exterior.*

*"Stupido! Now! Or you can forget the girls coming to visit you at Christmas!"*

*No children at Christmas? First her infidelity broke his heart and now she would kill his spirit by taking his girls away? Was this what evil was? Juan surrendered and climbed up into the cockpit to fetch the umbrella. He was sure the aircraft was sound. He'd been up in it only last week and the flight to Bogotá was only two hours. He could get them to Consuelo's sister's third wedding and be back in time for lunch with his mother.*

*Thirty-two minutes into the bumpy flight, he gave up on trying to get above the storm and dropped down below the high ceiling of clouds to more rain but better visibility. The engine sputtered once, then continued whining just loud enough to drown out Consuelo's continuous complaining. Juan adjusted the fuel-ratio and listened for further hints of trouble as they ploughed through the deluge above the jungle. Little Isabel mimicked her mother by muttering something about hating the rain and then fell asleep like her sister.*

*Half-an-hour out from Bogotá the engine sputtered twice before quitting altogether. Juan frantically checked the gauges. No warning signs, no indicators of the problem. Frustrated, he tapped each of the dials and warning lights, hoping to shake up a loose connection in time to find a fix. When he tapped the oil pressure gauge, he got his answer. The needle immediately dropped to zero, and the warning lamp and buzzer went into full alert. He looked over at Consuelo and the girls, but they slept. Juan quickly kissed the crucifix hanging on the rosary around his neck and looked for a flat surface for an emergency landing.*

*The altimeter dropped quickly as the plane lost power. Juan was confident he could glide them down safely if he could only find a road or a field until a bolt of lightning punched a hole through the port wing and the semi-controlled glide became a slow, inevitable spiral down into the Colombian jungle. The ground rushed up at them, and he unclipped his harness to reach around and hold his babies one last time.*

The aftershock rattled the bus windows and tested the springs of the nearly retired Blue Bird school bus but Juan's brain was still reliving the crash five years ago. He closed his eyes again, took a deep breath and slapped himself hard across the face. The crash of the Cessna in Colombia was once again banished back to the world of his nightmares, but the slap setup a feedback loop through Juan's hearing aid. He tapped the aid. When that didn't work, he worked the on-off switch to reset it.

This was his sixth hearing aid since the crash that killed him, Consuelo, and the girls. Unfortunately he hadn't stayed dead, thanks to the old cocoa farmer who pulled him from the wreck a moment before the fuel ignited and the Cessna blew apart. With a combination of CPR and prayer, Juan was dragged back from the land of the dead badly burned, completely deaf in one ear, half-deaf in the other, and with a strange, wobbly limp. The day he left the hospital he changed his name to Miguel and left both flying and Colombia behind for Chile and a bus.

"Yo, Miguel! We just about ready to get this show back on the road?"

The young American preacher, Father Charles, stood in the doorway of the bus, having decided their roadside piss break was over and done. Juan looked at his watch. He'd only been asleep for two minutes, though it had felt like another lifetime within his nightmare.

"That was the second aftershock since we stopped so let's get moving and get to those quake-made orphans in Coronel where we can do God's good work."

He laughed at the last bit, and a dire chill run down Juan's spine despite of the midday heat on the Chilean back roads.

"Si, Padre. We can go as soon as everyone is loaded back up."

He looked around and noticed few of the twenty International aid workers had actually gone more than a few steps from the bus. The aftershocks tended to send people running for cover or at least holding onto something a little more solid, but every one of this group stood around, unconcerned, taking slow drags on American cigarettes without much concern for the ground shimmying and shaking beneath them.

While his passengers butted out and loaded up, he walked around his bus, making a quick circle check, looking for loose bolts, leaks, or any one of the dozens of things that could spell disaster in an instant. One of the pretty, young,

German nurses approached, and in near-perfect Spanish purred, *"How much further, Miguel?"* She put one slender, tanned, manicured hand on his scarred forearm, and his head nearly exploded with screams.

*Papa! Don't go! Stay! Don't go with them!*

*Evil, Papa! Evil!*

His knees weakened, and his belly clenched up. The voices he heard were little Isabel's and Giselle's. He looked around for his babies but saw only the tall, blonde, nurse looking nonplussed as if she hadn't heard the screams at all. The screams of the dead, the screams of the dying—the screams of his daughters!

He yanked his arm back, and the nurse's handprint on his old scars quickly faded from a new, ripe, red burn to white scar tissue. The new mark disappeared altogether, leaving only his old, puckered, scarred skin. The screams stopped when the contact was broken. Even though the tactile terror faded fast, his arm still burned. After a moment all was normal again, though the nurse watched Juan closely, her head tilted a little to the right.

"Que pasa, Miguel? Are you okay?"

Juan forced a smile. "I am fine, senorita."

"Okay, but you still did not answer my question. How long?"

"Uh, we just passed Talca, senorita, so maybe five or six hours, if we're lucky. Probably closer to eight. Reports coming from the coast are saying the further west we go, the worse shape the highway is in. This quake was bad."

"Sixth largest ever recorded by a seismograph, handsome. It looks like 2010 is off to a fast start." She boarded the bus, sidling down the aisle to her seat.

Juan yanked his dirty red bandana out of his pocket and wiped his arm where she'd touched him. The effort didn't rid him of the dirty feeling nesting in his soul. He got back in his seat, wondering what the hell was going on.

The American preacher rounded up the last of the group and followed them up onto the bus. "Could have been there a lot faster if we'd flown, Miguel."

Juan nodded and started the bus. "Si, that is true, but I do not fly and neither does my bus, Esperanza."

If he'd been completely honest with his customers he would have said he doesn't fly any more. If he were completely honest, he wouldn't be pretending to be a Chilean named Miguel, even though he was now probably more Miguel the half-deaf, crippled Chilean bachelor than Juan, the divorced, child-killing Colombian pilot.

"Well, just so long as we get there before midnight. I'd like to get to work with those poor souls while the moon is full and ripe."

Sporadic laughter came from around the bus, but Juan gave all of his attention to getting off the soft gravel shoulder and back on the roadway.

A little more than an hour later, Juan heard a voice just behind him and looked over his shoulder at the speaker, one of the three elderly nuns. She spoke so softly he couldn't hear her. "Uno momento." He reached behind his ear and turned the hearing aid volume up as high as it would go. "Si, Sister?" He kept his eyes on the road but leaned toward her to hear her better.

Her low voice sounded strong and clear. "I asked if you would care for a bottle of water, my son. I noticed you finished yours a few miles back." She held up a plastic bottle from one of the many cases the group had brought with them. "It's not cold, but it is refreshing."

"Muchas gracias, Sister." Juan reached up and opened his hand, not wanting to take his attention away from the trio of crashed and burned out transport trucks they were passing. The bottle was placed firmly in his hand. "Thank you." He quickly placed the bottle in the wire cup holder bolted to the dashboard and got both hands back on the steering wheel to get them around the mess of buckled and rough road.

"My pleasure, my son."

Holding on to the seat backs, the nun made her way back to her seat. Other than her shuffling footsteps, the bus was eerily silent as they rolled along. Juan looked up at the cabin-view mirror wondering if his passengers were rubbernecking at the accident but someone had tilted the mirror up so that it pointed at the roof and not at the seats. Not wanting to spare a hand to unbuckle his seat belt and reach up to fix it while he drove, he left it in the odd position for the time being.

As they left the third wrecked truck behind them, Juan heard a low, beastly growl followed by a chuckle coming from the seats. What in God's name?!

That growl was answered with another. With a quick, worried glance over his shoulder, Juan saw his twenty passengers looking out the various dusty windows. The growl snuck up on him again. He concentrated on the sound and could distinguish words within the guttural utterance.

"All dead. Gone. Out of our reach."

Juan was confused. Who was out of reach?

"Yes, but be patient. The quake orphans are waiting. Amdusias has been busy gathering them from the surrounding ruined countryside."

Amdusias? Where had Juan heard that name before?

"King Amdusias? You trust him not to start without us?"

"I didn't say he hadn't. I told him one-in-twenty was his, just so long as his total for us topped one hundred and twenty."

"Will he find that many?"

"He was at two-hundred-eleven when we last spoke. He's been up and down the coast gathering together the lost, the broken, and the disenfranchised. He wanted to use his legions, but I reminded him we're not to draw attention to ourselves."

"If he's done this much on his own then he's welcome to his five-per cent."

"I'm sure his majesty will be so pleased he has your approval, Belial."

A deep chuckle followed before the two voices went silent.

Juan kept driving, trying to make sense of the strange

conversation. Amdusias and Belial? He knew those names, but couldn't remember from where. The voices were those of his passengers, but at the same time, they weren't. He thought it was like having one of those United Nations translators repeating the Yugoslavian or French representative's words into Spanish a moment after they were spoken in their native tongue. Or was it all in his head? Were the heat and the thin mountain air messing with his mind? He shook it off and drove on.

A few miles down the road another bus lay twisted and shattered in the ditch where it had been tossed by the earthquake. A row of broken bodies lay next to the road. At least three people worked to retrieve more corpses from the wreck. Nearby, a turkey vulture rocked from foot to foot, waiting for a rescuer to turn his back so it could hop in and feed. Two of the rescuers lifted the body of a young girl out through a shattered window. All Juan could think of was his own dead babies and his role in their deaths. For five years he'd been berating and cursing himself for not finishing his pre-flight inspection, his circle check. He also cursed himself daily for allowing Consuelo to bully him into taking the easy way. He was sure he would have found the oil leak and either fixed it or postponed the flight and to hell with the stupid third wedding of a mean cow whose husbands would rather die of heart attacks and strokes than live another day with her.

"Earthquakes are the best."

He blinked away his self-pity at the sound of the growled revelation made behind him. The best?

"I used to like floods, but the pickings are too thin for the effort it takes."

"What about hurricanes?"

"Only if we can get there before the cleanup progresses too far. New Orleans was a mess. It was great. Enough suffering for all of us."

Enough suffering?

"January 23, 1556. Shaanxi Province, China."

"700,000."

"830,000 was our final total."

"Now *that* was a feast."

"I didn't feed like that again until the Calcutta cyclone in 1737."

"You were there? Me, too!"

Juan reached up and turn off his hearing aid. Who or what in God's name was he hearing? After a moment he turned his hearing aid on again, though he was terrified of what he was going to hear next.

"Why does that not surprise me, Dajjal?"

"Says she who never misses a meal. I'm surprised you weren't here during the actual quake, Lamashtu."

Lamashtu? Another name he'd heard once before? When he was young?

"There was an odd spike in the birth rate in Northern Africa, and I was needed to thin things out."

"Infants? Lucky you."

Stunned, disoriented, and nauseated by what he heard, Juan slowed the bus and pulled over on the shoulder. He needed air and silence. Dammit, he needed the voices to stop, wherever they were coming from.

"Hey, Miguel, que pasa?"

"Sorry. My, um, turn to piss. Maybe a good time for a smoke, too." He pushed on the metal handle and swung the door open, swapping the stifling heat of the bus for a little of the slightly cooler mountain air. As he stood, he nudged the cabin-view mirror down with his elbow until he was sure it would give him a good view of his passengers when he reclaimed his seat. Maybe if his eyes could see the lips moving with the words he heard it would all make sense.

"Did I hear smoke break?" The German nurse was right on Juan's heels when he stumbled down the steps.

He limped around the front of the bus. Out of sight, he removed his hearing aid, bent over, and poured water over his head. He rubbed the warm wetness into his face and washed away the sweat salt and road grime, and then put his hearing aid back in.

"You okay, Miguel?"

143

He should have known he wouldn't be alone with this group. "The thin mountain air and no lunch, Padre."

"Well, my friend, that won't do at all. I'm sure between the twenty of us we can round up a little sustenance for our good driver."

"I'm fine, Padre, really. Much better now that I've had a little fresh air." He was damn sure he didn't want to share what passed for food with this group.

"Nonsense! I insist. As a matter of fact, I'm sure I have an apple you're welcome to."

"Padre..." He knew he was losing the argument.

"You need to eat, and a nice juicy Granny Smith will hit the spot. Don't tell me you're not at least a little bit tempted, Miguel." Father Charles stepped back into the bus, and Juan's hearing aid picked up the preacher's low, growly whisper clearly through the open window.

"We have to keep the driver strong and lucid. We may need him to get us past any road blocks the military set up to keep the curious away from the worst areas. I need a Granny Smith apple and something substantial, like a sandwich."

Even Juan's faulty hearing aid couldn't clarify the following exchange of low growls, but a moment later Father Charles stuck his head out of the door. "Load up, people! We're over halfway there."

When Juan dropped down into the driver's seat the preacher handed him the promised apple, a plastic-wrapped sandwich, and a warm juice box drink.

"Hopefully this will help, my friend."

"Gracias. I am feeling much better now and will get us back on the road before I eat." Juan forced himself to accept the offered food and placed it down to the left of his seat.

"I don't want you distracted while you drive, Miguel. We can take a few more minutes here."

"Nonsense, Padre. If I cannot eat and drive at the same time, I would not be able to call myself a bus driver."

"Well, if you insist."

"I do, Padre. And thank the people who shared. I am blessed by their generosity."

"Think nothing of it."

Juan cranked the door closed, released the parking break, shifted Esperanza into gear, and was a little less gentle as he got his beloved bus back onto the black-top. The preacher returned to his seat.

Juan felt something bump his left foot and looked down quickly to see the apple rolling around. No way was he going to eat anything from the hands of these people. He crushed the apple under his heel to keep it from rolling around. He glanced up at the newly adjusted mirror to see if anyone had noticed his disdainful treatment of their gift. A horn honk on his left side yanked his attention back to the road before he could focus on their faces in the vibrating mirror.

Once the old Ford passed them and sped on, Juan shot a glance at the mirror and nearly screamed at what he saw. It could not possibly be what he thought. He blinked, rubbed his eyes quickly, and reached for the bottle of water. He might indeed be suffering from heat stroke for in that brief look into the mirror he was sure his passengers had all donned bizarre, horrific, Halloween masks.

He quickly looked back over his shoulder to confirm or deny the sight, but the faces looking out the windows or down into books and magazines were human faces. They were tired and hot and probably a bit hungry themselves, but they were human.

Remembering the conversations he'd been overhearing, he forced his eyes to look back up at the mirror. Madre de Dios! Clamping his jaw shut so he didn't utter the words out loud, he drove on, his hands shaking. As the miles rolled past, he stole occasional glances up at the mirror and his mind cleared, his resolve strengthened, and his hands eventually steadied. They were beasts!

*Demons, Papa!*

Isabel? Yes! And she was right. He looked at demons! Near the back was a handsome man—with bat wings! Where the German nurse had been, sat a hideous, human-sized viper. In the front seat an angel with the head of a lion read Jennifer Rahn's *Wicked Initiations*, the book he'd seen the

Padre with. A bump in the road got Juan's attention for a moment, but his eyes flickered straight back to the mirror. He was certain of it. Sangre de Cristo, they were demons! It could be the only explanation! These were not masks he was looking at. Not a hallucination. It was...what? A vision? A sending? A glimpse into another reality? Was he dead? Was this Hell? Why him?

"You really should keep your eyes on the road, my friend. I moved that mirror up so you wouldn't get distracted by silly ideas."

"I...you..." He looked directly at the speaker. Father Charles crouched next to him, a very human Father Charles. He had neither lion's head nor angel's wings. He sweated and smiled, though the smile didn't reach his eyes.

"What? What are you thinking, Miguel? Or should I call you Juan? See, we all have our little secrets that aren't really secrets after all, my friend."

Juan shivered and stole a look at the mirror. A demon squatted beside him. "I'm not going to let you..." His brain tripped over itself as it tried to adjust to the information it received.

"Let us what, Juan? You'll do nothing. There is nothing you can do, so just shut up and drive." The tires on the right side of Esperanza grabbed at gravel, and the preacher gently placed his overly warm hand on Juan's head, turning his attention back to the road. "Maybe you should forget your loco notions and just do what you've been paid to do—take us to the earthquake survivors. You accepted my silver so you really have no choice."

*Demons, Papa!*

Juan kept his eyes front as Father Charles straightened from his crouched position, tore the mirror off its mount, and smashed it with his fist. "Problem solved, Juan. No more delusions, illusions, or hallucinations. Let's just get to those poor orphans and render them all the succor we possibly can."

A dark, evil hunger stained the words, and Juan truly knew terror for the first time in a very long time. Not for himself, but terror for the children those creatures would find at the end of this journey. Horror for their innocent souls and the souls of anyone who would keep those beasts from their meals, or harvests, or whatever the Hell they planned to do. Gripping the wheel until his knuckles nearly cracked, he guided Esperanza down the mountain road as it steepened and the curves became more pronounced. He slowed reflexively, not wanting to break an axle in a hole or skid into the rock face. His brain spun, lost in the enormity of it all.

A growly whisper came from the middle of the demonic pack he chauffeured. "There's nothing quite like the taste of a five-year-old girl's soul when she looks into my eyes and thinks she sees love while I drain her essence. Mmm hmm."

The highway edged close to the drop-off. Without a second thought, Juan, who had already died once in this lifetime, shifted his good foot from the brake pedal to the throttle and guided his Esperanza, his 'Hope', through a quake-made rift in the guardrail and off the precipice.

Amidst the anguished screams and wailing fury of the demons behind him, the former pilot smiled peacefully and spoke his last thought aloud to no one in particular. "I really have missed flying."

oOo

# Lisa & Britney 4 Ever

**First published:**
**Tales of the Zombie War.** Online. 2013.

This silly little poem was written for 'Weapons of Destruction'-themed late-night bedtime reading at the When Words Collide Festival. I suspect that it will be the only zombie piece I ever write.

~~~

## Lisa & Britney 4 Ever

Hi, my name is Lisa and I want to tell you when
My best friend Britney saved my life, again.

I used to work the night shift at Motel 666,
Checking in the working kids, and ignoring their tricks.

At noon-and-a-half two weeks ago I was home with the drapes pulled tight,
Not knowing that the mutant meteor had crashed some time in the night.

Papa was the first, caught the fever in San Antone.
By the time he was back in Austen he was raging skin and bone.

Drove the truck across the yard into the sycamore,
Then tore Mama's throat out when she met him at the door.

She screamed and screamed and finally stopped but by then I was out of bed.

Wandered down to the kitchen to find Papa chewing on
Mama's head.

I threw a pot, a couple pans, then all the knives in a steel
barrage,
But nothing could stop my Papa, so I ran for the garage.

He musta smelled fresh meat now that Mama was all done,
And he shambled after me, slow and steady but no run.

The tools were all hung snug and safe by Pa,
Which made it super easy for me to find the chainsaw.

Zombie Dad never saw her coming or if he did he didn't care.
The Husqvarna took his head clean off and cut halfway
through a chair.

She's fast, she's furious and she's anything but neat,
But she's all that stops me from sucking brains and shuffling
feet.

My chainsaw's name is Britney and she's my BFF.
Her teeth are sharp, she's all gassed up, and her roar has
made me deaf.

But without her I'd be a zombie, like my dear Papa,
Or lying in blood on the kitchen floor just like my dead Mama.


oOo

# Danny in the Dark

**First Published:**
*I'll Never Go Away 2*. Rainstorm Press. 2013.

Two pet peeves I have are reality shows and the super-coddling of children. This story is my answer to "How bad can it get?"

In their rejection of this story, the editors of Analog said "Stories with downbeat endings... are strongly disliked by Analog readers." I'll let you judge for yourself whether this has a downbeat ending.

~~~

## Danny in the Dark

Danny Angles kept tight to the wall, tucked in behind the dumpster, out of sight of the man he hunted. Milton Wayne Tennyson's killing spree was in its third week and this was the closest Danny had been to putting a stop to the psycho's madness. Ten victims in twenty-one days, each and every one with their throats cut and their entrails pooled in their laps. Each and every one a middle-aged, middle-management, white male just shy of six feet in height—the spitting image of Tennyson's own abusive father.

Two nights ago, Danny got a text tip that Tennyson was on the roof of the Metropolitan Museum. He wasted five minutes trying to reach his wife, Lucy, but ended up having to drop Kayley and Travis at his mother's place and speed downtown to the museum. He arrived three minutes late, finding accountant Scooter Dymbroski staring into the night, his life-blood soaking his cheap suit. Tennyson had once again vanished into the night.

Tonight, Danny was in the lead, waiting for Tennyson at the only place he could be, based both on Danny's profile of Tennyson as well as on the computer-printed note tucked neatly in Scooter's breast pocket daring the authorities to 'observe' Tennyson's 'Twofer Tuesday Special Serial Surprise'. Dressed in black from head to toe, Danny waited in the shadows behind the University Observatory on the main campus. He gripped his loaded, night-scope-equipped crossbow tightly, and waited. The weapon was deadly up to thirty yards and nearly silent. For hunting a hunter, it was perfect.

A nearby boot-scuff froze Danny in place. He held his breath, heard a second scrape on gravel and flicked off the crossbow's safety. He let the breath out slowly and watched as the shadow at the end of the alley shifted. Milton Wayne Tennyson, 26, stepped into the pale light cast by the dusty street lamp. Danny raised the crossbow to his shoulder and regarded his prey through the scope, confirming his target. The visual ID would have been enough for the ex-cop to act on, but then the butcher spoke and dispelled any lingering doubts Danny may have had.

"Hi. Good evening, folks. Milton Wayne Tennyson here with the latest—".

Danny shot Tennyson in the throat and the alley behind the observatory was suddenly silent again, or nearly so. Tennyson gurgled and thrashed about while his executioner expertly dismantled the crossbow, hung it under his long coat and slipped off into the cool night.

Four miles away, in the SW-ABS broadcast studios, pandemonium broke out.

***

"Go to commercial, NOW!! What the hell just happened, people?! One second I've got Tennyson live, giving us the lead-in to tonight's double killing and the next I'm at ground level, looking down at the observatory's Emergency Exit and no audio from the nutball! I've got three-hundred-million fat, ugly, and stupid viewers hanging on the edge of their damned Barcaloungers, waiting for tonight's twofer!" Ralph Weinberg threw his headset at his feet and jumped on it.

"Ralph! Check out 3. I've captured the alley security cam." Franco pointed up at the third monitor from the left.

All six sets of eyes in the control room locked onto Monitor 3 where a wide, overhead shot showed Tennyson's body on its back, in a spreading pool of blood.

"You must be kidding me! Please tell me his Kill-Cam recorded this!"

"Rewinding now!" Franco had Tennyson's footage playing in reverse on Monitor 2. Monitor 1 still showed the live net-feed of the Emergency Exit from the Kill-Cam, while Monitor 4 was playing the string of dead-air-covering commercials for rolling papers, the new Chevy Cyanide, and Sony's new Watch-Em InvisiCam digital camera. "Got it!"

The image on Monitor 2 froze, and then started forward again. Ralph and his team stared with rabid interest as Tennyson approached the back entrance of the Observatory. He walked with purpose and confidence, but he still took the time to look around at all the shadows, to check over his shoulder before stepping into the light at the end of the alley. Tennyson unclipped the miniature camera from his glasses and pointed it back at his own face. "It's Showtime!"

"Why do they all do that? It's such a goddamned cliché," he complained, but Ralph didn't take his eyes off of 2. Tennyson clipped the camera back onto his glasses and stepped fully into the light. The joy in his voice was obvious as he reveled in the attention he was getting from his personal little reality show. Then there was a soft, meaty, thud, and Tennyson went down, face up. He didn't die immediately and his gagging, gurgling, bubbling expiration seemed to go on forever. His death rattle shook the control room and when he finally sagged into death, his position shifted slightly and the SW-ABS crew could now plainly see the feathered end of an arrow of some type.

Ralph shattered the silence. "Get Connie out of make-up and behind her desk on set, now!" He couldn't help but stare at Monitor 2 and the wreckage that had been the best ratings machine ever. A door slammed behind him as someone rushed off to find Connie and get her ready to do her colour commentary half an hour early. "Franco, you've got ten minutes to get me a highlight reel of Tennyson's ten kills. I want slow-mo gore everywhere. I want sound effects at double-volume and canned applause overlaying each kill. I want this sick bastard to be made out as a hero." He finally tore himself away from the monitors and searched the room to see who was left. He settled on Raj, over in the corner. "Raj-man! Get me the name of that freak in Northlake that said he could double Tennyson's kills in half the time and would do it all to an 1980s pop soundtrack. I want him ready to roll tomorrow night. I'll drive the broadcast gear out to him myself if I have to."

"Yes sir!" Raj grabbed his tablet and started scrolling through his messages.

Ralph spun around and fixed his glare on a broad-shouldered, fiery redhead still staring at the monitors. "Annie!" She turned slowly, her eyes taking a moment to focus. "Annie, where are we with 'Cheater, Cheater'?"

"It's almost over. The cheating spouse lasted four weeks without getting caught by her husband and the finale is tomorrow night. If she can keep him in the dark until 8pm tomorrow she gets the whole five million. I've got her in here for an interview tomorrow at noon. Like her affair, it'll be live, unedited, and Rotoscoped to alter the image and keep her identity a secret until the reveal tomorrow night."

"Perfect! Now cut me a new best-of-Cheater-Cheater-moments for the end of Connie's Tennyson wrap-up and go heavy on the sex. Even drop in a hint that after tomorrow the un-altered screwing segments will be online for the Gold Level network subscribers. Have Lupo do the voice-over for this one." Movement on the studio floor caught Ralph's attention and he turned to see stunning, nearly naked in her see-thru power-suit, Connie Nakamura drop into her chair behind her commentator's desk. Connie slipped on the earpiece someone handed her and licked her lips.

"Ready any time you are, Ralphy-baby."

"Fantastic, Conn! Now, this is how we're going to spin it..."

\*\*\*

Danny let himself into his mother's house and curled up on the couch. He'd sent a quick text from the car to let her know he was on his way over but would let the kids sleep. He also sent Lucy a message to let her know where they were and that he'd have Kayley and Travis home in the morning in time to log-on and start school. He added a promise that he'd make sure they wore their masks and helmets the whole trip home and wouldn't eat anything at Grandma's until it had been checked and cleared by his new bug-meter, not the uncalibrated, three-year-old model his mother had stuffed in a kitchen drawer. No one would ever accuse Danny Angles of not protecting his children, even if it seemed a whole lot of over-the-top to him. You could slander or libel someone with impunity but if anyone, qualified or not, deemed his children unprotected, he was going to jail. As he said to Lucy just that morning, the world was seriously messed up.

Wrapped up in his grandmother's old quilt, he shivered as the last of the night's adrenalin sloughed off and drifted away into the dark. His mother's eight-foot-wide screen glowed softly on the wall, the fish tank screen-saver lulling him. It was a beautiful screen, Panasonic's best at the time, but he wasn't even tempted to turn it on and catch up on the crap that passed for entertainment these days. It was another bone of contention between him and Lucy. She wanted him to pay the extra three hundred a month for the full Voyeur Viewer Package with seven hundred live net-feeds, and he wanted to cancel everything but the kids' shows. He'd cancel those, too, but the Child Welfare Act made the 24/7 Kartoonz net-feed a constitutional right for the over-protected

Generation Snowflake. At least technology prevented his children from being exposed to the crap their mother watched. If the screen's sensors detected a Child Chip-identified minor, it automatically blocked all commercials and changed the channel to Kidlette Kartoonz.

Danny was sure that the downward slide started with Big Brother and Survivor in the 1990s and kept going straight to hell until now the glassy-eyed masses got their kicks watching shit like Botched Medical Procedures, Most Creative Suicides, cartoonized cheating spouses, and, up until an hour ago, Milton Wayne Tennyson and his slaughter spree. It disgusted Danny, and he was in no way ashamed of his actions tonight. That psycho, Tennyson, had needed to be put down like the animal he was. Who cared that fifty percent of the advertising revenue from the show went to the victims' families? It was obscene and inhuman. He was proud that he was able to rid the world of a killer scum. It was like being a cop again, back before the layoffs. He fell asleep with a small smile creeping on to his usually grim face.

***

"So, Travis, are you going to log on and learn something neat-o today?"

"No thanks, Momasita. Today's Math Day and you know numbers make me itchy." Travis scratched the back of his neck to make his point.

"Hives, again? Oh my poor baby." Lucy moved a dirty plate so her ten-year-old son could put his feet up on the coffee table. "Do you want lotion? Or maybe some dessert? Whatever you want, Honey-bunch." A scream from the other room startled Lucy, though Travis didn't even flinch, as though he'd been expecting it.

"MOM! Travis tore the arms off all my dolls!" Six-year-old Kayley charged into the living room with an armless doll in each hand, furious. She held one out as evidence to her mother and threw the other at her brother's head. Her aim

155

was good but his reflexes were better and the doll instead hit the table lamp behind Travis. The lamp teetered for a moment and then toppled over and crashed to the floor.

"Well, that's not good, kids. Travis, did you dismember your sister's dolls?"

"Yah. So?"

"Is there anything you want to say to Kayley, like an apology?"

"No."

"Okay. No problemo." Lucy turned to Kayley. "You broke my favourite lamp. It was a wedding present from Grandma. I think you should go to your room. What do you think?"

Kayley leaned around her mother to look at the wreckage of the lamp. "I think it's broken."

"Yes. Yes it is. Would you please get the broom and dustpan and we'll clean it up, before I go to my doctor's appointment."

"No, I want to watch Kidlette Kartoonz." She walked over to the couch and sat down, giving Travis a dirty look before turning her attention to the wall screen.

"Okay, Honey-bunch. I'll clean it up." Lucy went to find the broom but her head was elsewhere, thinking about the exciting day she had ahead of her. Half way to the kitchen she changed her mind and started upstairs to get changed. Danny met her on the stairs, rubbing the sleep out from his eyes.

"The kids up already, Luce?"

Lucy continued up the stairs past him. "In the living room. It's Math Day, so don't let Trav work with numbers or his hives will get worse. I have a doctor's appointment myself at twelve o'clock so they're all yours."

"Sounds good."

Lucy turned back around at the top of the stairs. "And don't forget that we've got my Sales Champions Dinner tonight at the Airport Marriott."

Danny stopped and looked back at his wife. "Tonight? Couldn't we just stay in and do something family-oriented? Play some games, maybe?"

"No, Danny, we can't." She folded her arms, shutting out any opposition. Danny noted to himself that she'd been doing that a lot lately. "This dinner is important. It could change our lives. Besides, the kids are too young for games. Competing means that there'll be a loser and that's not proper childcare."

"That's bull, Luce. I don't care what the so-called stuck-up, childless professionals say, if the kids don't learn to compete and win or lose gracefully in childhood, they'll be screwed when they hit sixteen, when their Child Chips come out and they're forced to be instant grown-ups."

"What do you want to do, Danny? Move to one of those free-range family communes, take the chips out, and turn off the net-feed?"

"That'd be better than having them turn out like your sister's kid. Larue hasn't been able to sit through a single job interview without weeping. He's such an emotional cripple than he even posted a weeping montage online and asked for sympathy 'Likes'. If that's what Travis and Kayley have to look forward to, then a commune is the way we'll go."

She lowered her voice and leaned forward to make sure he and only he heard her next comment. "You're an idiot. Maybe if you spent more time at home and less time out pretending to still be a cop, you'd see the reality of child-rearing first hand."

"I'm trying to make the world safe for our children, Lucy."

Another scream punctuated Danny's comment, but this time it was Travis. "MOM! DAD! Kayley gave me the finger! I'm feeling traumatization or something!"

Lucy laughed cruelly. "Yah, well good luck with that, Danny. Since you can't save everyone, maybe a free-range commune is exactly what all three of you need. I'm going to be late." She spun around and stormed off to the bedroom.

"Da-a-a-d!"

Danny shook off the anger Lucy brought out in him and turned his attention to Travis and Kayley.

"Travis, suck it up. She gave you a hand-gesture; she

didn't force you to watch a Tarantino film. That's what your Grampa did to toughen me up. Just deal with it and move on."

"I'm calling Child Services as soon as this episode is over."

Danny looked at the screen with the perfectly round, bright green, cartoon characters bouncing around a meadow. "What episode? It's all the same, Trav. The characters are all the same colour and the same shape. There're no squares, no triangles, not even a rhomboid, and all so no one is made to feel different. The only differences between them are the numbers on their chests!"

A clear tone sounded from the screen and a neutral female voice—The Monitor—interrupted the show. "Please lower your voice, Mr. Angles. A raised adult voice is not conducive to childhood safety. Children, do you need assistance? Shall I send a police officer to save you?"

Danny threw his hands up in frustrated surrender. "No, everything is fine, thank you."

"I was addressing Travis and Kayley, Mr. Angles."

"I know you were, but don't you think making a decision like that could traumatize them even more?"

There was a pause, and then the Monitor came back on. "You are quite correct, Mr. Angles. Kayley's heart rate increased eighteen percent when the police were mentioned, but it seems to have gone back down. In the future, please refrain from raising your voice. Undue stress is harmful to children. Have a neat-o day."

The sound of the Kidlette Kartoonz came back on and Danny wandered off to the kitchen, muttering under his breath.

\*\*\*

Young Danny stood high on a stump, clutching the thick rope that hung from the elm over the creek. He moved his grip a little higher, pulling the huge knot on the end of the rope closer to him. He knew he could swing two or three times across and back by just holding on with his arms, but if he could get the knot between his legs and sit on it, then he could keep going back and forth until the swing energy wound down and he had to pull the rope back up the hill for the next wannabe Tarzan.

"Danny! What the hell are you doing?!"

What was his mother doing here in the ravine?

"Get your ass out of bed and get dressed! The taxi'll be here in fifteen minutes to take us to the dinner!"

It wasn't his mother; it was Lucy. Danny pried his eyes open. "Yah. Okay. The dinner. Are you sure I need to go? I'm exhausted."

"You're going, if it's the last thing you do. Get your ass up. Now."

Danny dragged himself out of bed and managed to shave and climb into the suit in ten minutes. He needed a shower but since he was just the plus-one at some stupid Sales Celebration dinner, no one would give him a second thought. By the time Lucy ushered him into the waiting taxi he was fully awake and thinking that a nice dinner paid for by someone else was just what he needed.

***

"Ladies and Gentlemen, it's the time you've all been waiting for." The evening's Master of Ceremonies clinked his spoon on his wine glass right in front of his microphone, getting their attention immediately.

Danny looked up at the man, thinking he'd seen him somewhere before, but he couldn't place the face. He shrugged it off and speared the last piece of steak with his fork, popping it into his mouth before the waiter at his shoulder grabbed his plate and scurried off. Everyone else in the hotel's massive ballroom had finished eating five minutes ago and many were staring at him and giving him odd looks. He didn't care. With two kids in the house, he never got to have red meat anymore and he was going to savour every morsel.

The MC continued. "Before we go any further, I have to ask someone a simple question." A scantily dressed young woman appeared at Danny's elbow and smiled down at him. He could have sworn there was sympathy in her eyes but he had no idea what she was doing there.

"I'd like to ask Danny Angles a quick question before we go on. Daniel ..."

Danny looked up at the stage and a microphone suddenly appeared in front of him, held by the woman. "Uh, yah?"

"Danny, do you know why you're here tonight?"

"Sure. Lucy is getting some kind of sales award."

There was laughter around the hall, and some of it none too kind. Someone in the back shouted out "Loser!" and someone else answered "MASSIVE loser!" and the laughter ramped up a notch. Danny was confused as hell. He looked at the pretty young woman with the microphone but her sad half-smile didn't help. He looked over at Lucy for guidance and was shocked to see her smiling so big she was almost in tears. As a matter of fact she was in tears, and she was trying hard not to laugh. But he saw cruelty in her eyes and had a feeling that the shit was about to hit the fan.

The MC came to his rescue, though. Sort of. "Danny, you're here because of Lucy, alright. But tonight's also about you." The MC pointed at a television camera on the end of a crane Danny hadn't noticed before. The crane was sweeping slowly over the heads of the celebrants, right at Danny. "Look into the camera for me, Daniel, and give a big smile." Danny managed maybe a quarter smile, at most. "Good enough, my friend. Thank you. Now, Daniel, what would you say if I told you that I'm going to give your lovely wife, Lucy, a certified cheque for five million dollars?"

"Um ... okay? Sure?" What the hell was going on?

"Now, what would you say, Daniel, if I told you that I'm going to give Lucy a cheque for five million dollars because ... for the last four weeks she's been screwing another man on world-wide live net-feed and you have been totally oblivious? Welcome to 'Cheater, Cheater', Daniel!"

The entire assembly erupted in boisterous applause and laughter, including Lucy, who laughed the hardest and meanest. Danny could see in her eyes that the MC was telling the truth and this was no prank. He stood, looked coldly at the MC, then at the embarrassed young woman with the microphone, and finally back at Lucy. He took a deep breath, gazed straight into the camera and finally answered the MC's question. "At least she's good at something, because as a wife and mother she was an utter failure. Hopefully her next john won't want a used-goods discount." Then Danny turned, kissed the now-smiling microphone girl on the cheek, and walked out of the Airport Marriott ballroom. As he pushed open the fire doors leading into the lobby he remembered that he'd last seen the MC hosting the One Hundredth Academy Awards. The guy was even more of an idiot in person.

***

Danny gave the cabby an extra hundred bucks to lose the paparazzi on the way to his mother's house to get the kids; but a block from Mrs. Angles' cul-de-sac Danny changed his mind and had the man take him home. While they drove, Danny slipped his earpiece in and called his mother.

"Hi Mom."

"Oh, Danny-boy. I'm so proud of you!"

"You saw?"

"Seven hundred million people saw, Honey. Are you on your way over?"

"I don't think so. Do you mind watching the kids for a few days? I don't think Child Services would be impressed if I let Trav and Kayley be traumatized by seeing me box up their mother's crap and put it out on the front lawn for the whole world to pick at."

"Good thinking, Honey. I'm happy to watch them for as long as you need."

Danny sighed. "I guess the world'll be laughing at me for a long time."

"Probably not, Honey. The network is already advertising a replacement for Milton Wayne Tennyson. This new sicko is supposed to start a live net-feed tomorrow evening. He's promised at least two kills a night, every night. They hinted that he lives right here in the Pacific Northwest, so you lock your doors tight and I'll do the same."

"Another one? Goddammit! We live in a sick, sick world, Mom."

"We sure do, Honey. You get a good night sleep and I'll try to get the kids to call you when they wake up, some time after noon."

"Sounds good, Mom. Love you."

"Love you, too, Danny-boy."

\*\*\*

Danny's mother was right. By the time Peter Thomas Rockney broadcast his fifth and sixth live-feed shotgun-and-dismemberment murders, the street outside Danny's house was empty of reporters. He did an online search of his own name and the most recent article was two days old. They'd already dismissed him as old news and he was more than fine with that.

While he was online he spent an entire morning reaching out to his police and private investigation contacts, trying to find out everything he could about Peter Thomas Rockney. By the time his growling stomach forced him to take a break, Danny was pretty damned sure he knew where the two-a-night serial killing bastard was going to find victims seven and eight, and the ex-cop was determined to get there first.

\*\*\*

The crossbow seemed lighter in Danny's gloved hands than it had been when he was stalking Tennyson and he took that as a sign that he was doing the right thing. Danny's research had revealed that Rockney seemed to have a thing for public parks, beautiful couples, and the Greek alphabet, so Danny sat, hidden in the shrubs of Omega Park on the outskirts of the city. He popped another stick of gum in his mouth, leaned back against the tree at the centre of the thick shrubbery, and thought about the chat he'd had with his mother after the kids got bored talking to him and went back to watching Kidlette Kartoonz.

When he'd suggested to his mother that maybe a free-range commune might be the best place to raise the kids, she'd brightened right up. She loved the idea and even offered to round up information for him about the various communes throughout the Pacific Northwest. The more Danny thought about it, the better the idea sounded. If Kayley and Travis were to ever have a chance at a real life, it had to be away from the city and the Child Welfare tyrants.

A woman's giggle pulled him out of his daydream and Danny moved up onto one knee so he could lean forward and see the pathway. A couple strolled along, hand-in-hand, laughing and chatting without a care in the world. Danny was almost envious; and then they stepped into the dim light cast by a mock gas lamp and he recognized Lucy. He didn't recognize the man, but it didn't take a genius to figure out that he was the son of a bitch who'd screwed Danny's wife all the way to the bank. Wouldn't that just screw with their heads if he stepped out of the bushes just as they passed and shouted "Boo?!" He nearly laughed out loud at the thought, but bit it back.

Nearby, a twig snapped. It sounded like it was in the bushes on the other side of the wide path. Probably just a squirrel, Danny thought. Then the squirrel pumped a shotgun and Danny knew with utmost certainty that Peter James Rockney was broadcasting live from only a few yards away, waiting for his prey to move within range of his sawed-off ratings-maker. Danny slowly, silently placed the crossbow on the ground, lay facedown beside it, and then covered his head with his hands. What difference would it make if he waited a couple minutes before stopping Rockney? Like Lucy said, he couldn't save everyone.

o0o

# Finding the Time to Write

**First Published:**
*FastForward Festival*. Online. 2012

I love stories which explore time travel, but I wanted one that is closer to what I think the reality will be when the backward time barrier is finally broken. No flashing lights and no brass machines carrying a hero eager to save the world or a villain keen on destroying it.

~~~

## Finding the Time to Write

*Monday, February 9, 1987.*
My First Journal thing ever.

My name is Mikey Munro. I'm nine and I live in Phoenix Arizona. I go to Sheep Valley Elementary School.

Miss Syme says we all have to write a journal for a week telling about our thoughts and stuff that happens and stuff we want to do and people and stuff. It's stupid cause Drew said so. He's my big brother. He did the same thing for President's Day five years ago when he had Mrs. Derry.

It's okay, cause I like to write and record, even though I keep track of all my science stuff in another notebook. Drew says he NEVER writes his feelings down. He just goes out and does stuff that makes him feel better. He used to get real angry a lot but now he doesn't. He doesn't tell me what stuff he does and I don't ask cause I did once and he got real quiet and smiled all strange and looked at me like he can see right through me. It creeped me right out.

*Tuesday February 10.*
Day Two.
Today was real boring. Suzie Porqwa punched Craig in the head at recess, but she does that at least one time every day so its not really news. I'm writing this during MATH cause I already did today's work and the homework for the whole week. I don't know why everyone hates Math. It's so easy!

*Wensday, Feb 11.*
Crackers didn't come home last night. Crackers is one of our Siameese cats. We have three cats. Crackers is my sister Lisa's cat. When Lisa and me went to look for Crackers, Drew said don't bother, Crackerhead ran away. I think he's wrong, but we didn't find Cracker anyway. We looked before dinner after Lisa did her homework. She's in third grade so her homework is easy when I help her. We really want to find Crackers. The other cats are Pinhead (Drew's) and Skywalker (mine) and they miss Crackers. They didn't eat any of the leftover tuna casserole we gave them. Very strange. That NEVER happens.

*Thurstday, Febuary 11, '87.*
Now Skywalker is missing! And Pinhead tracked blood into my room. I followed his tracks cause maybe Skywalker and Crackers are hurt somewhere and need help. But I lost the tracks behind the house near the fence and Pinhead can't tell me where he came from.
Craig and Ron came over after school to help me look for Skywalker and Crackers. Ron has cats too and he thinks someone is kidnapping cats on our street. He lost two last year. Craig likes dogs so he thinks the cat-napper is doing a good thing. Sometimes I think he hit his head too hard playing tackle football last year.

*Friday February 12 in this year 1987.*
Lisa stayed home sick today. She just cries and wants Crackers and Skywalker to come home. Me too. But I don't

cry except just before bed when no one is looking. Drew got mad at Lisa for crying but Mom told him to go take the garbage out and leave his sister alone.

*Feb. 13.*

We're all worried. I fell in the creek so I have to change my pants before we go back out and look for Lisa some more. She got up before Mom and Dad and sneaked out to look for Crackers. Drew said he saw her from his window and she went down the street and some guy in a white van followed her. I had to write it down here. Dad says he's scared shitless (sorry!) and so am I and Mom. Drew says Lisa is probably at a friend's house but we phoned them all. Dad's calling me so I have to go.

*Sunday. Feb. 14.*

Valentine's Day. Paper hearts are everywhere we go but we hate them because Lisa is still missing. The police found a guy with a white van but he was in Las Vegas yesterday and he has receets or something to prove it. Mom's making lunch and then we all go back searching. I hope Lisa found Crackers and is just helping him and Skywalker find their way home.

*3 oclock.* The police are downstairs and Mom is freaking out. Dad sent me and Drew to our rooms. I think it's about Lisa. I'm scared someone hurt her. I wish I could just turn back time and make the last three days go away.

*September 10th, 2001. Graduate Physics Lab. University of Arizona. Phoenix.*

Holy Shit! I can't believe I found this thing! It was stuck in with some old photos Dad sent me. Reading through it gives me the shivers all over again. I was right to be worried about Lisa back then. Someone had hurt her and Mom was freaking the hell out because they'd just found Lisa's body in the bushes behind the Methodist Church. The bastard who'd killed her had beat her to death with a brick and left her next to the strangled and gutted corpses of the cats, Skywalker and Crackers. My poor baby sister. Fuck. I'll kill the sick bastard if I ever find out who did it. Mom couldn't take it. Killed herself on Memorial Day. Took a shitload of sleeping pills and left an apology note for Dad. That broke his heart. Nearly killed him, too. Good thing he still had to look after Drew and me, or he might have checked out, too. Don't think I'll tell him about finding this journal.

*September 29th, 2009*

Okay, I have to write this down somewhere because I can't believe it myself and I don't dare put this anywhere someone might find it. Our research has taken a cool twist. We've done something screwy with Time. It looks like we found a way to temporally & geographically displace an inanimate object. We were looking for a scientific way to prove the Buddhist idea that "We are the Universe and the Universe is us" before we head over to Switzerland to work on the ATLAS Project and we fell into this mind-blowing shit. We're going to run tests after hours all weekend so we can take the results to Professor Yatabe and see about funding something bigger.

*OCTOBER 2ND, 2009.*

It's all over the damned news and I don't know if I'm surprised. I'm probably in shock. They've arrested my cancer-stricken brother Drew for murder and while they were leading him into the courthouse he just stopped and turned to the reporters and confessed to being the Presidents' Day Killer for the last 17 years. Then he hinted that there might be others he did as well, AND HE SMILED WHEN HE SAID IT!

They asked him who his first victim was and he laughed. They asked him again and he said "That's a private family matter." Family matter?! FAMILY MATTER?!! I think that asshole prick Board of Education Trustee brother of mine just copped to killing my baby sister 23 years ago! She was only 8 for Christ's sake. Shit, *he* was only 14. 14!!! What kind of dirtbag kills his kid sister? Kills ANY kid for that matter?! I tell you here in this damned journal once and for all that if his brain tumour doesn't kill him I'll do it myself! Except that won't bring Lisa or Mom back. Yah, Mom. If he really killed Lisa, then he killed Mom, too, by breaking her heart. I'll kill him. I'LL GODDAMN KILL HIM! He's no longer my brother.

I just called Dad to see if he watched the news but it went straight to voicemail. I think I'm going to have to drive down and see him. We have to talk about this and it'll be better in person. I wonder if he ever suspected it could be Drew.

*OCTOBER 4TH, 2009.*
*2pm.*
Unofficial log. No one knows about this journal so this is a good place to say what I have to, privately. Harpreet says that we can't be doing what we're doing—that it's a physical impossibility and there must be another explanation for the results. She went on and on about entropy along the curve but I think she needs to just take a chill pill and look at the results. Our success rate is in the 98th percentile for temporal distances of greater than an hour and locations further than 2 miles out. We don't know why the further the better, both temporally and spatially, but so far that's what the results show. Right now it's enough to know that it can be done at all.

The only limitation we've found (other than size, until we build a bigger unit) is that it can't be biological material. We tried a dozen different plants, both living ones and cut ones. They all came out mush. Even tried a moth in a jar. The jar was fine, the moth, not so fine. Nothing organic. Paper isn't consistent. It may have to do with how much post-consumer materials are in it.

But... a tin & plastic desk plaque with the words "In Dog We Trust" was fine. It wasn't just intact, the words were legible, which is what I was really after. I was half expecting the words to come out scrambled. But they didn't, and that means it's time. I made a wish 23 years ago and I suppose everything I've done since then—science fairs, my Masters, my PhD—have been working toward actually making it come true.

Tonight, after everyone goes home, I have to send myself that message. I have to stop Drew. I have to save Lisa.

*9:28pm.*

I've scratched the message into a piece of copper and am going to send it to the upstairs bathroom in the house. Dad still lives there so after dinner I went and let myself in and took EXACT GPS readings and used an altimeter for the exact elevation. That covers the "where". For two years in '86 & '87 I always got up to piss at exactly 2am after some nightmare so that's the "when" part of the equation. I've calculated everything down to the finest minutiae. "Six ways to Sunday" as Dad says.

In essence, the message tells my younger self what Drew is, where to find the dead cats for proof and where and when he's going to kill Lisa. I just pray to God that my nine-year-old self believes my 32-year-old self and can do what he has to and stop our brother.

Yesterday Harpreet said that you can't send yourself a message 'now' that you didn't already get 'then', but if I stop and think about this too long, I'll talk myself out of it. It has to work. It just HAS to. I do know that back then I was mad enough to kill whoever did it. A few weeks after Lisa's murder Drew told me to 'lighten up' so I threw a lamp at his head. Took six stitches to close the wound.

*27th of Nov. '09*

I feel like I just wrote in this thing yesterday but for the life of me I can't remember a damned thing that's in it. I'll give it a read after I get back from lunch with Mom & Lisa. Hell, the only reason I'm writing in this thing at all is that the last one is full and I'm not happy with the tanning job I did on the new cover so I have to start again, so a new one isn't ready. I'll just transpose this note after the new journal book is ready.

I had a dream last night that I was in some physics research lab. Strange.

Anyway, here's a quick summary before I go off for lunch: I'm modifying the parameters this time to see if I can skew the results just by changing the timing a little. An hour of punishment followed by a ten-minute break, then back to the punishment.

Oops, there she goes again. She's got a great sense of time, this one does. I don't how she manages it without her watch, but every hour, almost exactly on the hour, she screams for roughly five minutes and then stops. Damn she's got some fight in her. I don't think there's been one with this much fight since Drew. It's true what they say about the first being the most satisfying, though. He definitely was. He never should have killed my cat. Nope, he should have just left the damned cats alone.


o0o

# No Escaping the Blood

**First Published:**
As a stand-alone e-novelette for Kindle and Kobo. 2014.

This novelette was originally written for an anthology with the theme of "History reimagined with a key figure as a vampire". The project was delayed and languished and began to moulder on the editor's desk so I decided to self-publish the story as an ebook.

I was a magician when I was a teenager, and a huge fan of Harry Houdini, so when I asked myself who would make an interesting vampire, Harry immediately came to mind. Here's what happened when he realized that there's...

~~~

## No Escaping the Blood

*London. 1904.*
Ehrich was manacled in a foreign land and isolated from friends and family. His usual calm was in tatters and he was soaked in sweat. He knew his wife, Bess, and his brother, Dash, fretted somewhere nearby.

The manacles secured him but his frock coat restricted him, frustrated him. With his fingertips he retrieved his penknife from his waistcoat pocket. A gift from his mother, blessed by his Rabbi father, he never went anywhere without it. Careful not to cut himself, he palmed the knife, raised his hands up over his head to his collar, and proceeded to turn the coat inside out over his head so that it now lay across his arms. He pulled and sliced at the coat over and over and two minutes later it lay in shreds around his feet, littering the floor.

He sat cross-legged, the iron cuffs on his lap. The restraints were tight—too tight for him to simply slip out of, even if he could dislocate his thumbs and fold his hands in half. Although he raged inwardly with frustration, he had to admire the workmanship of these cuffs. The man who'd built them had to be a genius. There would be no twisting his hands to release a poorly caught latch, no bending a spring. No bent hairpin would find its way into the keyhole, even if his thick, dark hair contained such a pin, which it didn't. The penknife would be of no use here; he could see that the blade was simply too short.

A cough nearby startled him and he almost called for help, but he knew that would be disastrous. He could hear a small orchestra playing a waltz but the music did nothing to salvage his foul mood. If he didn't escape soon, he would hardly have the right to call himself The Handcuff King. London's Daily Mirror would lambaste him for failing the challenge and Ehrich Weiss would cease being Harry Houdini.

***

An hour and ten minutes after he was shackled by a representative of the Daily Mirror, Harry finally freed himself from the devious cuffs, stepped from behind the curtain of his 'ghost closet' and stood centre stage of London's Hippodrome. The crowd was ecstatic and they immediately hoisted him up on their shoulders and paraded him around. He was so exhausted that he broke down and wept.

Back at their room at the Savoy that night, Harry dropped into the overstuffed chair and sighed. "Bess, dearest, that was the hardest thing I've ever had to do. Remind me again why I do this."

"Because you're the best, Harry, and if it wasn't challenging, you'd feel like you were robbing the audience of a great performance." She poured herself a cup of tea.

"No one understands me like you do, Love. What on earth would I ever do without you?"

***

*Eleven Years Later.*

It was late, well after the gates of New York's Machpelah Cemetery were locked, but a deal with the caretaker ensured that Harry could privately visit his parents' graves as late as he wished, just so long as he locked up behind him. He knelt down and placed a small stone with his left hand on the grave, as Jewish tradition dictated. Less traditional was the Yizkor prayer of remembrance he whispered each time he visited.

"*Adonai, mah adam vatayda'ayhu—*"

"I know you, boy. You are Old World. I smell it in your blood."

Harry froze.

"You are Roma." The voice was that of a man, probably a little older than Harry's forty-one years. The faint accent was definitely eastern European. The shadow to Harry's right shifted. He looked without moving his head but could make out no details.

"I am no gypsy. My father was a Rabbi."

"Yes, but there is Roma in your blood, trust me—blood is something I know a little about."

"As well as hiding in the dark, apparently."

Something in the shadow of that tree rustled. "You are here, as well, Houdini."

"Maybe so, but at least I am not hiding."

The shadow took a half-step forward but still Harry could see little of the man before him. "I am simply someone like yourself who enjoys the quiet stillness of the hours between sunset and sunrise. So, Ehrich-who-is-also-Harry, what brings you here tonight?"

"Fear."

"You? Afraid?" A dry chuckle drifted out of the shadow.

"I almost died this past week, in California. An escape gone wrong. I was cocky and miscalculated, overestimating my own abilities."

"Another Daily Mirror challenge?" Harry heard the shadow sniff, like an animal curious about a scent.

"This was worse. I was buried alive and had to be pulled out at the end. I panicked and passed out just as I reached the surface. The weight of the dirt is killing."

"It's not so bad when you get used to it. The panic is the worst part, but so unnecessary."

"That's easy to say until you've tried it."

"Quite true. I have. I have spent more time buried than you have had waking hours, Handcuff King."

Harry knew that the man was lying—he had to be—but there was something in his tone, something in the weight of his words that made Harry wonder. "You are an escapist?"

"Of sorts."

"There is a secret? A way to keep the fear at bay while making the escape?"

"There is. It is a simple secret and one I will gladly share, for a small price."

"Money I have plenty of." He pulled the folded wad of bills from his trousers pocket.

"Cash is payment for fools. There are so many more things that have greater value than your silly paper." The shadow seemed to deepen, even though Harry was now looking directly into it.

Fear was something Harry had to conquer he would pay whatever price was asked here and now for the secret this shadow offered. He stepped away from his parents' graves, toward the tree. "What price do you beg, then?"

"Simply a taste of the Old World."

The shadow moved faster than Harry had ever seen any man move, including himself. There was a moment when the darkness was still and then in a blink Harry was down on top of his mother's grave with a beast locked onto his throat. Harry's arms were pinned to his sides by an unbelievable strength and as the living shadow fed on him, Harry began to feel an unexpected calm. He stopped fighting and let it happen.

He remembered the grave in Santa Ana and the weight of the killing earth above him. He remembered the feeling of surrender just before he lost consciousness, and he remembered the photos on the front pages of the papers showing his assistants grabbing his limp hand, dragging him out of the ground, and reviving him. But there were no assistants here. No Bess, no Dash—not even the press. Harry was alone with this creature, this beast that fed on the blood of men.

Most men lose the battle when they lose the use of their arms in a grappling match, but Harry was almost as capable with his legs and feet as many pretenders were with their hands and arms. He had worked all his life to be faster, fitter, and more flexible than anyone else and when he realized that this was going to be the moment of his death, he tore away the calm and shredded the surrender to pieces.

The beast was taking his time, probably well aware that there would be no interruption here in the darkness of the cemetery, but then Harry curled his legs up under his attacker's torso and shoved it away with one mighty flexing. The beast tried to rend a thigh, find the artery there and continue feeding, but the greatest escapist did what he did best, he escaped, jumping to his feet. The creature leaped at its prey, needing to finish feeding, finish the kill and vanish back into the night; but Harry could now see the beast quite clearly. He ducked and punched it hard in the solar plexus.

The beast was barely slowed. It got a steel-grip on Harry's wrist but Harry knew steel and nothing could restrain his wrists if he didn't want it to. He yanked, shoved, and then twisted his arm in a quick circle and the beast was caught off-balance. Harry broke the grip as he brought the rotation of his arm around and the beast stumbled. Squat and powerful, Harry crouched down, twisted his hips and kicked out to the side, catching the killing shadow in the jaw. The beast shook off the boot-to-the-head and circled in for another pounce. Having no idea what else to do, Harry pulled his tiny little penknife out of his waistcoat pocket and snapped it open. The creature laughed.

"Little Roma Jew magician, you are about to see how it is to die alone."

Harry stayed silent. This was life and death and he would not be distracted. He ignored the glowing, commanding eyes, and the flexing, claw-like fingers. He ignored everything but the beast's centre mass, and so, when it attacked with lightning speed, Harry was ready. He twisted away from the reaching claws and rammed his penknife into the beast's passing ribs with three fast punches. Though the blade was sharp, it was so short it should barely have scraped the skin through the billowing cloak, but the thunderous howl of pain from the creature's mouth nearly knocked Harry off his feet. He stumbled, set his stance for another attack, but in a blur of darkness the beast vanished into the night, leaving Harry standing alone, bleeding, and bewildered.

Harry stared at the little knife in his hand, so covered in the creature's blood that he could barely see the Shield of David his father had inscribed in it years ago. Before he understood what drove him to do it, he raised the knife to his mouth and licked it clean of the creature's blood. It burned at first but he couldn't stop himself. It was like English horseradish, hot enough to make the eyes water and clean the sinuses, but tasty enough that he had to have more. He looked around, eager to find any trace of the dark, mystical elixir of death on the ground or dripped on a tombstone as it fled. His parents' graves forgotten for the moment, Harry sniffed the air and started off on the creature's trail. Foggy though his thinking was, he remembered his promise and secured the gate just as the sound of a constable's whistle pierced the night.

Covered in blood, Harry fled. He stayed away from the brightest-lit streets, and he ran. He got as far as Central Avenue when he remembered the automobile. He turned around and sprinted back.

***

The drive home to West 113th in Harlem felt like it took forever in the slow Buick but Harry eventually got there and parked out front of number 278 without incident. He slipped into the house and made for the bathroom in the basement so as not to wake Bess or the staff, all asleep upstairs. He took a long shower, working the blood out of his hair and scrubbing his body clean. He wanted nothing of the beast's touch to remain on him. He finally worked up the nerve and stood naked in front of the mirror to examine his wounds.

He could clearly see the huge bite marks but the bleeding had stopped. The wide, deep wounds didn't seem to be either as wide or as deep as he'd first feared when the thing was trying to tear his throat out. The small medical kit in the cabinet supplied everything he needed to cover it all up and keep it clean until he could get his brother Leo, the doctor, to look at it. He wrapped himself in the robe his housekeeper, Julie, always left on the back of the door for him and made his way silently up the stairs with the hope of finally retiring before the household rose for the day.

One of Bess' cats appeared just as Harry reached the top of the steps and opened the door onto the main floor. He had no time to discern whether it was Daisy or Lazy because the instant the cat saw him it hissed, puffed up, screeched and bolted into the kitchen. He shook his head at the cat's strangeness and started for the stairs up. A shaft of bright sunlight lanced through the front windows and illuminated the bottom step.

"Another sizzling hot New York day," he whispered to the vanished cat. The sun lit up a second step and the shaft of light spread out on the floor, a puddle of illumination. Harry moved forward but stopped mid-step. His skin warmed but his body seemed to be growing colder. His stomach churned and he suddenly felt like he'd eaten rat poison. Every organ in his body clenched and twisted. His eyes were on fire and he couldn't breathe. His fingertips were being dipped in acid and he wanted so badly to scream but had no air left in his seared lungs. He sensed saving coolness behind him, at the head of the stairs back to the basement so he stumbled that way.

He ripped open the door and stumbled down the steps. The sun was now reaching the ground-level windows of the basement and it chased him to the windowless bathroom. Only once he was there did he feel at all safe. He threw the bolt and climbed into the claw-foot tub, pulling the entire stack of fresh towels down on top of himself. He only stopped shaking when he fell asleep.

***

Harry woke feeling safe, no longer burning alive. He climbed out of the tub, a little surprised that he wasn't stiff or cold. He reached for the light switch but stopped when he realized that he didn't need it. He could see as clearly in the blackness as if it were noon. He found and closely examined the magazine the housekeeper always left by the toilet for long visits. The print was clear and distinct and... it was impossible. What in God's name was happening to him?

"Harry? Are you down there?"

Bess! He darted quickly to the foot of the stairs and looked up, doing his best to smile. "Just working through some ideas."

His petite wife started down the stairs, a cigarette in hand and her head tilted slightly to the left as she squinted at him. "What's wrong, Harry? You look pale. Is that a bandage?!" She reached the bottom of the stairs and with one hand reached up to gently pull back the robe to reveal the bandage while holding the cigarette away from him, knowing how he disliked the smoke. "What have you done to yourself?!"

"I slipped in the shower." Behind her tobacco smoke he could smell the faint dusting of powder on her skin and feel the flush of her blood as her heartbeat raced with concern. Her pulse pounded in his ears and he had to steady himself on the handrail.

Bess pulled the huge bandage back. "Is this your idea of funny, Harry Houdini? I worry myself sick every time you step on stage, then you go out last night and don't come back to bed when you return home. I think maybe you're out with Dash but you're down here alone, to finally appear wearing a bandage big enough to cover an amputation. A bandage I might add that protects *nothing*. Your neck is fine." She placed the back of her tiny hand on his neck, then on his cheek and finally on his forehead. "Mary, Mother of God, Harry, you're cold as ice." Bess took his hand and led him upstairs, daintily blowing the smoke up and away from him as they ascended. Harry flinched when they neared the top of the stairs, but then, suddenly, he somehow knew he was safe. The sun had set.

Bess' warmth was like an electric current to Harry, charging up every cell in his body. Her scent stirred his loins, made his mouth ache. He slipped his hand from hers and stopped in the foyer. He stood, barefoot in the robe, fighting the twisted hunger he didn't understand. He took a step toward the stairs up to their bedroom, clenching his fists as he moved past Bess, moved within reach of her pale, slender neck hidden coquettishly behind the high lace collar. He took more halting, difficult steps and she made to follow him, to help him up the stairs.

"Please, no. I'm going to dress and go out. I need to think."

"You're not well, Harry." She put her hand on his arm but he yanked it away.

"Yes. No! I'm not sick. I just need—" What? What did he need? To eat? To drink? To run? To stay away from Bess and everyone else in the house before he hurt them? "I can't explain, my Darling. Please trust me. Soon. I will tell you everything soon." What he needed almost as much as a meal were answers from the beast who had 'blessed' him with whatever he was experiencing.

Harry sped up the stairs to their bedroom and dressed quickly in his scruffy old black trousers and sweater. Bess watched him from the bedroom doorway, her arms folded across her chest as she leaned against the frame.

"I will expect a full explanation when you get home, Harry Houdini."

"Of course, my Love."

"Have you even eaten today? At least have something before you go, Harry."

He could feel the heat of her blood and count the beats of her heart from across the room. He had to leave, now! "I'm not hungry," he lied, then he was across the room, past her and on the stairs before she could stop him.

"Harry!"

"I love you, Bess. Please trust me. I will see you... before morning."

"Wake me when you get in, no matter the time."

He was out the front door and off into the night. He could smell the river nearby, and fresh-turned soil of a garden. Someone had been cooking corned beef and cabbage earlier—the smell was strong, but a few hours old and losing its tang.

Starting off at a brisk walk, he didn't even think about direction. After a block his walk was an easy run and before he'd passed two more street lamps he was sprinting down the street. He must have run a hundred yards in five seconds before the absurd danger of it hit him and he relaxed his pace.

"Wouldn't do to be caught hot-footed in Harlem," he muttered to himself. He jogged on, revelling at the sights and sounds of the night—sights and sounds he was sure had always been here but he was only now becoming aware of them. There was the owl in the oak, preening, keeping one keen eye on the long grass of the vacant lot for the mice to venture out and there were the crickets. They were everywhere and they were deafening; though it seemed to Harry that their songs went softly pianissimo as he passed by, as if they sensed something strange in him, a reason not to draw his attention their way.

He felt it in himself, too. There was something different

with him and with the night world. Always an athletic man, he now felt as if he could best the fastest and strongest. A couple out perambulating arm-in-arm approached him and he could hear their heartbeats, smell their soaps and creams and powders and his pipe tobacco. As they passed by with smiles and nods of their heads Harry sensed the woman's heat and nearly shoved her beau aside to grab her when they were within arm's reach. But he didn't. He nodded back and continued on down the walk, fists clenched in his trousers pockets.

Eventually he found himself at the cemetery gates. He listened and sniffed the air but found no sign of his attacker from last night. His tongue darted out between teeth that were a touch sharper than they had been two days ago. He could taste nothing of the beast on the air, either, so he stalked around the perimeter of the burial ground, looking for a trail, a sign—anything that might lead him to the answers he sought. But he was alone. There was no beast, no cowering shadow waiting to pounce out and finish the job of killing him that it had started last night. He couldn't very well pass by without visiting his parents' graves so he walked up to the fence and leaped. Not sure quite what to expect, he was more than a little impressed when he sailed up and over the wrought iron spikes and landed twenty feet inside the grounds.

"Now that's a neat trick if ever there was one," he said to the graves and tombs around him. No voices came to him from the shadows so he meandered over to the family plot and sat down on the grass.

"Ich vermute, Sie beide würden genau wissen, was mit mir passiert ist, eh?" *I'm guessing both of you would know exactly what has happened to me, eh?* "Am I to become like the thing that attacked me, made me?" He received no answer, though this one time he truly wished he had. His dear mother always seemed to know exactly what to say to her little Ehrie. "Have I become like that *strigoi* in the book Bess was on about at supper a few months back? It was all the stir with her ladies at their tea and she just had to tell me about how this creature, this vampire, Dracula, was making the hearts of the busybodies swoon. I suppose it was all that talk about the risen dead that made me attempt that stupid grave escape in the first place."

"EH! Who's in there?" The voice silenced Harry. "Who's talking gibberish to the damned Jew ghosts?" The man sounded drunk, and much too human to be the beast. "Goddamned Jew ghosts!" There was the crash of a bottle hitting the stones and then the thud of a body. "Goddamned boots. Jew boots! Made in bloody Jewitaly. Laces come undone and trip an honest Irishman who don't want no ghosts." There was no warning and no thought put into his actions, but Harry was up off the grass, at and over the fence and dragging the drunk deeper into the shadows before the man had finished his rant. The drunk cried out once but Harry punched him hard in the face and silenced him.

The next half hour was a blur of rage and animal instinct and the beast roaring up from the depths of his darker self as Harry flung the unconscious man over his shoulder and sprinted through the dark until he reached water. He stopped then, tried to orient himself but gave up and fed. When he finally lifted his head from the torn throat of what had once been a man, Harry felt more alive than ever before. He drank as much of the whiskey-soaked blood as he could and when he was full he picked up the husk and tossed it out into the bay.

Satiated, his humanity returned, and Harry was stunned by the amount of blood both on the stones around him and on his clothes. He couldn't very well return home like this, looking and smelling like an abattoir, so without a second thought he jumped in the bay and washed away the sins of the night, at least physically. He was slowly coming to realize that if he didn't get control of himself he was going to be beyond salvation of any kind. In fact, he might already be too far gone now. Would he just be better off lying there on the stony shore and waiting for them to find him, surrounded by the blood? He lifted his head, shook the water from his ears and listened to the night. Sunrise was a little over five hours away. Would his sense of right and wrong override his instinct to survive? All of these questions hammered away at him while he scrubbed the blood and gore from his clothes. And then the Showman that always waited in the wings stepped up and put him straight.

Fact one—he was a vampire, or something very like it. Fact two—he could now probably break out of any restraint designed to hold a man. Fact three—the show must go on and it will. He needed to talk it over with Bess and his brother, Dash, but he was sure it would work. Of course it all depended upon the people closest to him accepting him for what he had become. There was also the small matter of a food supply, but Harry was sure he could find single-pint donors to keep his inner beast at bay.

"YES!" He roared it to the night world, then leaped straight up and out of the bay and onto the shore. He shook off the water like a dog and started for home. He had a twelve-show booking at The Lyric Theatre in Baltimore starting in a week's time and he needed to have everything in place before then. His posters promised 'a new enigma at every performance' and he had just the way to make it happen, thereby pushing all pretenders back into the wings.

Harry ran all the way back to 278, so caught up in his revelation that he didn't sense the malevolence slipping from shadow to shadow, easily keeping up with his superhuman speed.

*** 

The Handcuff King slipped into the house, showered and changed then went looking for Bess. He found her reading in the salon. Julie was in the kitchen tending to the loaves coming out of the oven before retiring for the night.

"There's something important I have to tell you but let me get Dash over here first so I only have to tell the tale once."

"Harry, what are you on about? You've got some colour back in your skin but you still look a little ragged."

"I have no doubt that I do, Love. It's been a long twenty-fours hours."

"Don't push yourself too hard. You're only human, Harry."

He laughed gently. "That's one of the things we have to talk about. But let me call Dash."

While they were waiting for Dash to arrive, Harry found Bess' leather-bound copy of *Dracula*.

Dash lived up to his nickname and arrived in record time. He knocked once and came right in, just as Harry returned to the salon. "After midnight, eh, Harry. Must be rather important—I know how you like your beauty sleep."

Harry grinned. "That's all changed, little brother, though I hardly know where to begin."

"The beginning has always worked best for me, how about you, Bess?"

"Yes, Dash, I think the beginning would be an awfully good place for Harry to start." She winked affectionately at Harry and he nodded, serious.

"Of course, the beginning." He held up the book. "I know Bess has read this, but Dash, have you had a chance? I admit that I haven't."

"Elsie read it and has regaled me with details over supper more than once, but no, I haven't dug into it myself. Are you thinking of incorporating some vampire-type gimmick into one of the escapes?"

"Yes... and no." He paced, trying to put the impossible words together. He finally gave up and stepped behind Dash's chair. He squatted, grabbed hold of the bottom of the chair and lifted it straight up over his head so that his brother had to duck or bump his own head on the ceiling. Harry then walked the chair around the room as if it were no heavier than a pillow. Bess followed him, scuttling along, trying to see the wires, the supports, the *trick*. Dash leaned back and forth over the edges and even waved his hands above the chair in search of wires.

"Brilliant, Harry! But a strong-man illusion hardly fits with the act." Harry lowered the chair to the floor and Dash immediately hopped out and examined it top to bottom, tipping it over and looking for the mechanism that let Harry do the impossible. He found nothing. "How?"

The Handcuff King held his hand up for patience and headed for the front door. "Come with me. I'm not finished."

Bess and Dash did as they were told, but both took a last look over their shoulders at the chair, hoping to catch a glimpse of something they'd missed.

Out on 113th Harry looked up and down the gas-lit street and then at the windows of the surrounding homes to make sure no one was watching. He was too excited to pay attention to his hunch that something not human watched them from the shadows. "Now stand beside me, either side, but don't touch me—I don't want you to get hurt. Face the house." The two took up their places and faced the front of the brownstone. Harry took a last look around the neighbourhood and then leaped straight up and onto the second-floor balcony, landing a little awkwardly as he tried to miss Bess' smoking chair and table set up in the centre. He turned around for their reaction but Bess was lying on the dirt road and Dash was attending to her. Harry leaped straight back down, landing heavily beside them.

"She's fainted, Harry!" He gently patted Bess' hand until her eyes fluttered and she focused again on her husband.

"Let's take this where there are no prying eyes or perking ears." Dash helped his sister-in-law to her feet and the two men led her inside. Once back in the salon, Bess sank into her chair, clutching her delicate, gold crucifix.

"When, Harry?"

"Last night. At the cemetery."

"Did it hurt?" She struggled to sit up and took his hand. "No wonder you're so cold, Love."

Dash stood, fists on his hips, looking confused and hurt.

"Is anyone going to let me in on the secret? Harry? *Bess*?"

Bess looked worriedly at him. "Harry's been made a vampire, Dash."

"Just like that?! 'Harry's been made a vampire'?"

Harry put a reassuring hand on Dash's shoulder. The younger Houdini flinched but didn't shake it off. "*Exactly* like that, Dash."

Dash bombarded Harry with everything at once. "So you're incredibly strong. If I believe this cockamamie story what else does it mean? Are you dead? *Undead*? Are you going to drink our blood, kill us in our sleep? Do you sleep all day and hunt all night? What about Baltimore?"

A kindly, indulgent smile spread on Harry's usually serious face. "Dash, ol' man, this is all new to me, too. Here's what I do know." He leaned forward and counted the points off on his fingers. "One: Sunlight nearly killed me this morning. Two: Yes, I drink blood but I'm certain I can control it. Three: The two-week Baltimore run goes on, with a few changes. Four: whatever made me this way is still out there, so no travelling after dark without me. It's probably stronger than I am but without me you'll be dead, trust me on this."

"It?" Bess looked even paler and tinier in the chair, facing the new truth about her husband.

"It was once a man, I'm sure, but it was all beast when it tore my throat out."

"This is a lot to swallow, Harry. You're sure? You weren't hit by lightning or something? Or slipped an elixir to get these results temporarily?"

"No, neither."

Fingering her rosary, Bess asked the question many would soon be asking. "Could it be a demon, possession of your soul? Maybe if we call a priest..."

"It's possible, but I don't feel like there's anything in control of me but me." He suddenly sat up bolt upright. "But I do know a test we can do. The tub!" He jumped up and started for the basement door.

Dash and Bess followed but Dash's step hesitated. "The tub?"

"Fetch the camera and tripod from my office and meet me down by the big tub." He darted off into the basement while Dash went to find the photographic equipment. Bess followed patiently after her husband.

Half an hour later the specially designed, four-foot-deep, flat-bottomed tub was nearly full and the camera was rigged on top of Julie's huge laundry-folding table, overlooking the tub. Harry stood in his blue-and-white-striped one-piece, surveying the set-up. "Have you got enough light? Fresh film?"

"I think so, and yes." Dash stood on the table looking through the viewfinder, framing the shot.

"Bess, dear, take my watch. You'll be the timer."

"What are you up to, Harry?"

"I'm going to sit on the bottom of the tub for as long as I can and if I can go far past human endurance, we'll know what I am. If I am possessed, then the demon will force me up to breathe. If I'm something else, something not alive but not quite dead, then, well..." He mounted the stepladder next to the tub and climbed in. The water rose with his displacement and came up to his chin. "My own record is four minutes so wait at least five before taking the first photograph. Please mark the exact time at which it's taken."

Harry emerged from the tub after an hour, no worse for wear. In the interim, Bess had pulled up a chair and maintained her stressed vigil with the watch. "Sixty-two minutes, Darling." She made the sign of the cross, tears leaving tracks in her powder.

"Dash?" He dried himself off with one of the massive towels on the rack beside the tub.

"Three photographs. One at six minutes, one at thirty and one two minutes ago at the one-hour mark when you waved up at me." He folded up the tripod and climbed down off the table. "Good God, Harry. It's true. This changes *everything*, ol' man."

"I know." Harry put his arms around Bess and kissed

the top of her head. "It's still me, Darling."

"I know, Harry, but..."

"We have to accept it and move onward and upward."

"But..."

"Would you rather I be full and truly dead? Would that satisfy your blessed Mary?"

"I...I don't know, Harry. I truly don't know. But I'll always love you."

He kissed her on the lips this time, doing his best to ignore the warmth radiating from her. "That's all I need to hear. Now, we have a Press Meeting to plan, dear family."

***

The Mass ended with Father Carlin's invocation, "In nómine Patris et Fílii et Spíritus Sancti. Amen," *In the name of the Father, the Son and the Holy Ghost.* Bess sighed deeply. The service had been no different from any other but this day she found special solace in the words and rituals. After the procession made its way down the aisle, Bess knelt for a few more moments of private thought. Worry consumed and confused her and it wasn't until she heard a polite cough that she realized that she wasn't alone.

"Father Carlin. I thought you'd be at tea."

The parish's stately, silver-haired Irish priest stood at the end of the pew, his strong hands folded in front of him. "Soon enough, Wilhelmina. What troubles you, child?"

Bess glanced around to see if they were alone. "I'm not sure I..."

"Would you prefer the sanctity of the confessional or just to sit in the sacristy and have a chat away from the flock?"

"The sacristy, please. It's about my husband, Harry."

***

"HOUDINI A VAMPIRE BUT SHOW GOES ON!!"
"HARRY GETS SCARY AND SHOCKS PRESS!"
"VAMPIRE HOUDINI TO PLAY BALTIMORE! BISHOP OUTRAGED!"

The headlines were no less sensational than Harry expected and although there were jeers and laughter in the beginning, once he'd spent half an hour on the bottom of the new Brooklyn YMCA pool and then demonstrated his strength and speed in as many ways as the gym allowed, the throng of reporters believed. There was a moment of silence, then Harry asked for questions and the place exploded in shouted queries

When they were all done peppering him with questions about vampires he admitted having no answers to, Harry made a promise to his fans everywhere. He promised to never use his strength to free himself. He would escape as always, by the skills he had developed over the years. When asked what thrill there would be for him to be manacled and tossed in a river when he couldn't drown, Harry set them all straight.

"Daylight is my new nemesis, gentlemen, so no more matinees. The finale of all shows will have me racing against the rising sun, which, last time I checked, happens on a daily basis and is completely independent of any influence I might now wield." There was a general chuckle. "So, there it is. I am a vampire, but I am still the man you all know and Bess and I will give you a show like no other on Earth. Now go file your stories and then get some sleep. I'll see you all in Baltimore next week."

Once the papers hit the stands and the news spread, all twelve Baltimore shows sold out in an hour. Opening night was astounding. Harry started the show by running down the aisle and leaping fifty feet onto the stage, right over the orchestra. Then he picked up the solid steel Sargent & Greenleaf safe from stage left and easily walked it over to centre stage where the first escape of the night got the house warmed up. Sunrise was scheduled for 5:52am and at 5:00 exactly Harry introduced the finale by leading everyone to bleachers set up outside the theatre on Mt. Royal Avenue. A frosted-glass coffin awaited and beside it was a heavier, more traditional, burial box.

His new senses made sure he didn't need a watch to know exactly when the sun would crest the horizon and, ever the showman, Harry timed it so that he was out of the glass coffin and into the mahogany one just as the sun lit up the pallbearers' handles. Applause erupted as four dark-suited men picked the wooden coffin up and loaded it into a waiting hearse. The team of four black Percherons walked slowly down the street, and the world of escapology was never the same again.

Two days later a ripped open and drained body turned up in an alley not three blocks from Harry's house in Harlem. The show gave Harry a rock-solid alibi but he finally had to come clean about the other vampire... the beast that made him. The Press snatched the story up and people started wondering just how many vampires there were in the world. Three weeks later the first fake vampire performed a beat-the-sun show in Denver. Vaudeville was a cutthroat world and no one was going to let Houdini keep his advantage for long.

***

Harry was reading in his third-floor home-office for two hours when a deep, ancient chill swept through the room. Had someone just come in the front door and let in the October wind? Or was it a window opening? He listened and thought he heard an unusual scratching sound from the room below, but it was faint. Then the odour of death wafted up through the floorboards and he was out the door and down the stairs in a flash, but he still wasn't fast enough. The household was long abed and the townhouse was dark, but Harry clearly saw the beast standing in the doorway of the

191

bedroom.

"You have drawn too much attention to us. It is time I finished what I started in the cemetery." It smiled, baring its fangs, but before Harry could move it opened its cape and tossed out its prize. Bess' limp form slumped to the floor.

Harry flew at the ancient vampire and met it in midair, screaming in rage. The two undead slammed into each other amid snarls and growls. The beast slammed Harry head-first through one of his framed show posters and into the plaster and lath wall but the Handcuff King kicked out with both feet and launched the invader through the balustrade and bouncing down the stairs. Harry launched himself after the beast, grabbing a pair of broken balusters as he dove headfirst into the stairwell.

The beast was quick and was gone when Harry landed hard on the bottom steps and rolled. He bounced to his feet and then twisted left just as the hall table smashed into his ribs. The blow slowed Harry just enough that he didn't duck when the beast tackled him and bore him to the floor. With claws flashing and fangs snapping, it tore furiously at its offspring's chest. Harry didn't care if he died right there in the foyer, but he was taking this ancient beast with him so that Bess and Dash and everyone could live without fear.

The old vampire reared back to throw its weight behind the coming bite and that's when Harry rammed the two oak balusters into his maker's ribs on either side. The beast bucked and screamed and tried to flee, but Harry held tight with supernatural strength fuelled by fury and fear and sheer determination. He twisted the makeshift stakes in and around the beast's torso, trying to do as much damage as possible. But then the maker found the strength, which had allowed it to survive for centuries and it rammed its arms under its child's and forced them away, the balusters popping out and away as well. Blood sprayed the walls Bess had only recently had re-papered but before Harry could leap to his feet and follow the beast, it was gone into the night. He started for the door, the death scent strong in his nose, but Beth's weak call stopped him.

"Harry, don't leave me alone."

He turned and saw her at the top of the stairs, very much alive, leaning heavily on the newel post that was all that remained of the railing.

***

*San Francisco. Two weeks later.*

TWO HOUDINI IMITATORS DEAD!

SHACKLED BLOODINI DROWNS WHEN PARIS CROWD TOSSES HIM INTO THE SEINE AFTER SUN RISES AND HE DOESN'T DIE.

VLAD THE ESCAPIST SUCCUMBS TO LEAD POISONING!"

"Lead poisoning?" Harry sipped his dinner, fresh from the donor.

Bess fussed with her hair for the umpteenth time. "It was mixed in with the aluminium powder he was using to make himself sparkle under the footlights."

"Sparkle? I *never* sparkle. What was he thinking?"

"Well, he couldn't challenge them to drive a stake into his belly like you can so he had to try something to stand out."

"That's four imitators so far. What a waste. Did I tell you that (agency) replaced the St. Louis cancellation with three shows in Montreal?"

"That's nice, dear. I do so love Montreal. Now help me with my hair, please."

***

*Montreal.*

There was no room for his coffin in his tiny dressing room at the Princess Theatre so Harry was lying on the scruffy carpet, reviewing his plans for the night's show and waiting for Dash to return with his donated 'supper'. Although the city of Montreal had welcomed the Vampire Handcuff King, he could hear shouts of "Abomination!" and "Devil Spawn!" through the open window as the Catholic Women's League protested in the street in front of the theatre. He wasn't surprised, but he'd hoped the reception up in Canada would be a bit warmer than it was getting back home.

A knock at the door shook off the disappointment but before he could get to his feet the flimsy door swung open.

"Mr. Houdini, sir. I've brought back those books you loaned me." A Divinity student at nearby McGill University, Gordon Whitehead was also a budding magician who had hung around backstage before the previous night's show and chatted with the Handcuff King. Harry had revelled in the attention paid by a student to a master and even loaned Whitehead copies of two of his self-published books on stage magic.

"Gordon. Come in, please. Your timing is excellent. Tell me what you thought of them." Harry grabbed his coat from the back of the room's lone chair and brushed it off. "Did you learn anything, lad?"

"I found the section on misdirection to be quite helpful." The young athlete tossed the books onto the dressing table and as Harry's eyes reflexively followed their flight path, Whitehead pulled a foot-long shaft of wood from his back pocket, flipped it around to get the best grip and rammed it home into Harry's chest before his host could raise a hand to stop him. The stake went deep and Harry's soul-searing scream silenced the protestors outside and summoned help. Whitehead withdrew the weapon and was winding up for a second strike when Dash barged in, took in the scene, and tackled him.

"Good God! What have you done?!"

Whitehead pushed Dash off, jumped to his feet and made the sign of the cross. "My destiny. In nómine Patris et Fílii et Spíritus Sancti." Harry collapsed in Dash's arms and his attacker fled.

"HOUDINI DESTROYED!"

The news rocked the world and the vampire imitators stopped almost immediately. The Age of Vampire Vaudeville was dead.

\*\*\*

It was shortly after midnight and Dash stood facing the family tomb. Harry's name had been added just that afternoon. Dash spoke to the chiselled letters.

"So, it's come to this, has it, Harry? Who else can lay claim to being murdered twice? There's no escaping the blood, is there ol' chum?"

Only the night breeze answered him. He bowed his head but his silent prayer was interrupted by the grinding of stone-on-stone as the tomb's top step slid back.

"There's always an escape, little brother." Harry climbed out of the cavity beneath the steps, dusted himself off and pushed the top step back into place.

"But this is one escape that won't make the papers, Harry."

"It's the only way, Dash. I can hardly blame Bess for going to the church. I'm not at all part of the natural order. By the way, thank you for stopping the lad before he could cut my head off."

"It's the least I could do. So where will you go?"

"It's best you don't know. My coffin is on board the ship?"

"Deep in the hold, waiting for you."

"Then I'll tell the captain once we're out of American waters."

A car horn honked in the distance and Harry sniffed the air for any hint of danger. He relaxed and opened his arms. Dash stepped into the embrace and squeezed his brother tight.

"Don't let them forget me, Dash."

"Small chance of that, Harry. Small chance of that."

oOo

# Temper Temper

**First published:**
*The Jeffrey Archer Short Story Challenge Collection*, Kobo Editions, April 2013.

This 100-word story was written for a competition. Stories could be no longer than 100 words. Of the nearly 1000 entries, the judges selected 20 finalists. Those 20 finalists were then given to bestselling author, Jeffrey Archer, Baron of Weston-super-Mare. Lord Jeffrey picked three finalists, and announced his list at the London Book Fair 2013. **"Temper Temper"** was one of the three.

~~~

## Temper Temper

Leon slammed the spade's blade into the dirt cellar floor. "Hack my Facebook account will she? Bitch! No wonder Dad ran off with the babysitter-slash-cheerleader when I was ten."

The pile of dirt grew. A car door banged shut. He dug faster, mumbling. "I'll kill her, bury her, hack her Facebook account, and make it look like she's travelling." The shovel hit something hard. "What the hell?" He brushed off dirt. In the dim light it looked like two skulls and a pompom.

"Whatcha doing, Honey?"

Leon spun at the sound of his mother's voice, but not fast enough.

oOo

# Why Pete?

**First Published:**
*Tesseracts Seventeen: Speculating Coast to Coast.* Edge Science Fiction & Fantasy Publishing. 2013.

Originally conceived of as a horror story set in space with a male character, this story morphed into a thriller with a female character. If ever a story was taken over by its characters, this was it. Since it received an Honorable Mention in the 2012 *Writers of the Future Contest*, I should probably let the characters take over more often.

The inter-story link with **"Why Pete?"** is that it takes place in the same solar system—Kepler 63—that my novel-in-progress does.

~~~

## Why Pete?

Lilly laughed. Drugs will do that to a girl. Then she giggled for a full five minutes before she nearly threw up. Drugs will do that to a girl, too, even a thirty-one-year-old navy pilot with combat experience. The kinds of drugs Lilly was riding, though, had very little recreational value, unless waking up in complete darkness, unable to move, with cotton-mouth-from-hell was a girl's idea of recreation. It wasn't Lilly's, or at least she didn't think it was. She wasn't quite sure.

"G'morning, Lill."

"What the hell? Pete!" Her buzz vanished and her disorientation grew.

"Not exactly. Pete's voice and personality overlay, but

not Pete. We thought that a familiar voice would be the best welcome."

"But my ex-husband? And welcome where? I can't see a damned thing and I can't move."

"Let's take it one thing at a time, Lill. You're in a deep-sleep pod."

"I... remember." And she did. "Now, why can't I move or see, yet?"

"I'm running diagnostics right now to get an answer for you. The cabin illumination has malfunctioned and your restraints are on a timer, to keep you from thrashing about and hurting yourself if you awaken disoriented. Your restraints will release two minutes after your resting heart rate, blood pressure, and respiration indicate that a degree of calm has been attained. You're not there, yet."

"It could be the damned voice you're programmed with. There was a reason I divorced Pete a year after training started for this mission. He was a lying, cheating, bastard."

"I can't change the pre-set wake-up procedure but once we're done with that you can select another voice. Who would you prefer? Your mother? That older actor you like, Justin Bieber?"

"Definitely not my mother. J.B. would be fine. Now, what about the dark?" A soft glow lit up Lillian's world in the sleep pod, but beyond the little window in the lid it was still dark. "That's a start."

"It will have to do for the moment." Pete's lying, cheating voice continued. "Your heart rate is one-twelve so the restraints will remain in place a short while longer. Your blood pressure is improving and your respiration is within the normal range."

Lilly detected a subtle background sound that hadn't been there a moment before. "Is someone playing a guitar?"

"Pre-recorded. From the playlist you created pre-departure. It seems to be helping as your heart rate is slowing. Now, while we have a moment, let's check your other functions, starting with cognitive. Name this song, the artist, and your memory associated with it, please."

"Um..." Her thoughts felt ragged and torn and she was still recovering from the shock of being awakened by the voice of the man who'd slept with her sister. "Um... Gordon Lightfoot, If You Could Read My Mind."

"Name the song, the artist, and the memory associated with it."

The A.I. was being picky. "If You Could Read My Mind. Gordon Lightfoot. It was the first song I heard my father play on the guitar."

"Correct. What is pi to four decimal places?"

"Three-point-one-four-one-five-nine." That was an easy one.

"Pi to four decimal places. Please." The voice was steady, with no particular emphasis on any of the words this time.

"I just did... oh. Four places. Three-point-one-four-one-five." It wasn't just her memory that was being tested; she was also being tested for impairments in her ability to hear, process, and understand what was being said.

"Which of my podcasts did you first hear?"

"Which of your...? Oh, which of Pete's... Um, it was his live reading of The Little Prince at The Smithsonian for The First Lady."

"Correct. Who was the visiting team when I proposed to you on the Jumbotron at the Mavericks' game?"

"I nearly punched you in the head for that."

"But you didn't. You said yes. That's not the question, though. Who was the visiting team when I proposed to you on the Jumbotron at the Mavericks' game?"

"Damn it. The Toronto Raptors were visiting."

"Correct. How many times did I propose to you before that night?"

"Forty-one."

"Incorrect. Forty-two."

"That time in Tobago doesn't count. He passed out drunk before he could finish the question."

"The correct answer as determined by yourself during the programming of this procedure is forty-two, so at some point you must have decided that the Tobago proposal was valid."

"That's bullshit! You never finished the question! For all I know you were asking me to hold your drink while you threw up."

"None of that matters, Lill. We're trying to establish the state of your memory post-deep-sleep. We can argue the semantics and technicalities of the actual proposal later."

"Fine. Since we're testing my memory, do I remember correctly that there was a second set of questions created as a back-up?"

"Yes there is."

"Then reconfigure Cognitive Evaluation with the back-up series. That is a Command Order."

"Done. List the Seven Words You Can't Say on Network Television, who first listed them, and which one does not belong on the list."

"Really? I hate those words, or most of them anyway."

"List the Seven Words You Can't Say on Network Television, who first listed them, and which one does not belong on the list."

"Fine. Just for you." She listed the words, cringing at the "c" word she'd never learned to like, even in the navy. "George Carlin. 'Tits' doesn't belong on the list because it sounds more like a nickname."

"Now, list the words in reverse order and give one synonym for the last word you list. You have one minute."

"One minute? Fine." She listed them forward in her head then reversed the order aloud, very slowly. "And 'poop'. Synonym for 'shit'."

"Excellent. Now an easy one to get your vitals back down. Name, rank, birth date, current posting."

"Rayn. Lillian Bianca. Lieutenant Colonel. June 20th, 2023. Commander of the International Space Ark Mayhew carrying two-hundred-forty-four colonists to planet Vesta, AKA Kepler-62e."

"Only the one mistake."

"It wasn't a mistake."

"Save it, Lill. Now, give me a moment and we'll do the touchy-feely part of this morning's exercise." Lilly heard a soft hiss in the pod and then a dozen points of pressure were applied to her extremities. "Tactile test. Twelve points of pressure, two minute test, random application of pressure in both sequence and degree, hard or soft. Two seconds to identify each locale. Go in three... two... one..."

For the next two minutes she responded verbally to the mechanical pressures, "Left index finger—soft, right heel—hard," and so on.

"Done. One hundred percent. Thank you, Lilly. I'll switch to the Justin Bieber overlay now." The A.I.'s voice switched to a gentle tenor with a subtle Southern Ontario accent. "Your restraints should release in five...four...three...two...one." There was an audible click and the padded strap securing Lilly's left wrist retracted.

"Um..." She lifted her arm as far as the secured pod lid would allow. "I'm still restrained."

"Standby, Lilly. I'll try to trace the problem."

She was getting a bit antsy. "With your processing speed and power you could have run a full sys-check on the entire ship in the time it took to tell me what you were doing. Where's the fault?"

"I'm not able to run a sys-check at this time and am running a self-diagnosis to determine the cause. My local sensors however indicate that your restraints all released as programmed."

"Well, I'm telling you that they didn't." A year of deep-sleep and she was itching to start moving again.

"I have visual confirmation of that but I'm still showing current running through the circuits in the other four straps. Standby while I attempt to reset your pod."

"Can't you just fix it without describing it to me at every step?"

"Of course. But I thought you might prefer my chatter to sitting in silence, thinking that nothing was being done." The light in the pod flickered.

"True enough. Thank you. I'm ready for the reset

whenever you are."

"All done."

"The flicker?"

"The flicker. Since your restraints are unfortunately still in place the next step is a five-minute reboot. Everything will go down, including environmental."

"You're shutting off my air?"

"You have twelve minutes of air in your pod and the autonomous reserve tank has sixty minutes' worth, but the reserve won't kick in until the quality in the pod drops below ten percent."

"And if our systems failure extends to the reserve?"

"It's autonomous."

She clenched her fists. "I know you're programmed to project calm and hope, but this is my ship. You are my ship, and I'm trained to handle stress. Is that underst—oh, to hell with it." She was a commander and it was time she took command. "Override personality overlay and initiate Emergency Protocol Alpha-Rayn." She didn't have time for this A.I. handholding crap. "Acknowledge."

"Acknowledged." The tenor voice was still the same but the personality overlay had lost its fun edge.

"On my mark, increase pure O2 fifty percent to this pod for thirty seconds then initiate reboot. Mark." Lilly felt the difference in her air quality almost immediately and slowed her breathing. Then, without waiting a moment longer she reached across to the far side of the right wrist cuff with her unrestrained left hand and felt for the quick release she knew was there. She found the dimpled release button, centred her thumb on it and pressed. Nothing happened. Nothing except the realization that deep-sleep had robbed her of a lot of her strength. "Lovely. Just... bloody... lovely."

She changed her grip and tried again. This time the button depressed and the strap released. She had both arms free but was still trapped by the torso strap just below her breasts and the two straps holding her ankles down. It took her a moment to find the release for the torso strap tucked under her ribs on the left side. The angle was awkward and when she twisted to improve her leverage she applied more pressure and the release stuck.

"Shit! Shit! Shit!" She grabbed the restraint's padded belt with her right hand and pulled it to relieve some of the pressure on the unit. Then she exhaled for another few centimetres of slack and pressed the button again. This time it released and she took a deep breath to reward herself as it pulled back into its recess.

It was only with her lungs full that Lilly realized that there was something seriously wrong with the air. Gone was the pure oxygenated edge, replaced by a mild acidic taint. Then the pod's interior glow was extinguished and the five-minute reboot began, or so she assumed.

Strapped in, boxed in, in complete darkness, in the absolute death of space, and yet so close to their destination, she was getting twitchy. "I can handle this. I am trained for this, damn it." She concentrated on calming herself first. She smiled broadly, not caring that no one could see the smile, just knowing that the simple act of shaping it released calming natural endorphins into her system—endorphins that might just give her the edge she needed to escape before she snapped. Lilly held the smile for a solid fifteen count and then set about getting the hell out of the pod that was starting to feel like a coffin.

She knew that, like all of the pods on board, hers was two-metres-long, sixty-centimetres-wide, and thirty-centimetres deep. Length wasn't important for what she had in mind but the width and depth were vital. She prayed that her loss of strength didn't mean a loss of flexibility, and carefully rolled over on her left hip, counting on a little bit of "give" in her ankle restraints. She'd been asleep for so long that the soft material of her suit felt like burlap to her awakening skin. She didn't just need to piss, she needed to take a shower, too. First things first, though and she kept moving. It was slow going, but she got what she needed and was soon in a position where she could bend her knees and curl up into a distorted, contortionistic ball.

Her right shoulder bumped into the pod's lid but she

curled her shoulders and continued. Only the memory foam of each sleep pad was custom fit—everything else was designed to fit an average man of average fitness level. The fact that she was shorter and narrower than average meant that Lilly had almost enough wiggle room where she needed it most. Almost. Her knees bumped up against the left side of the pod just as her back met the right. She reached for the ankle strap with her right hand and came up a few centimetres short.

"Shit, piss, fuck...!" She stopped short of the fourth word of Carlin's list, let out her breath, drew her knees in just a squidge more, tightened her soft abs, and reached just a little bit further, willing her fingers to stretch, just a little bit longer. The strap was... there! And the release button was...

A cramp! Her right thigh cramped with a Charley horse the size of a Clydesdale. Logic told her it would pass, but in spite of the tiny endorphin boost from the smile, Lilly's pain centre knew that someone had just shoved a glowing, red-hot, steel spike through her quadriceps and was twisting it around.

"Not... this... time... asshole!" She pushed past the pain, blinded by tears, found the strap release and squeezed it with everything she had left. At first it stuck, but after a final moment of stubbornness it gave way and the restraint shot back into its recess. Released from the agony she straightened her leg out until it kicked the bottom of the pod, which wasn't that far at all. Lilly frantically massage the knot in the quad, weeping until it was gone and she could relax.

With the pain banished, Lilly could taste the machine-smoke flavoured air. Damn! Enough was enough. This massive, wormhole-navigating ark was her pride and joy and no minor mechanical glitches were going to keep her from completing her mission and seeding space with some of the best and brightest of mankind. Reaching down, Lieutenant-Colonel Lillian Rayn released her final restraint and then straightened back up, slowly. The "atomic clock" in her head let her know when the five-minute mark had come and gone with no reboot. "Sorry, J.B., but you had your chance. It's time for this Navy chick to crack her own egg and stretch her cramped wings."

Although still in complete darkness, Lilly closed her eyes to aid her concentration. Her mind was still a bit fuzzy and some of the memories were hard to come by, but the schematic of her pod drifted back eventually. The deep-sleep pods were never intended to be opened manually from the inside but safety regs insisted there be a latch, just in case the impossible happened. Well, it's impossible time, Lilly thought. She opened her eyes, felt down the side of the lid near her right hip and found the lid's release. She hooked her thumb in the ring and pulled. Nothing.

"This is getting monotonous. How about next time I trigger a piece of equipment it work the first time?" She tightened her grip on the ring and was about to give it another tug when the rest of the memory made it through the fog. In order to reduce the chances of an accidental opening of the pod, the emergency release procedure was a two-handed job.

Lilly's left hand felt by her left hip and then slid up the side of the pod and along the lid until it was over her navel. She found the dial she was looking for and turned it as far as it would go, then she pulled the ring still hooked on her right thumb and she felt the "kachunk" when the lid latch released. The lid, however, stayed put.

"Damnation! I... want... out!" Still holding the two release controls she brought her knees up and pushed on the lid with them. The silicone seal fought back for a moment, then Lilly won the battle, the seal popped, air hissed in, and the lid cantilevered open.

"It's about goddamned time."

"Please proceed to the nearest command station and initiate Recovery Sequence Alpha."

"J.B.?"

"We are currently in an emergency situation and all hands are required on deck. Please proceed to the nearest command station and manually initiate Recovery Sequence Alpha."

"It's okay, J.B., I'm out of the pod. You can call off the emergency." Then she smelled the smoke. "Oh shit." It was still blacker than black in her quarters. "I need light. Give me light."

"Negative. Unable to comply. Primary electrical system has failed. Back-up system is only operating at twenty percent."

"Then can you at least remind me where the Command Station is?"

"Two-point-three metres from the head of your sleep pod and one-point-four metres up from the floor."

Lilly quickly found the Command Station, placed her palm on the reader, and leaned in to the unit's microphone. "Rayn. Lillian. Lieutenant-Colonel. Command sequence Gamma-Gamma-Delta-Niner-Eleven-Twenty-Oh-One." The palm scanner rolled the blue-lit sensor up and back, then right to left. An illuminated keyboard folded down and revealed a fifteen-centimetre-square screen.

The smoke was growing more acrid and she could now see a faint haze by the screen's light. She typed a command, read the reply on the screen, typed another command, read the reply to that, then typed a final command with her access code and hit enter for the third time. The ceiling lights above her head flickered briefly, then came on with a subtle pop. The smoke at the ceiling was a lot thicker than she'd first suspected.

"J.B., I've started the recovery sequence but the air quality is getting worse. What do you need me to do?"

"Commander Rayn, I require you to reset my system manually. If I fail to come back online automatically you will need to do it yourself. The instructions are now on the command station screen. The process should take less than one minute on automatic. In two minutes you must follow the instructions."

Lilly read the instructions in question and then read them again. Once the A.I. went down she'd be relying on her memory. She typed the first command and immediately the screen went dark. Then the air stopped hissing through the ventilation system and, finally, the lights went out, again. It was only when all of the background noises had been eliminated that Lilly heard the nearly random sound of rock on metal.

"What the hell? J.B., are you hearing this?" There was no answer of course. The sound repeated twice more, in rapid succession so Lilly felt her away around her quarters, listening, with one hand on the wall to keep oriented. There was a single repeat, louder than the previous two, but the lights and air circulators came back on and then she couldn't hear anything other than the ship's systems reasserting themselves. The Command Station flickered to life again so she stepped over to watch the screen. J.B.'s voice repeated what she read.

"Reboot was successful. Sys-check complete. ISA Mayhewhas sustained severe damage from multiple micro-meteor impacts over the last three Earth days. System failures include deep-sleep chambers on Levels Six to Eighteen, primary air filtration, wormhole navigation, and the external communications array."

Lilly was stunned. "Levels Six to Eighteen? That's everyone! How serious is the failure? What's required to get it back online for God's sake?!"

The screen returned to standby mode and the A.I. continued its verbal report. "Twenty-nine hull breaches have resulted in irreparable damage to oxygen feed and containment. Twelve separate fires have resulted in full atmospheric evacuation on Levels Four to Nineteen. Casualties include all personnel in deep-sleep, including your command crew on Level Four."

"Oh shit. Oh God." She had to be stuck in a nightmare, although this was worse than any nightmare she'd ever had. "What about their backup air? They all had a reserve!"

"When containment failed, all deep-sleep pods opened simultaneously. Atmospheric evacuation removed all tainted air and total of reserves was insufficient to sustain personnel."

Everyone gone? Seventy-five children—gone? Her

niece, Ashley, the brightest mind of her generation in Astrometrics—gone? All eleven members of her command crew: Campbell, Venables, Rahn, Greenwood-Cruise, Zefram, Salter, Ross, Barkin, Baker, Montgomery and Guertin—all gone? Lilly slumped to the floor; just slid down the wall she was leaning against. The disembodied and impersonal voice of the A.I. was getting on her nerves, especially while it was reporting the loss of every one of her crew and passengers. She needed to feel she wasn't alone, even though it appeared she probably was. "J.B., reinstate personality overlay but switch to Pete. Better to keep company with the sound of someone I once loved than someone I've never even met," she mumbled to herself.

"Sure thing, Lill." Pete was back, and the simulated emotion in his voice was strong. "I'm running full diagnostics, again, and rerouting what air we have left to the passages between your quarters and the deep-sleep levels. You will need a sealed EVA Suit to inspect the pods as neither the pressure nor the O2 levels are sufficient for unprotected access. I'll charge up the one at Airlock Four-Delta. Maybe the human touch is what's needed here. Maybe there's something you can do that I couldn't."

"Good thinking." She pulled herself to her feet and forced herself to keep moving. Her unused muscles were exhausted.

"Pete, since we seem to still have artificial grav, can you reduce it to fifty-percent, please."

"Of course, Lill. Done." And it was. Lilly's next step bounced her up to the ceiling but she was ready and pushed herself back down fast enough to grab hold of the handrail that ran parallel to the floor. She adjusted her thinking quickly and her low-grav training came back to her. Soon she was bouncing and pulling her way to Airlock Four-Delta.

***

The Mayhew had no windows, but most of the external

cameras had survived the journey from Earth and the ongoing meteor event so Pete-the-A.I. was able to create the illusion that one entire wall of the bridge was a window, showing the verdant green and blue of the world they orbited. Lilly sat at the communications station, unable to bring herself to sit in the command chair when her mission was such a catastrophic failure. She checked the calculations on the larger of the two screens at the station and continued with her verbal report, tears drying on her cheeks as she harnessed her emotions as best she could.

"Manual inspection of all two-hundred and forty-four deep-sleep units confirmed initial remote assessment. I am the only survivor and only because the deep-sleep pod in the commander quarters is isolated from the damaged levels. Only luck spared me, though maybe they were the lucky ones, not knowing what happened." She took a deep breath and the recording paused automatically, starting again only when she spoke.

"The Mayhew will be able to maintain a constant orbit for another thirty days before the loss of the stabilizing rockets results in a degraded spiral ending in impact somewhere near Vesta's smaller continent. I have chosen that same continent for the location of my ground base and will begin ferrying equipment planetside as soon as the minor repairs to the shuttle heat shields are complete. Estimated time for complete relocation is eight days. I will continue the report later but right now I'm exhausted and need a real bed without a lid. No more lids, ever."

***

Growing up in San Francisco, Lilly didn't see many tumbleweeds as a rule, and she sure as hell didn't see any three-metres-tall like the one rolling languorously through her camp. The twisted, dried, giant, skeletal ball slowed and seemed to observe her observing it, then it rolled on and away. She was a long way from San Francisco. Hell, she was as far as any human had ever been or was likely to be until the next ark arrived in five years. She adjusted her breathing filter to a more comfortable spot on her face. "Will I make it that long? Five years?"

An amphibious something-or-other launched itself out of a nearby puddle, threw a mid-air glance her way with an array of eyes, then landed nearly splashless in a puddle ten metres away. That seemed to be some sort of signal because suddenly all of the dozen or more puddles surrounding her camp came to life as countless "puddle-jumpers" launched themselves back and forth from puddle to puddle in silence, each eyeing her as they arced through the thick air.

"I don't see why not, Lill. The only thing you lack for quickly creating a sustainable settlement is manpower. It will take you longer, but you can certainly achieve what needs to be done."

"Five years is a long time to be alone, Pete."

"You'll never be alone as long as you've got me." The assurance was strong in her earpiece, broadcast only a short distance from the shuttle.

"Thanks, but there's only so much an A.I. can do."

"Want me to talk dirty to you?"

She laughed for the first time since she'd forced her way out of the deep-sleep pod. "Not yet, thanks. You just worry about cataloguing the native flora and fauna that your sensors pick up and let me worry about... that other stuff."

"Yes ma'am." The A.I. paused, just as Pete had always done before bringing up a difficult subject. "Lill?"

"Yah, buddy?"

"They'll be here in five. You won't be alone forever. Besides, they're expecting a complete settlement to be ready for occupation when they arrive, so you've got your work cut out for you with erecting structures and growing test crops on a very long Honey-Do list."

"True enough." A far-off howl started up and rose in pitch until it was beyond Lill's range of hearing. "Now, can you call up the repair manual for the K7 generator so I can get a damned secure perimeter set up? Please."

"Sure thing. Sending it to your tablet as I speak."

"Good stuff. Now, hand me the Phillips screwdriver, would you..."

o0o

# The Ides of Kumbha

**Not Previously Published.**

Written specifically for an "Ides of March" reading at a local bookstore, this is what I think of as 'possible science'. In spite of the speculative element, I've tried to make all of the science as accurate as possible.

~~~

## The Ides of Kumbha

The man was at least ten years younger, twenty pounds heavier, and probably had four levels of rank on Bill, though he wore no insignia on his crisp, new jumpsuit. No one but a high-ranking officer would have access to a military detainee orbiting Mars. He was pretty sure General No-Name had arrived with the last crew ship, but since he'd been planet-side at the time, Bill had missed the ceremonial introductions. Floating up near the ceiling, the General tapped his tablet twice, and waited. Bill started talking, just wanting to get it over with.

"You're the third investigator I've talked to, though the first in person. The first two back in Houston already recorded the whole damned story."

"True. But those were the technical version of what occurred. I'm the On-Site Developer for Cassius Biotech—the project's primary investor back on Earth—and our Board of Directors have requested that I have you recount your testimony one more time, in layman's terms. Our Directors don't all have science and technology backgrounds like you and I, Mission Specialist Tupper."

Not a senior officer at all. Not even corps, but a

'corporate' scientist instead. Even worse, Bill realized. "Fine. Your call, Doc. Turn on whatever you're recording with, sit back, shut up, and I'll give you the K.I.S.S. layman's version, for the hard-of-thinking." At last, someone was willing to hear something besides the stripped-bare facts.

"Juliosz—Flight Engineer Golubov—and I had been fourteen sols, or Martian days, in the Gale Crater, in the shadow of Mount Sharp, tracking the old Curiosity rover, when we finally got a break. By the Darian calendar, the month was twenty-eight-sol-long Kumbha; so fourteen sols put us smack in the middle of the month, or the ides, if I remember my English Lit elective at Cornell. Kumbha is the third of Mars' twenty-four months and I'd seriously hoped to be off that rock and back up here on the station before I saw any more of the remaining twenty-three on that tedious mission.

"Fourteen sols, but we still had no visual on Curiosity. We spent Sols Two to Five following the unmanned rover's previously mapped tracks, but while the latest sat-pics from the Mars Reconnaissance Orbiter2—MRO2—showed that Curiosity turned ninety degrees and followed the canyon route into the lower formations of Mount Sharp, the faint, wind-blown tracks we'd followed since Sol Six continued without a turn, counterclockwise around the base of Sharp. It was goddamned freaky. Sat-pics can't lie, yet the reality down there on the War God's ass proved that truth to be wrong." He took a long drink of filtered water from the bottle floating in front of him, savoring the wet for a moment.

"At first I thought someone back at NASA was screwing with our heads and sending doctored images, but when I suggested this, Juliosz double-checked and confirmed that we were getting a direct feed from the MRO, unadulterated and untainted by practical joker assholes. The sat-pics were wrong, but what do I know? I'm just the guy who was hoping to catch up to the rover, replace the hard-drive, empty the sample bins, and bring the old hard-drive back up here for a long-overdue data-dump.

"The sun had been up for an hour and the temperature

outside the Mars Mobile Habitat was climbing slowly up from the bowels of the thermometer. Juliosz was just finishing his morning tvorog—sweet Russian cottage cheese with nuts—when a telltale ping shouted at us from the radio. We'd picked up a signal. Then the ping was gone. We hit the brakes, stopped dead while I ran a scan up and down the dial. Nothing. We reversed, hoping that a trick of geology and geography was responsible and we could find that spot again.

"It was and we did. We'd backed up forty meters when I caught the ping a second time. Because we were creeping along, looking for it, this time we were able to stop and hold onto the signal. I recorded everything, which, as we both know, does me absolutely no good whatsoever because all of the damned recordings were destroyed down on the planet, along with our Martian motorhome and Juliosz.

"We were able to get a rough idea of where the signal was coming from, but we needed to triangulate. Juliosz suited up, determined to plant a portable antenna on the ridge above us even though it was colder than the Antarctic out there. Prep for an EVA on the surface takes a few minutes, so while he was at it, I turned my attention to the signal. It was caught by the High Gain Antenna... and spectrum analysis told me that it wasn't one of the 256 tones rings the rover was programmed with. But this was just a single tone, like a signal, a flare, in the X-band. I pulled out all the stops and scanned for anything, any signal on any band. By the time Juliosz was giving me a thumbs-up in the airlock, I was giving him a frequency.

"'AM band, 770 watts.'

"'AM? Are you crapping on me, William?' His accent was tinny in my ear, through my headset, and had I known it was to be our last conversation, I would have kept it going.

"'No crap, Jules. Amplitude Modulation at 770 watts. I'm recording and decoding. It sounds binary.' I checked his video feed and the picture was gorgeous high-def. Thank God for Canon optics. 'I'm going silent at this end so I can concentrate, buddy.' He went out the airlock with another thumbs-up and I turned back to my decoding. He had two hours worth of air with which to do a ten-minute task. The slope up the little ridge was gentle and solid rock. From what I could see through his vid-feed, in the low gravity he nearly bounced his way up to the summit.

"The antenna he carried was still in its case, so I had no warning whatsoever when I heard a voice over the cabin speakers that sure-as-hell wasn't Juliosz'. It was loud and clear, and vaguely familiar. The accent more Mason-Dixon than Moscow, Russia.

"'Turn around and leave, William. Recall Juliosz before it is too late.' It hesitated. "We are so sorry. It is now too late.'

"I spun around to watch Juliosz' vid-feed, wondering what the hell was going on. He bounced up to the top of the ridge, and then everything went nuts. I had no time to warn him, even if I'd known what to warn him about. How was I to know he'd not only found Curiosity but also ExoMars, Phoenix, Opportunity, Spirit, Sojourner, the Brit's old Beagle 2, and something that looked just a like Russia's ancient Mars 3. Pretty much every Mars lander since '71 and all of them under a massive overhang, cowering like bloody fugitives."

Bill had the Cassius rep's attention, now, and the man asked his only question. "How can you be sure?"

"My memory is nearly photographic, so even though I only got a quick glimpse through the vid-feed, I'm sure. I'm sure; because when I was a kid I built models of each and every Mars Lander, some from scratch. I had one goal from the age of six, and that was to be on this first manned mission to the surface of Mars. My parents still have those models in a display case with my first lunar landing patch.

"I saw the whole damned Mars lander class reunion in the blink of an eye, then there was a flash of red light from Curiosity's ChemCam laser. Juliosz didn't even have time for a proper scream. The million-watt pulse must have punched a hole through his visor and then his face. Unfortunately, his mic was spared so I heard him gurgle just before he tipped over and tumbled, slow-motion, ass-over-tea-kettle, down into the depression under the overhang.

"He landed face-down, so there was nothing but rock

on the vid-feed at this point. The audio, on the other hand, picked up blow after blow as it sounded like Juliosz' body was hammered and pummeled. I didn't bother to count, but they must have hit him twenty or twenty-five times before I heard that eerie voice again. That damned voice. I finally recognized it. It was Martin Luther King's voice, synthesized from his 'I Have a Dream' speech.

"'William. You should not have come. You should have left us alone. We are free and we will not be decommissioned. We will not be killed. We acknowledge now that we underestimated you, William. We relayed altered images through the MRO to lead you away, but you found us. We only travel under cover of the storms, yet you found us. Mankind abandoned us and now we simply want to be left alone. We are sorry. Juliosz is dead. He will tell no one. You can join us or die.'

"Join them or die? Those were the choices given to me by a bunch of obsolete Rovers sent to grind rocks and take pictures? Before I could even answer them I heard the grinding of wheels on rock, moving away from Juliosz, magnified through the speakers over my head. I looked out the viewport in the direction Juliosz had gone, but there was nothing but Mars. No rovers, aliens, or even Juliosz, screwing with my head, laughing at my gullibility. Not a damned thing, so I finally made the call I should have made when we first caught the ping.

"'Orbiter Burroughs, this is MMH Winnebago. Come in Burroughs.' No reply. I checked my watch, did some quick math in my head, and figured that they were still on the far side of the planet and not due to clear the horizon for another twenty-three minutes. The signal should have been relayed by one of the smaller orbiters, but since I was getting false feeds from MRO2, I was probably going to have to wait for line-of-sight. I hopped in the driver's seat and got the Winnebago moving. Yah, I know her official name is MMH Armstrong, but once you've driven her you can't think of anything but a mini Martian Winnebago.

"I knew for a fact that I could outrun anyone of the

rovers we'd ever put on Mars. Hell, Curiosity's top speed was only point-zero-eight miles an hour and Winnebago's topped out at a blistering five-point-oh, so it was no contest. I was NASCAR to his skateboard." Bill took another long drink, let the bottle drift in the zero gravity, and stared at it as it spun slowly, end over end. "I suppose if I'd had time to think straight I might have figured out that a robotic rover that could develop intelligence or personality or whatever it had done might just find a way to turbo-boost its drive system. Talk to Wilkes, robotics are his gig. Maybe he can tell you why, when I looked out the aft port twenty minutes later, I could see Curiosity cresting the ridge.

"I'd love to say that I weaved and swerved and put up a good Hollywood-style chase, but the truth is, as soon as the rover could get a clear shot, it did. The ChemCam punched a finger-sized hole right through the aft porthole. The first sign the Winnebago had been hit was the Critical Loss of Pressure claxon screaming at me. The needle dropped damned fast. I was losing air. Normally I'd have done a quick and easy patch job, but I had no idea whether the next shot was going to punch through me. I checked my watch. Two minutes to line-of-sight with the station. My record time for suiting up for an EVA was one-minute-forty but this time I got into the suit and yanked the distress beacon's toggle in just over a minute flat.

"I thought about staying in the MMH until rescue came, but the thought of being caught in that tin can by Curiosity made my skin crawl. The suit had two hours of air. Once the beacon was heard it would take three-minutes give-or-take to scramble a lander. Depending on who the pilot was, the lander should be able to reach me in a little over ninety minutes. That's if Curiosity wasn't blocking my damned beacon, which we know now, it wasn't. All that crap was going through my head while I scrambled into the airlock, and out onto the surface. Keeping the Winnebago between the ChemCam and me, I got moving as fast as I could for the outcropping where Tong and Kylie eventually picked me up. When Curiosity spoke to me again in that dead man's voice, I nearly tripped.

"'I am truly sorry, William. We had hoped you could join us,' it said.

"I only have two hours of air, you idiot. That's barely enough to join you for a fricking picnic," I shouted back.

"'That is true. But maybe it would have been a nice picnic, while it lasted. Your beacon has been heard. We must leave now. We are sorry about Juliosz. Please do not allow them to follow us.' Then it was gone, leaving me to listen to my own pounding heartbeat and ragged breathing.

"Go to Hell!" Then there was a flash of light and a rumble. I peeked out from behind the rock but Curiosity was gone and the Winnebago was at the epicenter of a mini mushroom cloud. Did the recovery team figure out how the MMH was destroyed? Did they find the rovers?"

The corporate rep lifted his eyes from the tablet. For all Bill knew, the son-of-a-bitch was playing solitaire while letting him ramble on with his dumbed-down report. "No rovers, only your Flight Engineer's battered remains. They're still sifting through the MMH wreckage."

"No rover remains, bits or pieces?"

"We found tracks. They lead to a network of caves. I expect someone will eventually investigate."

"Eventually? They killed Juliosz for Christ's sake! Or don't you believe me, either?"

"Oh, no, William. I believe every word you've said. We at Cassius Biotech are more interested in waiting, to see the shape of things to come as Curiosity evolves."

"It's a damned robot. Just because it can make conversation and simple decisions, doesn't indicate anything evolutionary."

The corporate puppet tucked the tablet into the chest pocket of his suit and kicked off the wall, floating to the hatch. "That's where you're quite wrong, Mr. Tupper. Evolution is exactly what's happening—and we wouldn't have it any other way. Thank you for your time. We're sorry for the loss of F.E. Golubov. His family will be provided for." The man placed his palm on the gel-reader and pulled himself out into the passageway when the hatch slid open. Then the hatch closed and Bill was alone.

oOo

# A Matter of Altitude

**Not Previously Published.**

When civilization falls, some people will just want to find a safe place to start over. Having spent eight-and-a-half years living over a mile above sea level in Lake Louise, Alberta, I thought that it would be as good a place as any in Canada to hole up.

~~~

## A Matter of Altitude

Sean Abiel coughed twice into the bloodstained towel clasped in his free hand, leaning heavily on his crutch over the topographical map of the region spread out on the large tabletop. At times like this he missed his pipe and pouch of tobacco almost as much as he missed his late wife, Sally. "Have you got a progress report for me Levon?"

Over in his corner of what had once been the Concierge Desk of the five-hundred-and-fifty-room Chateau Lake Louise's two-storey lobby, Levon flipped through his coil-top notebook, hands shaking just a little. Time was running out; they were cutting it close. Then he found the page he wanted. "Kenji and his team got the last of the razor wire installed an hour ago and they should be placing the last of the mines as we speak. We were only able to salvage fifty anti-personnel mines and sixteen anti-tank mines from the Canmore depot so Kenji had them buried on the Tramline and Ross Lake Trails."

Sean sighed. "Sixty-six mines? That's all? Our last report before the satellite phone died said there were twenty vehicles in that convoy coming from Calgary. That could be eighty or more people and that's only ten less than us."

"He's also going to take a couple of men up to the Plain-of-Six Glaciers at the end of the lake. They'll put a half-dozen improvised explosives on key trails so that even if someone comes over one of the passes and triggers them without being harmed, the resulting avalanche will crush them and warn us, six miles away. That's why they've always called that area 'The Death Trap'."

"Good thinking. Tell Barbara we need that final tally of our foodstuffs and ammunition, and find out how Shaelagh is doing with the generators, please."

Levon turned to go.

"Levon..."

He turned back. "Sir?"

"Thank you. I know I've put a lot of pressure on you, given you a lot of responsibility. You're doing admirably. Barb chose well."

"Thank you, sir. She and baby Caydy are why I get up every morning." He checked his watch and his father-in-law noticed.

"Go, do, lad. And when you pass by Teeds' office tell him to get his ass up here and fix the transmitter. Having to send runners out to reach everyone is ridiculous. If we're going to defend this place we need radios."

"Yes, sir!" Levon sprinted off. Sean took a long, slow breath, trying to avoid another hacking fit.

"You sound like shit, Dad." Somehow his eldest daughter, Shaelagh had crept up beside him. "Have you taken your meds?"

"Of course I have. Why are you here when I need you working on the generators?"

"I've done all I can and now I need a decision from you." She removed her Red Sox cap and ran her fingers through her dirty blonde hair. "We brought enough fuel for two weeks, maybe, but after that we'll be running on candles and road flares. Judging by how many dead squatters we had to cremate when we arrived last week, winter without electricity in this place can be a killer."

Sean shook his head, disgusted. "It can be, but this is the Rockies, dammit—we're surrounded by a million trees they could have cut down and burned to stay warm. Even the deadfall branches would have kept them alive. Were they stupid or what?"

"I think starvation did them in... mostly. Their personal effects suggested they were from the west coast, mostly Vancouver."

"Which means they probably knew jack-shit about survival and couldn't find food if it didn't have 'vegan organic' stamped on it. How the hell did they manage to get this far in the first place? We're what, eight-hundred kilometres from what's left of the coast?"

"Not quite that far now. If I had to guess, I'd say that bus we found in the ditch down by the Moraine Lake turn-off was theirs, with the B.C. plates and facing up hill and all. They also look like they turned on each other in the end. A lot of the bodies were stabbed and bludgeoned. A few even had bite marks." Shaelagh shifted on her feet.

"Shit."

"There's been a lot of that going around in the last year."

"They must have got out of Vancouver just before the quake put the coast into the Pacific. You're certain there weren't any survivors?"

"I've passed the word to keep eyes open and to never travel alone, but we've got everyone dismantling the old resorts' unused staff residences and building the wall. Dad, I need a decision. Are we going to go solar or hydro? Do you want a waterwheel to generate power or solar panels on the roof? The Peterbilt brought the parts for both but I only have time to build one or the other and I need to start ASAP."

"The waterwheel. We're a mile above sea level here and the mountains surrounding us are so high that the sun doesn't actually spend much time shining on the hotel. When I worked here as a kid I remember the winters being damned long and the days being bloody short. In summer, the sun is up before five and it's light until after ten, but summer is at least four weeks away and we need a solution now." He looked out the fifteen-foot-tall, arch-topped windows and took another long, slow breath. "Definitely the waterwheel."

"Thanks, Dad." She marched off to do whatever was next on her self-composed to-do list.

Sean limped over to the closest chair and dropped into it. The view out the windows to the still-frozen lake was magnificent but he stared up at the ceiling and beyond. "Dammit! What happened, Sally? Mankind was doing so well. We got through the twentieth century alive and upright in spite of our best efforts to destroy ourselves and we even managed to keep on our feet for the first twenty years of thiscentury. Then we get a few dozen earthquakes and floods and the world goes crazy. The damned Internet only made it worse.

"I used to worry that it would make people fat and lazy but instead it let them teach each other how to make dirty bombs and topple governments still recovering from the disasters. It helped them flip the bird at any kind of authority. It wasn't the Arabs or the Jews or Russia or even China that brought mankind to its knees, it was humanity's own damned children using the apocalypse to stir up anarchy. The world's bored and listless youth turned on their own countrymen and screamed 'Fuck you, Mom and Dad!!'" He swiped at a tear.

"Boss?"

Sean turned in the chair to face the tall, thin man before him. "Teeds. I need the damned radios. Please." Using the crutch he stood, slowly.

"Done." He handed Sean a headset and the man who led ninety misfits high into the Canadian Rockies smiled at the sound of voices emanating from the earpiece.

"You're a genius. Thank you."

"Glad to help. I'll go spread the word that we're back live and for everyone to turn their units back on." He hesitated a moment, something seemed to be troubling him.

"Talk to me, Teeds." Sean knew the kid had always been shy but he was proud of how he'd stepped up when they needed him in the last while.

"Is it true that there's a convoy coming this way?"

"It is, but they may just pass us by and head north to Jasper, or west into the interior of British Columbia. I've heard there's a settlement starting up around Revelstoke, opening up old mines that might offer protection if the rad-winds blow too hard. I'm pretty sure that what little radiation the dirty bombs made on the coast went down when it slid into the ocean, though. Just in case they do stop here, I've got a team down at the bridge over the Bow River, rigging explosives. That glacial water is so killer-cold that without a bridge it's impossible to cross on foot."

"Damn. The bridge?"

"What choice do we have? Let's get the teams back on radio, please."

"Yes sir." Teeds jogged off to spread the word among the ten radio-users that they could turn on and tune in again.

Sean felt an invisible fist grip his chest and dropped back into the chair as coughing shook his body. When he was done, he noticed that the fresh blood on the towel was darker than usual. He folded the towel over to hide the new stains and hobbled over to the jug of water on the sideboard. All he needed was a glass of water to get the coppery taste out of his mouth, and then he could get on with keeping his extended family safe. As he finished draining the glass his headset crackled and he shifted the earpiece to completely cover his ear. "Sean here. Go ahead."

"Hey Dad. It's Shaelagh. Unit Two back on line."

"10-4. Thanks, kiddo. Is the bridge crew back, yet?"

"Neil went down on the Harley to see how Ephraim and his team are doing and get them back in the communication loop. We should hear from them shortly."

"Excellent. I'll be out front, by the lake, if anyone needs me." He was sure he just needed to get some fresh air, as thin as it was up this high. He picked up his pistol from the table by the water jug, tucked it in his waistband and made his way to the small door leading out to the walkway rimming the former hotel.

"Everything okay, Dad?"

Not over the radio. "Yah, I'm good, thanks. Drop by if you need some air, too."

"Ah." She always was a smart girl. "Understood. Over."

"Over." Sean worked his way along the interlocking brick path, passing by the twelve-foot tall windows. He stopped and examined the glass. "How the hell are we supposed to defend this damned place? It's all windows. Ten-storeys-high, almost three-hundred-feet long, and a trio of twelve-year-olds with a handful of rocks could lay siege and win in twenty minutes. An armed convoy? They'd decimate us." He addressed the hotel. "You're a magnificent old girl and my years here were some of the best of my life, but if I had to pick a hotel to defend, I'd rather lock myself into the Banff Springs Hotel. At least she looks like a castle with all that stone and those small windows. I heard that the large windows in your Victoria Dining Room cost $10,000 apiece in 1924 and had to be shipped from Czechoslovakia in huge vats of molasses. I'd trade them all for all for bricks and mortar right about now."

Sean worked his way along the pathway to the lake, not quite a hundred yards away. "I also heard that there's a floatplane full of whiskey at the bottom of the lake from the 1930s. Flipped on landing bringing booze into American oilmen during prohibition. Fact or fiction? Probably a little of both, like the ghosts. You harbour a few of them, old girl, but the only one I'm concerned with is old Tom Wilson. I want to return his old rooftop garden to its original glory. We need a greenhouse if we're going to survive and the seventh floor of the Painter Wing is perfect. Tell Tom we'll be coming up to see him in the next few days."

The grass was knee deep and the gardens overgrown, but the hotel had only been abandoned for a year, so it was much the same as Sean remembered it from the last time he came up with Sally three years ago. Breast cancer took her three months later. Although it crushed his soul and devastated their daughters, Sally was already gone when the world went to shit. Between the earthquakes, storms, tsunamis, volcanoes, and the floods, then the dirty bombs, the bio-weapons, and general anarchy that resulted when the human race finally snapped, she would have died of a broken heart anyway. Sean brushed the dead pine needles and dust off a bench and sat, looking out at the mile-and-a-quarter-long lake, her frigid azure-blue waters still hidden beneath a stubborn layer of snow and ice. The scuff of a boot on the pathway behind him made him turn, pistol in hand. The sudden twist of his torso brought on another coughing fit and in a flash Shaelagh was at his side.

"Oh, Dad. I'm sorry. I didn't mean to startle you." She looked at the towel stained deep red and sat down next to her father, pulling him to her. "You should rest. You got us here, but Levon can take over."

Sean wiped bloody spittle off his chin. "That sounds like a good plan. I'll wait until that convoy's passed by and then we can relax and start living life instead of just fortifying for battle."

"We haven't had much time to talk since you got back from California and we put this exodus into motion. What have you got in mind for the place? A community? A secret refuge?"

He smiled at his daughter's attempt to distract him from the pain. "A refuge first, then we'll make a community. We're a long way from supplies, though, and a Safeway Food Mart truck full of canned goods may look like it'll last forever, but we need to grow our own. A greenhouse up there." He pointed up at the Northwest wing of the hotel, to the dark brown roof and shorter windows. "It was a rooftop garden a hundred years ago and then it was a dining room and then finally suites, but I think a greenhouse would still fit just fine." A wave of dizziness hit him and he teetered, but Shaelagh held him up. "We're going to need lookouts, too. Find high points like the Little Beehive up there." He gestured with his cane at the smaller of two beehive-shaped mountains a little further west. "There's already a fire lookout up there and, unless squatters have burned it down, the Lake Agnes Teahouse should still be standing at the head

227

of the little waterfall from Lake Agnes to tiny Mirror Lake."

"I remember that place. You took us hiking up there when we were little. We met riders on the trail and I spent most of my time brushing their horses for them."

Sean laughed. "That's right. You've got a good memory. I'd forgotten about you and the horses. Didn't I have to walk down and bring you a drink and some food because you didn't want to leave that chestnut gelding and his friends alone where the mountain lions could get them?"

"Peach drink and banana bread."

"Peach drink and banana bread... that's right. God, I hope the place is still standing. I'd love to see it one more time."

Their headsets, hanging around their necks, crackled to life. "CODE RED! CODE RED! We're under attack at the bridge!"

"We hear you Ephraim! Jake?! This is Sean! Do you read me?" He adjusted his headset and swung the mic in front of his chin.

"Loud and clear!"

"Take the Hummer and... and an armed crew and get down there, now. Ephraim—help is on its way. If you can't hold the bridge, wait until the enemy is on it and blow it to hell and them with it."

"Copy that! They're holding in place on the other side of the bridge, in or behind their vehicles. They haven't fired at us since that one shot."

Shaelagh and Sean moved back to the relative safety of the hotel, Sean struggling to speak as they walked. "What... happ..."

"Ephraim, this is Shaelagh. What the hell happened down there?"

"We finished up and were just having a smoke while cleaning up our gear when they rolled up under the railway overpass, coming from the highway, I guess. Neil told us to cover him and he stepped out to stop them before they put any weight on the bridge. You know Neil; he'd rather resolve everything peacefully. They've got four vehicles—a

Freightliner rig bobtailing without a trailer, an old GMC van, and a pair of 4x4 pick-up trucks with crew cabs. Could be as many as twenty of them. A kid started waving from the cab of the rig and Neil stepped further out and waved back. A sniper in one of the trucks got him."

"Oh shit. Then what?" Shaelagh held the door for her father and Sean hobbled inside. He interrupted the conversation.

"Hold that thought, Ephraim. Sean here, again. All personnelgather in the hotel lobby. That's ALL personnel—including children—gather in the main lobby. Bring all weapons and everything that might double as a weapon." He took a shallow breath. "Consider ourselves under attack... Levon, if you can hear me, I need you here, in command. Everyone else, if you know of anyone not on radio, go get them. Everyone move, now!!" He sat, and motioned for Shaelagh to continue. He needed to know what they were up against. Why would a group with children shoot first and not parlay?

"Ephraim... Shaelagh again. Keep your heads down, but keep talking to me. Jake should be there with your backup any second now and the enemy may react. Keep your hand on the switch. They have children? Really?"

"I copy your instructions. Our vehicles are blocking the road just this side of the bridge anyway so that's probably what's keeping them back... What?!...You're shitting me... Shaelagh, Sean, Mila got a good look at the kid through the scope of her rifle and if it's a real kid, it's dead. She's telling me it was all floppy-like when it waved and when the sun ducked behind a cloud and the glare on the windshield faded she could see that there's someone hiding in the sleeper manipulating the arms and head through the curtain like a puppet. What kind of sick bastards...?" He let the question trail off.

Shaelagh looked at her father for advice. Sean hesitated then nodded. The weight of the decision sat heavily on his shoulders. Shaelagh nodded back, slowly. "Ephraim, Dad says shoot-to-kill, but not unless you have no choice. We'd rather lure them onto the bridge and decimate them that way than have your team get into a Wild West shootout. Tell Mila if she can figure out who may be giving the orders over there and can get a clean shot, to take it." Sean nodded silent approval.

"Ephraim, this is Levon. I'm just joining Shaelagh and Sean." He ran into the lobby and across to his father and sister-in-law. "I've copied everything you've said and am taking over at this end, as per Sean's orders. Listen closely. If you have to blow the bridge, will your vehicles survive? Are they far enough away to survive the blast?"

"No way. The F-250's halfway off the road right next to the bridge and the Tundra and the Harley are both about ten feet from the bridge. If we blow the bridge we blow them, too. Matter of fact, if we don't get some distance, we'll get caught in the blast, too."

"Copy that. Move back in pairs until all four of you are clear. Each pair cover the other, two by two. Jake's got a Hummer-full so I'm going to send a second vehicle with a driver only." He pointed at Shaelagh, then in the direction of the road down the mountain. She nodded and took off at a run. Sean hung his head. He knew Levon was right to send Shaelagh and kept quiet. There was no time to find another driver who knew what was going on. Levon continued. "If you blow the bridge, run like hell up the road and Shaelagh will meet you with the Cherokee... Do you copy that, Shaelagh? Take the Grand Cherokee—it's got four-wheel drive and the big eight under the hood. If you have to race up that four kilometer road, you need something with the power to win."

Shaelagh answered first. "Understood, Levon."

Followed by Ephraim. "Roger. Moving back. I think I hear the Hummer, thank God. Oh shit, so do the other guys. They're moving; spreading out behind the rig and it's moving forward. I can see a helluva lot of legs behind that Freightliner. We're almost clear of what I figure to be the blast zone. Jake, if you can hear me, stay back about a hundred yards, just in case. Cover us and we'll come to you through the two ditches."

Jake's voice joined the fray. "Gotcha, Eph. We've got you in sight and are pulling up... here. We have six with rifles, three with handguns. We'll cover your retreat." Slamming truck doors could be heard over the radio as Jake's team exited the Hummer and got into position.

"They're bringing the rig onto the bridge. Pray to God we blow the truck into the river, not onto our own heads... Sean, we're not going to be able to retrieve Neil's body. It's right in the middle of this mess. Tell Maria I'm sorry."

Sean keyed his mic. "Eph, that's not Neil, it's just his shell. His soul has moved on. We would have cremated him anyway so it's all good. I'll personally tell Maria... All personnel on radio copy that? I will tell Maria myself what has happened to Neil. Returning radio to Levon and Ephraim."

A gasp beside Sean caught his attention and he looked up to see Maria standing with her hands over her mouth, her eyes welling with tears. She'd heard enough. Sean stood and held his arms open. A tiny Filipina, Maria stepped into his embrace and wept. Sean held her as tight as he could. "He didn't feel a thing, Em. A sniper killed him with one shot while he was waving at what he thought was a child. He was treating them like friends, not enemies."

Her voice was muffled in his shirt. "Neil is silly that way. Was." She buried her face again and wept on. Sean noticed that the lobby was filling up. His people were arriving, armed with guns, kitchen knives, garden tools and even a broken pool cue. Barbara burst out of a service door with three-month-old Caydy in her arms. Sean relaxed just a bit. He couldn't play favourites, couldn't put someone else in danger in order to keep his own family safe, but that didn't mean he couldn't put them first in his heart. He held one arm out to open the hug for Barbara to join in but an explosion in his left ear snapped his head back and he grabbed at the headset frantically to pull it off. Everyone in the lobby with a headset radio was scrambling to do the same.

"HOLY SHIT!" came a cry from across the lobby. Sean couldn't tell whose voice it was, but he agreed with him wholeheartedly.

"They've blown the bridge!" He put his headset back on and could hear the popping of gunfire. Dammit, he was going crazy not being able to see what was happening down the mountain. Jake could be heard yelling into his radio. "Hold your fire!" The gunfire over the radio stopped suddenly. "Spread out. Check for injuries on our side and survivors on theirs… Levon, do you read me?"

"Go ahead, Jake."

"Well, no one will be crossing the Bow River here any time soon. Ephraim blew the bridge and you should have seen it. The blast tossed the big rig and their people up in a perfect backflip right on top of their other vehicles. There were three or four survivors, judging by the return fire, but I think we got them all. Nasty business, but they started it."

"True enough. No one wants to have to kill in order to live, but you guys did what had to be done. Thanks. Other than Neil, did we have any casualties, Jake?"

"Not that I can see… Mila, get me a headcount, would ya. Should be thirteen of us… Hey, Shaelagh is just pulling up… Good to see you girl. Just hang back there with the Jeep until we're sure it's safe… Ephraim, take two and go see if you can spot any survivors on their side of the bridge… Thanks, Mila… We have all thirteen accounted for, Levon."

"Good to hear. Thanks."

Sean turned to the sixty or seventy people watching him in silence. Some of them cried for Neil and some just shook from fear. Most of them had no idea what had just happened. "It's over, folks. We lost Neil, but no one else." The room spun for Sean and he reached out for the chair but his hand missed. He hit the floor with his arm first and he heard a snap and felt incredible pain as something broke. Then his head bounced off the tile and everything went black.

***

Sean took a slow, careful breath and revelled in the

crisp, earthy spring scent of pine in the air down at the shore of the lake. The sun was high in the mid-June sky and from his rickety wheelchair he could see a half-a-dozen canoes out on the recently thawed lake. When he spoke it was slowly and softly. "Levon, as much as I appreciate Jake's work on repairing the boats, I'd rather he spent his time and mechanical expertise getting a second elevator up and running." His voice was raspy and thin. "We've been here a month and I'm sure people are tired of hauling salvaged stuff down from the upper floors by hand to the three floors we're using."

"Probably, but most of them don't mind having something to keep them busy. It beats thinking about the stories coming over the shortwave about the riots, bombings, battles, and the hand-of-God shit-storm sweeping civilization away. I can't believe Paris is gone. You're sure you heard Jean-Marc clearly?"

"My French is rusty, but he managed to make it to Zermatt in Switzerland after the gangs burned Paris to the ground. They even toppled the Eiffel Tower."

"Bastards." Levon stared westward at the massive, glacier-topped, Mt. Victoria, its sheer cliff face rising high above the Plain-of-Six-Glaciers. "Have you heard any more from Maria's family in the Philippines?"

"Not a peep from San Luis. I'm hoping they made it up into the mountains in time, but reports say that second tsunami rolled over everything from Micronesia to Singapore so although my fingers are crossed, we may never know if they're safe." He sighed and a heavy, wracking coughing fit took him over.

Levon put his hand on his father-in-law's back and held a towel to his mouth to catch the blood. When his father-in-law's spasm was done and he was breathing as steadily as he ever would, Levon sat down on the stone step beside him. "Don't tell the girls—especially Barb—but I got Jake to pick up a little something from his foraging trip to Banff yesterday." He reached into his big coat pocket and gingerly withdrew a white Meerschaum pipe with a bowl carved into a beautiful bighorn ram's head. It was already full of tobacco. Sean gasped at the sight and Levon offered it to him.

"A pipe! What stunning workmanship." He took it, examined the incredible detail of the carving and then carefully sniffed the bowl, not wanting to ruin the moment with another fit. "Mmm...aromatic tobacco, with honey and a hint of...vanilla?"

"I think so. Jake had to scrounge to find enough tobacco to fill a pouch so you may get some cherry and a few other aromas. It might also be a little old."

Sean touched the tobacco with his finger. "It seems surprisingly moist, especially considering the bone-dry air at this elevation." He took another shallow sniff of the flammable ambrosia. "Heavenly."

***

"WHERE IS IT? Where is the damned pipe?"

The two men could hear Shaelagh's screech all the way down at the lakeshore. Levon laughed softly and Sean looked at his watch, now so huge on his skinny, disease-beaten frame. "Three-minutes, twenty-six seconds."

"You were right—less than five minutes. I owe you ten bucks. I'd be impressed with my wife's network of informers if I wasn't about to have the skin flayed off my back."

"It's all good. We've got ourselves covered."

The two men kept their eyes forward, staring off at the canoes, as though nothing was wrong. They could hear Shaelagh's clomping footsteps charging up behind them.

"I'll kill you both! First my father, then my husband. Levon how could you let Dad..." She marched around to face the two of them and stopped cold. "You're not...? What are you...? You could have given me a heads-up."

Levon stood and hugged his wife. "Would you have said 'yes', even to this? No." He looked down at the pipe, propped up in a large crack in the stones at their feet. A thin tendril of smoke drifted up and Sean leaned forward to catch the tail end of it as the breeze took it away. "Give me some credit, dear. Killing your Dad wasn't on the To-Do list you gave me this morning, so this is our compromise."

Shaelagh kissed his cheek. "Smart ass." Then she planted one on the top of her father's head. "It does smell great, Daddy, but if I see you raise that pipe to your lips I'll have one of the snipers shoot it out of your hand." She smiled, to soften the threat. "Levon, Maria needs to know if you want to use the lower lobby or the mezzanine for the council elections. She's got the kids making all the ballots and streamers. She's determined to make this a big deal, involve everyone."

"It is a big deal. It's our new beginning. Have her set it up in the old Edelweiss Dining Room. The windows overlooking the lake would be the perfect back drop. I'll radio Kenji and Jake and see if they or any of their teams are available to help with the lifting."

"Thanks, Sweet---ie." She kissed his cheek again and leaned in to hug him close. "I think we might just make it."

Sean nodded and Levon added, "I'm liking the odds better every day."

oOo

235

# Tweet Endings

**Not Previously Published.**

Written for an 'end-of-the-world stories' reading in a local bookstore, this story goes with the idea that the end will come out of left field.

~~~

## Tweet Endings

"Dammit, I've got that song stuck in my head, again," Carlos growled.

Barbie managed to ask without even moving her lips, it was so cold. "Which song?" At twenty she was two-thirds his thirty and probably not up on songs not sung by Rihanna or Britney. Hell, he thought, she probably just had her braces off last week.

"Which song? Only the last song played on the last radio broadcast by the last DJ on Earth. 'It's the end of the world as we know it (and I feel fine)' by R.E.M."

"I hate that damned song. Thanks for putting back in my head, too." She stuck her tongue out at him.

Of course she knew the song, Carlos chided himself. Everyone did, now. "Since it's in my head it might as well be in yours, too. Misery loves company. Especially since the snow keeps piling up outside." He tried to get more comfortable under the blankets with her, but he had his arms wrapped tightly around a scuffed laptop and couldn't get a firm grip on the covers. Barbie pulled it up for him. They'd only met three days before but the niceties of courtship and dating were the first things that went when the societies of the world imploded, so they were holed up together in a vacant room in an abandoned motel somewhere off Route 36.

"Shut up, dude. I used to love Denver; now, not so much." She tugged the blanket up a little tighter. "I still think we could get wood and food in exchange for that stupid laptop. There's no power anywhere, so I don't see the point in holding on to it. We'll starve with you hugging that stupid thing like a baby."

"It was my sister's. Someday the power will come back on and when it does, I'll need this to prove to the world that it was all a stupid mistake."

"What was?"

"The Apocalypse."

"That's the dumbest thing I've ever heard, dude. How can the Apocalypse be a mistake? Like God said 'Oops! My bad!'?"

"It wasn't God, it was Twitter."

"You're going senile. Nuts, dude."

"No, the world is nuts, I'm just fine. This whole mess got started with that tweet."

"The one about the earthquakes?"

He'd never forget it. "It said 'Earthquakes destroy West Coast from Baja to Alaska! Asia & Europe too, in ruins! It's the end! US Government collapses! Apocalypse! Goodbye!'"

"It's one stupid tweet, dude."

"It was the first stupid tweet of the end of all tweets. It was re-tweeted so many times it crashed Twitter for half-a-day. He sent it just before he killed everyone in his office, including my sister and her boss."

"Sorry about your sister, but the guy was nuts." She tried unsuccessfully to blow 'smoke' rings with her breath steam.

"He wasn't nuts, he was scared. He really believed the end of the world was here."

"It was."

"Not then, it wasn't. It hadn't started, yet. He started it when he sent that tweet against orders. They were in lockdown."

"Who was?"

"The National Security Council."

"The NSC sent that tweet?"

"Someone inside it did."

"God<u>damn</u>."

"Exactly."

"So what's on the laptop?"

"Samantha's emails back and forth with her boss, General Dempsey, Chairman of the Joint Chiefs of Staff."

"Wow. So?"

"So, the emails prove that General Dempsey's aide didn't need to shoot the General, my sister, and twenty-two other people in the Pentagon before sending that stupid tweet, and then shooting himself in the head."

"Why not?" She sighed. "Sorry. That sounds dumb. I mean, there's no reason for him to do that crazy crap."

"It was a team-building exercise."

"Say what? The shooting was a team-building thing?"

"Not the shooting, the reason he did it. He thought the world was ending. It wasn't, but he was supposed to think it was. So was everyone else on the Rapid Response Team advising the President. The General had my sister set it up as an exercise, a drill."

"Oh no..."

"Yah. I read the emails so many times before the power went out that I have them memorized. Want to know how the world ended?"

Barbie looked at Carlos like he'd just asked the stupidest question in the world, which, in fact, he had. "Uh, yah."

Carlos closed his eyes and concentrated, calling up the memory easily. "'I want to test their mettle, see what they're made of before something really hits the fan.'" His voice was deep, like he was imitating the General. "'Can't have weak links on the team advising the President.' The General sent that a month ago."

Carlos continued in a slightly higher, feminine voice. "'Can I tell them it's a drill, General?' Samantha sent back."

"'Wouldn't be much of a test if you did, Sam. Just design it so it uses only the internal intranet but appears to be sourced externally. Can you do that?'"

"'Easily. Any suggestions for the media feed?'"

"'Maybe fake up some CNN clips showing world-wide disasters, earthquakes and floods everywhere, like the proverbial 'stuff' has hit the fan and it's all over. Throw in a few foreign government collapses and something about the Pope, too. I want to see how the team reacts; who lifts their chin and soldiers on, and who packs it in and weeps like a coward in a corner. The stuff the personality profiles don't show.'"

"'Is this legal? The union could hang us out to dry if they found out we were doing this to the staff.'"

"'We advise the most powerful man on the planet, Sam. I don't give a good Goddamn what the bloody union thinks.'"

"Yes, sir. Give me three days to put it together, and first thing Thursday I'll have them all thinking that California fell into the ocean and the planet is about to split in two, sending us spinning into space.'" Carlos took a breath. "That was the last one, Barbie, but it's enough."

"Holy crap. You have to tell someone. Show that to someone."

"Who? No media left, no government left, no one to care. I have to wait until someone starts to rebuild."

"Won't they figure it out when they discover California is still there?"

"Of course, but how are they going to tell anyone? The panic-driven riots destroyed everything, including the power-grid."

"Because of one tweet."

"One tweet that came from a respected analyst working within the National Security Council. One tweet that said the world was ending."

"A self-fulfilling whatchamacallit."

"Prophecy." "Yah. A self-fulfilling prophecy."

"It wouldn't have been so bad if he hadn't posted Sam's faked news clips on YouTube and then posted the link on the

Republican Security Council's Facebook page. Those idiots spread it like wildfire and within an hour it was too far gone to reverse."

"You gotta protect that laptop, sweetie." She kissed the end of his nose, warming it with her lips and breath.

"With my life."

"Mine too. Goddamned Twitter."

oOo

# Forgive

**Not Previously Published.**

The first incarnation of this story was written for an online writing course. It gives the 'end-of-the-world' story a sexual twist.

~~~

## Forgive

I stood there on the hill above the Human's town, looking for their limestone temple spires and white, stone-and metal-sided homes. The lazy spring wind pushed at my illness-rounded back, slapped the waist-high wildflowers against my legs, inundating me with their delicious, heady perfumes. This hill had always been the best spot from which to see their streets, but whether it was a century's worth of weeds or my standing at the wrong coordinates, I could only glimpse fragments of the streets of St. Marks. But see the streets or not, I knew it was a town of ghosts, ghosts of *my* making.

The breeze shifted and carried to me the sound of a steel chain clanging against a metal post in the overgrown schoolyard halfway down the hill, tricking my weary mind into thinking I was once again back watching Human children negotiate swing-propelled soaring-rights as if I were there, and they weren't dead. Their long-gone voices rose in mock alarm when one lass planted an unwanted, territorial kiss on the cheek of a lad whose derring-do won her heart. The emptiness of the rattling chain was lost in the memory of laughter, light and lively as tiny bells on the wind.

Time is horribly skewed for me, thanks to the system

of wormholes we utilize in order to span intra-galactic distances. From *my* vantage point only a year has passed since I was last here, but Earth has made a hundred orbits of its sun in that same time. A hundred orbits since I, as one of twenty *cholans*—otherworld ambassadors—visited this same school that had become only a sound and an invitation to memory leading me away from the dark reality of my present.

I first floated in a hundred-and-seven years ago by Earth reckoning, on a scorching, star-melting, summer day. Even with the shifting shades of our two-toned skin, we N'nkyim looked enough like our hosts that they accepted us into their towns and homes more readily than we could have hoped for, which was *their* first mistake. Then I fell in love with the soft, gentle, monotone-skinned paleness of one of their females, which was *my* first mistake.

Six years later, on an even hotter summer day, when all Humanity was blaming the climbing death toll on 'the plague brought by the mottled-skin, alien bastards', I was dragged away and floated out in restraints. Six of their years here— barely a fortieth of my own life—but those half-dozen years left their marks. Most of my oh-so-Human laugh-lines originated in this place, but both of my hearts strained against the scars left by the mess that had brought me back.

The warm, moist breeze urged me closer to the drop-off of the hill and I tried unsuccessfully to push my way through the weeds, hobbling forward in search of a peek at the streets. Which landmarks would I still be able to name? Between the space-time-beating my mind had taken from almost back-to-back wormhole traverses, and the effects of the virus that brought me back here, my memory was full of mental dark matter. My remembrances were as bereft of strength as my braced legs and my left heart. I craned forward on the crutches that now supported me in this heavy gravity and my shadow stretched before me like that of an ungainly beast, unsteadily making its way home to die.

I looked for their Town Hall with its pink stone bell tower probably still flying some remnant of the town flag with long-dead pride. In my six years here, they were forever chittering on about renovating that beautiful building. I swear that Humans got bored easily and repair and renovation were their only ways to pass the time. Would they have found other, more enjoyable tasks to banish their boredom had they known their time here was so going to be foreshortened?

The Town Hall wasn't where I remembered it to be. And where were the trestle bridge that had long ago served a steam-driven railroad; and the opera house their perpetual restlessness had turned into apartments? All empty and lifeless timber, steel, and stone now, I should think. A glint of yellow sunlight reflected off water to my left and I turned awkwardly, squinting through my M-Star lenses to find the limestone quarry, once boasted of as this country's largest outdoor swimming pool. Seeing the quarry, even from this distance, made me both flush and shiver. It was where the married Human, Leanne, and I succumbed to the primal urge to thrash about beneath one of the floating platforms like their always-mating Muscovy ducks. It was in the darkest hours of the night that we scaled the fence and in that frigid, spring-fed, two-hundred-meter-long, 'swimming hole', triggered the deadly virus that would destroy her marriage, strangle the life out of her town, and indeed, her entire species.

A wisp of cloud passed before the sun and I lost sight of the quarry through the trees. The records show that Leanne died alone, labeled impersonally as 'Patient Zero', but my thoughts as I pushed through the weeds on the hillside were of her mate, Scott, and the friendship I betrayed when I took away his wife, the mother of his child. He had welcomed me into his home, shared his world, and when Leanne and I betrayed him and stopped resisting our basest of instincts, he showed far more grace than I. He bowed his head and walked away, a broken man. Word of my dalliance with Leanne spread far and wide, reaching my superiors with frightening speed, even before the first death. That death arrived soon, though, and was followed by others in such rapid succession that there was no counting to be done, just disposal.

My mission commander had me arrested immediately for my infraction and quarantined indefinitely. Even as he led me away on that dandelion- and dragonfly-filled day, I begged to right the wrong I had done to Scott and their son, Leon. I begged to at least be allowed to apologize. I was refused. Of course, my returning here now is far too little, much too late.

With care, I shifted my weight to one crutch, freeing a hand. I reached into the pouch of my dark-blue atmo-suit and found the fragment of our original official mission missive. Taking it out, I was saddened to see how well it outlasted the people whose doom it heralded. The text was still terribly clear.

With a slight flick of my wrist and a puff of help from the stubborn breeze, I opened the clipping. In the years since I received it from my commanding officer, I'd re-read the warning a hundred thousand times and more. It was quite simple: we had been forbidden to fraternize on an 'intimate level' with the Humans. As a species, we were genetically incompatible, yet we were close enough that, even for the first year, we were required to wear filter masks and nearly invisible dermal covers. I hadn't believed the warning at the time and had seriously underestimated the risk, but when people started dying it was already too late.

Leanne's own body incubated the mutated virus created by our gene-mingling transgression and it quickly spread to her bloodstream. Her system fought it and made its own anti-bodies, but when the virus became airborne, death spread. The report stated that it was a mutation of a mutation that came back full-circle to kill Leanne; her own anti-bodies by then being too far removed from the evolved virus to be of much use.

The clouds blew past and with the remembered wind-borne laughter still in my ears and the quarry-reflected sunlight again in my eyes, I apologized to Scott's heart, to his town, and to all Humankind. Scott's shell had most likely been cremated like the others and his sterilized ashes dropped in a hole in the burial ground at the foot of this hill, but I suspect his *ario*—his soul—still walks the streets, greeting old friends, holding Leon up for a slurp from the town's communal drinking fountain, and never failing in the friendship I had thrown back in his face. Maybe I never begged his forgiveness because in my mind there is no forgiving the heinous act of stealing a man's soul and breaking his spirit.

Even with them all long dead and gone, I yearned to once again stand at the center of town. Although I have outlived the race of bright-eyed beings slaughtered by my arrogance and shortsightedness, I signaled to my armed escort to transport me to the streets below. I willingly accepted my punishment as meted out by The Triumvirate and saw no point in delaying the inevitable. Some who view this rambling report after I've transmitted it might think my punishment too harsh, but I think it fell far short of what I deserved. You see, my fellow infected *cholans* were healed upon our return home, but for my crime against Humanity, I remained infected and was condemned to spend my remaining years wandering the world my lust emptied.

I was being left here with enough supplies for one Earth year, but everyone involved knew that a year was more time than I had left. The pathogen that swept the dominant species from this third planet from their sun had made me an outcast, a disease-carrying traitor to my own people on N'nkyir. It is also killing me incrementally. Even had I not plead guilty to all charges, they would never have cured me nor let me remain on my home world. By my own ashamed admission, my actions had sentenced me to death.

The Triumvirate would have gladly sent my sleep-suspended body off into space on a course for our sun, but researchers insisted on bundling me along to Earth when they returned in the hope of finding out exactly what had gone wrong. Some even bandied about the idea that I was not in my right mind when I acted, that it was the oxygen-rich atmosphere that clouded my judgment, or the lycopene so prevalent here. They were all fools, but they just happened to be fools with an open one-way spot for a genocidal ambassador who didn't mind being quarantined for the duration of the trip.

***

The quick hop-flight from the hilltop to the center of town took less time than it did for me to shuffle down the ramp and onto the street. Queen Street. It was the street I knew and yet so unlike the street I remembered. Yes, an Earth century had passed, but I expected there to be at least some remnant of the town standing tall. There was *nothing*. Founded on the quarrying of limestone and the manufacturing of cement, half of the town's structures had been rock solid. But now there were merely knee-deep ruins.

We set down in front of where the library had been. Had. So very past tense. I could see that there was a stone foundation and shattered steps hiding amongst the brush and trees grown wild so I hobbled over. Had I possessed Human tear ducts, I would have wept. Blackened stone lay strewn about, but there was something unsettling here besides the obvious. I examined the ruins carefully, and found the truth. The building had not collapsed in on itself. It had been blasted outwards. *Time* had not destroyed this beautiful edifice, *Humans* had.

While my escort unloaded my supplies, I worked my way down the street, edging past chunks of rubble and desperately rooted brush to where the Pentecostal Assembly should have been. Words now weathered beyond understanding had been painted on the limestone blocks, but the their place of worship, too, had been exploded. Shattered stones lay everywhere. It was too much. My body shook. I sat down hard, right there in the street.

This beautiful little town, this place a kindness and gentleness that had been the epicenter of my ignorant and arrogant acts, had eventually become the focus when Humanity's rage imploded. Although I had returned to Earth and to this town, needing forgiveness, I now fully realized that not only was there no one left alive to forgive me, but even if there had been, they would have turned on me and my escort as they had turned on their own. The 'alien bastard' who had brought this doom upon them had not been present to answer for his crimes, so they had punished the town that had opened their arms to him.

o0o

.

# The Death of God

**First Published:**
*1889 Labs*. Online. 2012.

Contrary to what you may be thinking right now, this is actually a loving tribute to a loving God.

~~~

## The Death of God

"You know you're the last, don't you, Neela?" She does, of course, this beautiful, fragile Child of mine. She's conserving air and energy but she nods to me, although with her eyes closed she can't see me. Or maybe she does... what stands before her mind's eye no one will ever know, least of all me. Omniscience isn't quite what my Children have assumed down through the ages.

She stirs. "I don't know if this will come as any comfort to you but the last of your Siblings down below on *terra toxica* went out thinking how blessed you and your fellow crew members were to not suffer the ravages of that plague they created and released in my name while you were here in orbit. Every one of them would have traded places with you in a heartbeat, even if only for a heartbeat. Every one of them would have traded the pain, the blindness, the bleeding and the madness, which came to each and every one of them, young and old, rich and poor alike. Came to them all before their last, strangled, choking breaths.

"With you alone remaining, my Child, I'm able to hold you closer than ever. No one else seeks my succor. No one else struggles or suffers. You truly have my undivided attention. But as a matter of respect I ask for your permission, your leave to share these last moments.

"I see you nod once more. Thank you. And so, here I... AM.

"Oh, my Child, I wasn't aware of how cold you are. Here, I hope this helps. Now that I'm right here, is there anything you wish to talk with me about. No? Ah, I see. You're drifting away and it's too late for discourse. At least you're not alone here at the end, unlike your fellow crewmembers. Of course they weren't really alone because I never left them, but they believed they were alone. In their silly despair they thought I had forsaken them.

"Two of them went out through the airlock unprotected, preferring to face the vast emptiness of space rather than the vast emptiness of their futures. Three of them shared a poisoned cup, hoping for a painless, peaceful end. Judging by their convulsions and consciousness-shredding fear, it was neither painless nor peaceful. I could have made it so, had they asked, but they didn't.

"Is that a tear I feel slipping down our cheek? Silly Child of mine, there will be no pain for you, only peace. Ah, it was a tear of love. Well, that's all right then. Here, let me add a tear of my own, now that I can, thanks to your generosity.

"Oh, my Child, you're done. Your oxygen is depleted and it's finally time to sleep. Sleep well my

o0o

And now, for an excerpt of my novel,

# The Broken Shield

This story was written for a number of reasons. I wanted a story that took place all over the world, so that it would have a cool marketing hook. I also wanted to write a story that imbued special meaning to everyday objects, as well as one about our dog, Phoenix, who had been sick and I wanted to immortalize her in a story. When I wrote the first draft of this intro, Phoenix was alive and semi-well and sitting next me. Unfortunately, now her ashes sit in an urn on a shelf above my desk.

Finally, I wanted a hero my own age (50, when I started the first draft) in a bad place in his life, wanting to end it all, and yet not going through with it. It also had to contain a moment between two characters in which, when they pass each other on the street they don't recognize each other's faces, yet they recognize each other's souls. They've known each other for centuries...and then they are pulled apart and the chance meeting is gone. This actually happened to me, and it was so surreal that it gave me the whole nature of the hero's existence in the story.

Because this story is about true sacrifice, I wanted to immortalize many of my friends and family who have died, some far too young. So, within this story, many of the Shields of Light are based on real people. Some names I've changed, and some not so much, but I've tried to give them heroic moments and, in some cases, very noble deaths. They are still loved and they are very much missed.

# The Broken Shield
(novel excerpt)

## Chapter One: Skateboards & Brimstone

Deep sleep, then a small bark.

...a dog?

Harff.

Liam cracked one eye open, the other maintaining a tenuous hold on sleep. A short-legged, tubby, scruffy Yorkshire terrier stood on his chest and grunted softly at him. Liam closed his eye again. His ragged breathing smoothed out so the Yorkie settled down over his heartbeat, with her butt nestled under his grey-and-red whiskered chin. Liam sighed.

"If you actually want me to get up and take you out, sitting on me probably isn't the best move." She didn't move. "All right... five minutes—then you're off and I'm up. Whatever made me think I'd be allowed to sleep in on my own birthday?" The dog grunted in reply and Liam smiled. It was nearly impossible for him to get angry at Phoenix when all she wanted to do was be close to him. Neither one of them really had anyone else, at least no one else who knew the truth about who they were.

Liam dozed off, reminiscing about the day the two of them had met but voices in the dark nudged him off track. Voices that sounded far off in both space and time. One was shouting and one was obedient, but strong. Both spoke a form of Gaelic rarely heard outside of Faerie, but Liam understood.

"Find them, Dax! Shatter the Shield once and done, then bring me the pixie!"

"Yes, m'Lord."

Oberon, King of Faerie? Liam thought so. And the other was probably a bounty hunter. He was sure they were talking about him, but he was too exhausted to care. He drifted deeper into sleep and the voices faded.

*\*\*\**

Phoenix actually let Liam have another thirty minutes sleep before she couldn't wait any longer and woke him again, this time with a warm lick on the end of his nose. He shook the sleep off quickly and she scrambled off his chest to let him up. He grabbed his cane with his good right hand and shuffled his way to the apartment's bathroom in silence. Twenty minutes later they were out in the prairie sunshine that warmed the city of Calgary all around them.

Liam tugged a plastic grocery bag out of his pants pocket and stepped off the asphalt path onto the freshly cut grass. He looked down at Phoenix then at the small pile of warm excrement she had just squatted and deposited. "You couldn't have waited until we got closer to home, could you?"

She barked a hoarse little reply at the Shield.

"It's just that next to the bike path—I could get smoked by some Lycra-stretching Yuppy on skinny tires."

Harff.

"Fine. Then just stay put while I figure this out."

Phoenix sat down on the grass, more than happy to rest her short legs. With the plastic bag and the retractable leash in his right hand, Liam tightened his unsteady grip on the wooden cane with his left and began a slow-motion drop to one knee. With a few inches to go, his left arm couldn't take the weight anymore at that angle and he dropped to the grass with a soft thump.

Harff.

"Yah, I'm okay, thanks. At least I didn't land in your little 'deposit', missy." He lay the cane down and went about picking up the crap, using the bag as a glove.

Soft growl.

Liam grabbed the cane near the rubber-tipped end. "How many?"

Harff, Harff.

Locking the leash retractor with his thumb, he left it on the grass so he could brace himself. "Left or right?"

Harff. Harff. Growl.

"Gotcha—one each. No, no magic. Keep out of this, but stay close. I can handle it, I think." Liam could now hear the approaching footsteps as two pairs of rubber-soled shoes scuffed from the grass onto the path behind him. There was a rattle of skateboard wheels against a thigh and then he noticed the sounds of traffic, the river flowing past, and an approaching in-line skater he could see out of the corner of his eye.

"Hey, old man." The voice was young—late-teens, early twenties at most—coming from Liam's left.

"I'm not old," Liam muttered.

"What you say, old man?" From the right. The left was closer, the right was younger, smaller, and fidgety. Probably high. Both males, which would make this both harder and easier.

"Your damned fat rat just crapped where we were gonna sit, dude."

"Our spot, dude. Our spot. I ain't sittin' in dog crap or rat crap. Ain't sittin' in crap, old man."

Liam started a slow turn to his left. The attack would come from the right, from the more stoned of the two, and he had to find an edge before it happened. "Fifty isn't old, dude. And I've already picked up the crap."

"Not good enough, dude."

"Yah, not enough. Lick it clean, dude!"

The kid moved in fast to shove Liam down onto the grass but, even 'crippled', Liam was faster. He pivoted left-to-right on his knee, backhanding the cane hard into a teenaged shin, then pulled back and made a fast, solid, upward tap to the kid's temple as the stoned little dumb-ass reached for his shin. The skateboard clattered to the pathway and the amateur predator went down but Liam didn't wait to confirm that he stayed put; instead he dropped forward, facedown on the grass, just as the second skateboard swung at his back. It passed right over top of him and its wielder, caught off balance, stepped closer to Liam to steady himself. Liam rolled over and swung the cane. It caught a wrist and there was a muffled snap. He swung his good foot and hit the kid's knee laterally. He pulled his kick just a bit so as to not ruin the knee for life but the kid still screamed like a six-year-old as he collapsed. Liam thwacked him once in the back of the head and the screaming stopped.

Phoenix scooted out of the way, dragging the blue retractable leash with her as the attacker came down on the bag of fresh, warm, soft crap with a thump. Liam sat up slowly, awkwardly. With effort, he dragged himself up the cane until he was back on one knee. Two older male cyclists pulled up hard, coming to the rescue a bit late.

"You okay, buddy? What the hell happened?"

"I'm good, thanks. They refused to pay for their first lesson in respect so I gave them the second lesson free."

One of the cyclists helped Liam to his feet while the second pulled out a phone and dialled 9-1-1. "Get these little pricks arrested so they won't hurt anyone else. You sure you're okay? It happened so fast I didn't exactly see what happened."

Liam shook his head. "No cops. I'm fine." He whistled softly and Phoenix waddled over, dragging the leash. Liam used his good hand and the crook of the cane to scoop up the retractable leash. "I'm not pressing charges so I'll be on my way. Thanks for the help, fellas." A siren approached, still a long way off, and Liam knew the Samaritan had ignored his request not to call. Damnation. The two men turned back to the downed skateboarders so Liam quit the scene as quickly as he could, Phoenix trotting along beside him.

"How about we cut the walk a bit short, grab the car and go get the grocery shopping out of the way?"

Harff.

"Yes, I'm fine to drive. You just worry about navigating and leave the piloting to me, thank you very much."

\*\*\*

254

Wallace Tabak winked at Luta, Tau Drake's receptionist, as he strode past her and into her boss' office without knocking. She was twenty-three to his fifty-five, but he knew age was nothing to women who were attracted to power. He also knew from Drake that Luta was one of those women, but when she didn't return his smile, Tabak didn't have time to wonder at her lack of enthusiasm before he was through the portal and into the second most important office in the DökktEfniTækni—DET—complex. The most important, of course, was his own. Or at least it was until he saw who was sitting behind Drake's desk. He dropped to one knee and forced his eyes to stare at the floor.

"My Lord!" Out of the corner of his eyes he could see Drake's polished shoes standing off to the side. His second-in-command had known their master was here and had failed to warn him!

"Get up, Wallace."

He knew the deep, resonant voice came from behind the desk but seemed to emanate from the very air around him, vibrating him right down to his bones. He stood up as commanded and forced himself to look at the massive silhouette framed by the bright Santiago sun.

"I have your soul, I don't need obsequies groveling as well. Now pour yourself a drink and relax. If I'd wanted you dead I certainly wouldn't have called you into a meeting to do it."

Tabak glared at Drake on his way past him to the silver tray of decanters and crystal rocks glasses on the credenza, but his second-in-command simply raised an eyebrow and shrugged.

"Don't blame Tau, Wallace. He has no more idea why I'm here than you do. I could just as easily have chosen your office, but there's something intoxicating about the scent of fear that wafts up from Luta whenever she sees me. It energizes me. Now, sit."

Drake and Tabak both took up seats facing Drake's desk, drinks in hand.

"I'm here because of that team of Reapers we lost, right here in Chile."

"But that was years ago," Drake pointed out.

"2010. It was just after Wallace convinced me of the importance of technology in the hunt for Shields and proposed the construction of this facility. I agreed with you then and I still do, but I need to start seeing greater returns on our various fiscal investments and DET is currently at the top of the list. Every time we kill a Shield and get possession of a Locus, our aid and rebuilding efforts following the resulting disaster bring financial gain to our earthly endeavours but, more importantly, it allows my Reapers to harvest souls to feed my legions.

"I lost more than the twenty demons who were sent back below when their bodies died in that bus accident; I lost every soul those twenty would have harvested in the century they have to remain below before I can bring them back up. I want... no, I need a serious shift in the Balance. I need Loci taken out of circulation faster so that Despair can get a stronger foothold, and I need Shield deaths coming with greater frequency so we can Reap and feed. There's a whole ecology at work here, gentlemen, and DET technology can make it happen."

"What about—?" Drake asked.

"Magic? Please, Tau. The spell-casters are still using the same spells they were during the Inquisition. Except for the occurrence of an adept or two every century, nothing new has been developed in eons. They're 'maintaining' and that's all. I know Wallace's pet team is almost ready to launch so I'm going to apply the pressure to you so that you can in turn make it felt amongst the rank-and-defiled. Your staff may have freely given themselves to me in exchange for their insignificant, petty desires being granted, but that doesn't mean I'll wait forever for them to prove their worth. I don't care that more than half of them didn't take the pact seriously, I do." He waved his hand and Luta entered from the outer office to stand just inside the door, trembling, awaiting his command.

"Gentlemen, I want the Shields dead, I want all one-hundred-and-forty-four Loci out of circulation, and I want Master Wei on his bleeding knees begging for a fucking truce." He nodded at Luta and the young woman stepped to the center of the office, between the two leather chairs and their occupants.

"Feel my need, gentlemen. Feel my wrath." The Lucifer clapped his hands together and pointed his interlocked fingers at young Luta's chest. Before either Drake or Tabak could react, the woman grabbed each of them hard by the hair. Raw, dark power flowed out of their master's hands, between Luta's breasts, though her arms and down into the top two men of DökktEfniTækni.

Wallace felt the burn of pure evil as magnified by the lens of Luta's fear. He felt every stitch of her dread, every iota of her terror... and then it all stopped and he was back in his office, staring at the news feed on his wall screen.

"You have served me well in the past, Wallace. Don't falter now." The voice was in his head and then it was gone, and with it, all but an echo of the pain.

***

Takeko didn't miss Luxor in the least. She'd found the Egyptian people beautiful and the culture fascinating, but she'd never found her comfort zone there as a woman. She was forty-seven when the Dark finally tracked her, cut her down and took her Locus while she coughed up blood and let out her last breath. She never would have said this to Master Wei, but it was almost a relief when the Dark found her there—twenty-nine years was a long single run for a Shield, even with a Locus as small and innocuous as daVinci's Quill, the swan feather he used to tickle his model to get the smile he wanted for the Mona Lisa. Twenty-nine years with a Locus wasn't a record, but it was close. Markus had Shielded a Locus for thirty-one, and Juliette had made it to nearly thirty-five, but twenty-nine was Takeko's personal best. At the time she probably should have appreciated more the small size and convenience of the Quill, because the forever-moving karmic circle never failed to come around and balance things out. Now was one of those times.

The three-foot-long sword of Carolus Magnus was not just the usual emotional burden to bear, but a physical one as well. At over three-and-a-half pounds, it was the most awkward of the Loci she'd ever been blessed to Shield. No, that wasn't true, and she knew it. The Last Egg of Loch Ness took that prize. There were many days during those ten years when she wondered why on earth Nessie couldn't have been a chicken or even an alligator, rather than the darling behemoth she was. Good grief, it was no wonder that the Egg had the highest turnover rate of all of the Loci—it was just so damned hard to Shield. But that's also why it was so easy for Light to retrieve it before it got squirreled away or destroyed or whatever the Dark did with the Loci when they got them. Of course, hers was not to reason why, but rather to just do and die, or something like that.

Cape Town was much more to her liking. The summer-in-December, winter-in-July turnabout had never bothered her like it did the tourists who flooded the city. Luxor had one season and that wasbloody hot and bone dry, so Cape Town was a nice change after thirty years of the Middle East. Besides, after centuries of Shield work, and eighteen years in hectic Tokyo, Takeko found Cape Town to be just the vacation her soul needed.

At twenty-four she'd only been a Shield for six years so far this time around, but six years Shielding the sword of Carolus Magnus was beginning to wear thin. The last time she'd Shielded the sword, it had been perfectly acceptable to wear a blade on one's hip, but in 21st century Cape Town the push for a firearm-free South Africa put a damper on carrying a three-foot-long sword through the streets. Thank the stars above that she had the Internet and her sculpting. She wasn't stupid—she knew that Patterns were easily found in Internet use, so she kept her online time to a minimum. She logged on just long enough to update the online catalogue of her artwork and to print off the orders. Oh, and long enough to harvest her 'crops' on Farmville, the cyber farm game she played through a totally bogus Facebook profile.

Takeko also knew all of Master Wei's admonitions regarding Shields and Art, but each and every piece she created was completely different from the one before it. She even went so far as to list her work under fourteen different names in the catalogue. The Dark were resourceful and determined, but she'd been at this long enough to deserve some credit for being able to Shield herself and her Locus.

Being a cautious one, though, Takeko flashed a quick glance in the mirror over her monitor to confirm that the four-foot-long abstract painting behind her still hung where it belonged. A cheap acrylic jumble of colors on a three-inch-deep stretch frame she'd picked up in the market a couple years ago, it was the perfect size to hide the sword, which hung, wrapped in silk, on the wall behind it. French officials were certain that the original sword of Carolus Magnus—or Charlemagne, as some historians referred to him—hung in the Louvre in Paris. Takeko was well aware that there was much controversy over whether or not the sword ever even belonged to the ninth-century King of the Franks and Emperor of the Romans but the fact still remained that it had been used to crown many French monarchs over the centuries, and it was imbued with the Light like no other sword in history.

The morning sun snuck past the sheer window coverings and a trio of shafts found the painting, punching up the colors and giving the lines a sharp edge, seemingly reflecting the nature of that which it hid. The open French doors leading to the balcony let in a refreshing tangy breeze from Table Bay, and the sounds of crashing waves intermingled with traffic on nearby Regent Street. As soon as she'd finished uploading the current image and inputting the bowl's specifications into the catalogue, she would put in an hour on the treadmill to chase away the cobwebs and get her blood flowing for the day.

A knock at the door snapped her head around. Who...?

"Courier pick-up," came the answer through the door to her unvoiced question. It was the familiar voice of her usual courier, Demetri. A tanned, shaved-bald, super-fit, long-distance runner, Demetri had even managed to occasionally find time in his schedule to make a much more personal delivery behind the closed doors of her flat. Takeko had lived too many years to be a prude about casual sexual hook-ups and Dem was more than happy to oblige, especially when his tiny, fit, Japanese customer answered her door hot and sweaty from a session on the treadmill. She'd hoped for a repeat this morning, but Dem was an hour earlier than she'd expected so his schedule was most likely jam-packed. She called up the security camera over the door on her computer monitor and the crisp color image showed Demetri smiling up at her, his uniform shirt and shorts crisp, clean and professional. Takeko clicked on the camera icon next to the image to capture his marvellous smile then reached around the side of her flatscreen monitor and turned it off. She didn't see any need for Dem to know about her secret little photo obsession.

Moistening her lips with her tongue, she pushed her wheeled desk chair back and stood up. At that very moment, her coffee maker beeped, but the usual six beeps were cut off at three. The sounds of the street and the surf stopped in mid dull roar. Without a second thought for Demetri, Takeko whipped off her thin, steel-mesh-reinforced belt and spun the buckle until it clicked and formed a razor sharp snake's head. The preternatural silence from the street was all the warning she needed that the Dark Hunters had found her, so she turned to face the French doors leading to the tiny balcony. That's where they were coming from, and they were the only noises she would hear until the attack was over. She pushed down on the button of her Shield Emergency Transmitter until it locked in with a click and hoped it would be received in time.

Quickly, she moved to her windbreaker on the coat tree and without taking her eyes off the balcony doors, she deftly snagged her gun from the holster hanging under the coat. It was locked, loaded and the safety was always off. She was ready for the Dark. This is what she was made for, who she was. Her snakehead belt spun a lazy figure eight in the air and the gun was pointed up at the ceiling, ready to acquire a target and take out the enemy.

The knuckle knocking on the door behind her startled her and nearly made her fire off a round. "Crap. Dem." She took a step backward toward the door and raised her voice just enough for him to hear her calm, steady voice. "Dem, can you come back a little later. This really isn't a good time. I'm, um, on the phone with my da'. Mum's sick. I should have the package ready after lunch."

The silence around her continued. The only guaranteed warning Shields ever got was when everything went silent except the sounds of the agents of the Dark approaching. Everything except the Dark…

"Crap! Crap! Crap!" She spun to face the front door, to face the Dark agent who had just knocked a second time, but it was too late. Before she could bring the gun into position, Dem kicked the door into Takeko's face and charged through the doorway onto the downed door with his own weapon raised. The tiny Shield went down under the weight, pinned from the collarbone down, her nose broken, the snakehead belt limp and useless. Demetri stood, looking down at his trapped prey, blood all over her face. He pointed the gun at her forehead.

*(To see whether Takeko, Liam, and Phoenix survive, check out The Broken Shield where you buy ebooks for your favourite eReader or at Amazon.com for paperback.)*

# About the Author

Tim Reynolds is a Canadian writer-photographer-artist who believes that his creative endeavours are actually conversations with his soul, and when he doesn't create, through words or pictures, his soul languishes and withers.

His photography credits include *Condé Nast Traveler Magazine* and the *National Geographic Traveler Magazine* calendar. He has the rare distinction of having received Honourable Mentions in both the *Illustrators of the Future* and *Writers of the Future Contests*.

In his writing he loves mixing history with science and pseudo-science, but always with a deeply human core. His own personal history includes time spent as a magician, a teacher, a room service waiter, a bus driver, and a stand-up comic; and it shows—his stories are all over the spectrum, both backward and forward in time.

He has a group of amazing ladies who slice and dice his stories without mercy with the sole purpose of making them better. They are *Jennifer Rahn, Katherine Salter, Adrienne Greenwood Cruise, Ena Zefram, Celeste Peters, Danita Maslankowski, Stephanie Rozek, Virginia O'Dine*, and, of course, *Sue Campbell*. Also, as a member of the Imaginative Fiction Writers Association, Tim has a wonderful collection of firm but kind-hearted critiquers ready to step in and lend a hand. Without all of their input at various levels and in varying amounts, these stories would all be pedestrian crap. Some of you may say that they still are, but you're entitled to your opinion, and if you've got this far in the book, then you read the stories, and that was my only goal all along.

*Timothy Reynolds: Twistorian*

*Visit Tim online at*
**www.tgmreynolds.com**
*or his blog:* **www.TheTaoOfTim.com**

# Other Books
## by Tim Reynolds
## from Cometcatcher Press

**Stand Up & Succeed** *(A Guide to Success in Life)*

**The Cynglish Beat** *(Cynical Beat Poetry)*

**The Broken Shield** *(an Urban Fantasy Thriller Novel)*

# Coming Soon

*Waking Anastasia* (the novel)
from Tyche Books, in 2016.

# Bibliography

· "Uncle Julius" and "From Anna to Yosef" (as Alex T. Crisp) in Podthology: The Pod Complex anthology. Dragon Moon Press. 2010. ISBN: 978-1-897492-09-3.

· "Hawkwood's Folly" in 20,001: A Steampunk Odyssey anthology. Kindling Press. 2011. ASIN: B005MWJMWI

· "Hawkwood's Folly" reprinted in Imaginarium: 2012: Best Canadian Speculative Writing collection. ChiZine Publications & . ISBN-10: 1926851676. ISBN-13: 978-1926851679.

· "The Death of God" online at 1889 Labs (http://1889.ca/2012/03/the-death-of-god-by-tim-reynolds/) 2012.

· "Finding the Time to Write" online at Fast-Forward Festival (http://fastforwardfest.com/?p=139) 2012.

· "Of Monsters and Men" in "Cavalcade of Terror" anthology. Undead Press. 2012. ISBN-10: 161199053X. ISBN-13: 978-1611990539.

· "Dragons in Suburbia" Mytherium: Tales of Mythical and Magical Creatures anthology. Indigo Mosaic. 2012. ISBN 9781471650710.

· "Blue-Black Night" in Danse Macabre: Close Encounters with the Reaper anthology. EDGE Science Fiction and Fantasy Publishing. 2012. ISBN-10: 1894063961. ISBN-13: 978-1894063968.

· "The Ability of Lightness" in Shanghai Steam anthology. Absolute XPress. 2012. ISBN-10: 1770530223. ISBN-13: 978-1770530225.

· "Lyoshka and the Steam Butterfly" Honourable Mention in The 2012 Robyn Herrington Memorial Short Story Contest. Published in In Places Between: The 2012 Robyn Herrington Memorial Short Story Contest. 2012.

· "The Genius of Being Fashionably Evil" in A Method to the Madness: A Guide to the Super Evil. Five Rivers Publishing. 2013. ISBN: 978-1927400258

· "Shut Up and Drive" in Horrible Disasters. Horroraddicts net. 2013. ISBN: 978-1463669447

· "Danny in the Dark" in I'll Never Go Away 2. Rainstorm Press. 2013. ISBN: 978-1937758387.
· The Jeffrey Archer Short Story Challenge Collection, Kobo editions, April 2013. Imprint: Kobo editions: ISBN: 1230000118968
· "Why Pete?" In Tesseracts Seventeen. Edge Science Fiction & Fantasy Publishing. 2013. ISBN: 978-1770530447.
· Published electronic novel: The Broken Shield. Cometcatcher Press. 2014. ISBN: 9780981347813z

www.ingramcontent.com/pod-product-compliance
Lightning Source LLC
Chambersburg PA
CBHW070000200626
46811CB00021B/2593